Could people tell how tur...
she was?

Dancing was sexual, of course—a civilized mating ritual....

But Beth had never felt it as vividly as she did swaying in AJ's arms, with the jazz heat of the band making her body throb. The sax groaned like sex cries, the drums pulsed in a get-some heartbeat. The congas came after her, demanding satisfaction now. She was surprised people just didn't give up all pretense and go for it on the floor.

There was something so sexy about a man who could dance. It meant he was in touch with his body, with her body.

And the way AJ was moving now, promising all kinds of sensual delights, she could hardly wait to hit the sheets.

Blaze™

Dear Reader,

I don't know about you, but I'm a mess of contradictions. On all those personality/style thingies, I am split down the middle. One minute I'm semioutrageous; the next I'm desperate to melt into the wallboard.

So I really can relate to Beth—the shy, repressed writer trying to be an out-there sex columnist. Then she meets a man who accidentally turns into two people himself—her lover and her boss.

These two truly need each other to be whole. AJ helps Beth blend her contradictions, and Beth shows AJ the warm guy behind the distant loner he thinks he is. She's the bridge over the moat guarding his heart.

Needless to say, this was a powerful story to write. I hope their story touches your heart. I'd be thrilled to hear from you. Write me at dawn@dawnatkins.com or pop over to my Web site, www.dawnatkins.com.

My very best to you,

Dawn Atkins

P.S. AJ is perfectly pictured on the cover by Greg Miller, the winner of the Blaze Cover Model Contest. I am honored to have this gorgeous guy grace my book.

Books by Dawn Atkins

VERY TRULY SEXY

Dawn Atkins

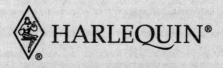

TORONTO • NEW YORK • LONDON
AMSTERDAM • PARIS • SYDNEY • HAMBURG
STOCKHOLM • ATHENS • TOKYO • MILAN • MADRID
PRAGUE • WARSAW • BUDAPEST • AUCKLAND

ISBN 0-373-79159-3

VERY TRULY SEXY

Copyright © 2004 by Daphne Atkeson.

Dear Reader,

Take a *good* long look at the man on our cover this month. Isn't he fabulously sexy? His name is Greg Miller, and he's the winner of our exciting Blaze Cover Model Contest. He and his wife won the grand prize of a romantic weekend at the Park Plaza hotel in New York City.

Last year we asked you, our readers, to tell us why your guy should be on the front cover of a Blaze novel. You responded with letters, poems, photos and e-mails about why the man in your life is a hero. And why he's also hot, romantic and sexy...

We had so many great men to choose from, it was difficult. But in the end we judged that Greg was the perfect man to appear on the cover of *Very Truly Sexy* by Dawn Atkins. I think you'll agree he fits the story well!

Thanks to everyone who entered our contest. And thanks for making Blaze such a hot series favorite!

Cheers!

Birgit Davis-Todd
Executive Editor
Blaze

To David, for loving the many faces of me
And to my best friend Gwen…you know why

1

"OKAY, SARA, DESCRIBE the first time you were intimate with Rick. In detail, please. No twitch is too tiny, no moan too minor."

Beth Samuels adjusted her steno pad on her lap, clicked on the mini-recorder she used to back up her note-taking, then leaned back to listen, her stomach jumpy with tension. Her Chinese Crested hairless dog Spud, as relaxed as Beth was nervous, shifted his barrel body against her hip, cozying up for a snooze.

"Were intimate?" Sara teased. "You mean *had sex*, Beth. If you're going to write about it, you're going to have to say it." Sara dipped an Oreo into the whipped cream garnish Beth had added to the circle of cookies for their snack-and-chat.

"I'm adjusting, okay? I said *twitch* and *moan*. What do you want?"

"More than that, sweetie."

Beth clicked off the recorder, dismayed by the challenge she faced. She had to go from easy-breezy entertainment writer to nitty-gritty sex columnist practically overnight. Well, by the next magazine deadline anyway. She wasn't that experienced at *having* sex, let alone writing about it. That was where her sexually accomplished friend Sara came in. If she would only cooperate.

"I'll make it work, don't worry," Beth said firmly. She would not let her readers down. She cherished her "On the Town" column, where, as her alter ego, E.M. "Em" Samuels, she scoped out entertainment venues, analyzing every nuance with as fresh a wit and focus on detail as she could manage. The column was her window on the world and it made her feel valuable and very alive. The money mattered, too, but not as much as the joy of the work.

"So, about Rick and that first time," she said, resituating herself, making Spud groan in his sleep. She snapped on the recorder again. "Was it on your first date? Why or why not? Did he suggest it, or you? Did you make out at length or did it just happen?"

"You mean, did clothes whip away, condoms appear and bodies magically meld?" Sara smiled. She'd told Beth more than once she was too dreamy about these things. "Sex doesn't have to be pretty to be good." She dipped an Oreo into the Grand Marnier frappé Beth had concocted as part of the evening's refreshments, then gestured with it. "People jiggle and wobble."

Beth lunged forward with a napkin to catch Sara's flying drips.

"Zippers snag," Sara continued. "Condoms fly across the bed. Bodies squeak and thrusts get off-tempo. But if you have the right attitude, everybody has a good time." She pushed the soggy snack into her mouth with a triumphant finger.

The drip danger gone, Beth relaxed against the sofa. "I just don't like the awkward parts."

"What you didn't like was sex with Blaine."

"Our sex was okay."

"*Okay* and *sex* should never be in the same sentence." Sara hadn't made a secret of disliking Blaine, though an I-told-you-so had never crossed her lips. Sara was fiercely opinionated, but a loyal friend.

"You have to take a different approach, Bethie, if you're going to make this work. Less lace, limos and gimlets and more 'Ten Tips for Better Blow Jobs.'"

"I'm not writing for *Cosmo*," she said, distress shooting through her. "It's still *Phoenix Rising* magazine. I'm just going to spice up the entertainment reviews with a little sex."

Though that wouldn't be as easy as it sounded. Or as easy as her managing editor, Will Connell, thought it would be. *Just take your notepad in for the post-date entertainment,* he'd said to reassure her. *What's the problem?*

The problem was that, for her, there was no post-date entertainment, though she wouldn't share that fact with Will, who treated her like a treasured niece. She was as likely to take Sara with her to scope out new bars, restaurants and clubs, as to take a man. She hadn't actually had a date since Blaine left, nearly a year ago. Maybe she was still recovering. Or maybe dating just seemed like too much trouble.

Sara tried to set her up from time to time, but Beth preferred cocooning in her cozy house with her pets, watching Doris Day-Rock Hudson romps while munching on low-fat caramel rice cakes and diet cream soda—low-cal snacks so she could afford an occasional cookie-frappé splurge with Sara.

But now *Phoenix Rising* was about to be gobbled up by a magazine conglomerate and Will was trying to save as many sections, columns and jobs as he could, including her own, God bless him.

"So pick up a guy and write about your own first time," Sara said, twisting a cookie apart to scrape the frosting off with her teeth. "Pop a toothbrush and some Trojans into your clutch, hit a singles' spot and— poof—a sex column."

"That's you, not me," she said, absently running her fingers through the silky fringe of a throw pillow, vaguely soothed by the tickling sensation.

"Maybe that's not sweet, shy Beth, but it sure as hell could be hip cosmopolite Em."

"I think I'll stick with my very own personal sex-pert—you. Just help me through this rough patch, Sara."

"And you think it's going to smooth out?"

"I can only hope." *We're in a reality TV world, Em,* Will had said. *Readers are bored with their own lives, so everyone else's fascinate them.* And nothing was more fascinating than sex. She sighed.

"Okay," Sara conceded, evidently reading her gloom. "I still say you need the adventure, but I'll tell you about the first time with Rick if it'll help you."

"Start with the highlights, please." Boomer, her St. Bernard, lifted his chin from the floor, as if interested in the scoop, and Ditzy, her teacup poodle, jumped onto Sara's lap.

"Is this animal story time?" Sara asked. She glanced up at the archway into the kitchen. "Even your cats are listening in."

Beth glanced up at her black-and-white spotted cats, Frick and Frack—watching closely from their favorite perch—then at Sara. "At least cover Ditzy's ears. I think she's still a virgin."

"Listen and learn, furball," Sara said to the dog curled in her lap, then shifted her attention to Beth. "Okay, the highlights. First off, Rick has the most amazing tongue. He did this swirly thing in my ear, and then below, where it counts, and, let me tell you, I thought I was having an out-of-body experience and a vision quest—where an animal guide tells you the meaning of your life, right?—in one big whammo."

Beth swallowed. "Um, that's impressive." The tops of her ears burned and she felt funny listening to something so intimate, but it had to be done. To distract herself, she scooped a dab of whipped cream from the cookie plate onto a finger, then let it drizzle sweetly down her throat.

"Impressive? It was mind-altering, mind-boggling, mind-melding—all that and more. After I stopped hyperventilating, I returned the favor, doing my very best work…."

Beth took careful notes while Sara described what her best work entailed, uncomfortable with the way her body began to feel like a marshmallow over a low flame—toasty warm on the outside and all melted on the inside.

A little bit later, Sara finished describing her second orgasm and paused for air. They both took big gulps of the orange-flavored frappé, thinking over the story. The drink was supposed to be research for the column Beth had planned on froufrou drinks. But now that her focus had to be sex, the cocktail review would be merely a sidebar.

"Great detail, Sara," she said. "But let me ask a few general questions. Do you always carry condoms with you in case the man isn't equipped?"

"Absolutely. Safer sex is everybody's job."

"But doesn't that make it seem calculating? Have condoms, will have sex? Doesn't it take away the excitement?"

"No more than having a fire extinguisher suggests you're planning a kitchen fire. It's a precaution. It's being prepared. Weren't you a Girl Scout?"

"That makes sense, I guess. Next question—what makes you decide to sleep with a guy?"

"Lots of things. If he makes me laugh…if he's a good dancer…if he looks good…if he seems sweet. With Rick, it was his body temperature. He was so warm, I just knew he'd be sensual in the sack."

"You slept with him because of his metabolic rate?"

Sara shrugged. "It's just sex, Beth, not the meaning of life."

"It's never that simple for me."

"That's because you angst over it instead of just letting it happen."

"Men don't react to me like they do to you."

"If you'd wear something hotter than a jumper, take your hair out of a braid and not look so serious all the time, you'd have better luck."

"You mean, if I were a different person. I'll settle for pretending to be you for a while. Plus I picked up some books."

"You're *reading* about sex? Jeez, Beth."

"What can I say? That's me."

"You underestimate yourself. You're a sensual person. Look at you in your silk pajamas."

Beth rubbed the smooth, cool fabric that covered her legs. "Yeah? So?"

"And look around. Your living room has deep colors and tons of textures." Sara gestured at the framed weavings—complex fibers in teal, silver and burlap-brown. "Plus, you love music—that whole wall is filled with CDs. Scented candles are all over the place in, what do you call them, aroma groups? Aroma *groups,* for God's sake. Fresh flowers in every room. And look what you did to our simple snack. Not only did you make a lovely frappé instead of breaking out the Diet

Coke, but you added whipped cream to my Oreos for a taste nirvana.

"You've got all the senses fired up—sight, touch, taste, smell, sound." She counted them off on her fingers. "Of course, sex does all that and more. It's a sensory jackpot with moans for music. You've just been neglecting that angle."

"I suppose so." Beth had worked hard to make her home comfortable and satisfying. She noticed she was still fingering the pillow fringe for the simple pleasure of the feeling.

"You just need a guy who can tap into all that sensuality and, ba-da-bing, you'll be as hot as your column."

"Believe me, if I find this mythical guy, you'll be the first to know. For now, let's go back to Rick's magic tongue. Would you say the secret is in the actual swirl, the heat and moisture of the tongue, or the pressure of the tip?"

"Good Lord, Beth. You need a man."

THE NEXT MORNING, Beth hurried her dogs back from their walk, anxious to get started on her column, her head full of Sara's sexploits and her own doubts. Sara was right that her column would be stronger if it were based on her own experiences, and it would be nice to meet a guy with racy techniques like Rick's tongue swirl, but what were the chances of that happening anytime soon? Blaine hadn't even been much of a kisser, alternating a thin-lipped maneuver with an open fish-mouth.

But they'd had fun together, she reminded herself, not wanting to malign her good memories. He'd stayed up on trends, loved going with her to check out new restaurants, bars and after-hours spots. He'd been a good conversationalist and had appreciated all the lovely touches she'd provided to their times together. They'd seemed completely compatible.

Until he left. With her confidence.

Oh, and her savings. But she tried not to think about that. Too humiliating.

Inside the house, her dogs extracted their personal favorites from the large wicker basket of dog toys, while Frick and Frack observed the doings from their positions on their tall scratching pole. Beth tossed the toys and looked around her living room, thinking about what Sara had said about her place.

She'd only intended to create a comfortable haven for her and her pets, but the result was a feast for the senses, now that she thought about it. And she'd done it on a shoestring budget, too. The overstuffed sofa was as comfortable as a glove, but with an appealing rough weave. The cherrywood cocktail table and matching end tables were deeply stained and gleamed like liquid, and the carved wooden upright lamp was as curvaceous as a living form. These were amazing steals from an estate sale. The framed weavings Sara had admired were vibrant against the wall she'd painted an accent plum color. She'd worked out a trade with the artist—doing some publicity brochures and newsletters for her.

In contrast to the soft warmth of most of the room, elegant glass vases of various shapes, colors and heights filled her knickknack shelf. Treasures from garage sales and eBay. She varied the scents of the candle clusters based on her mood, which Sara teased her about.

She breathed deeply of the white gardenias, red hibiscus and yellow honeysuckle blooms she'd arranged in vases in her living room, dining room and kitchen.

They were all from her yard. The aroma and bright colors made her feel good. She extracted a bloom and stroked her cheek with its petals, shivering with the delicious tickle. Maybe she was a sensualist, after all.

Her previous lovers hadn't tapped into her sensual side, that was certain. Not that she'd slept with many men in her twenty-seven years—three, counting Blaine. They had all been good intellectual matches for her, which seemed more important than sex, which she'd viewed simply as part of the package. Maybe she was wrong.

Maybe she would explore sensuality versus sexuality in her column. Which she had to get to work on. Now.

"Enough, guys," she said, refusing the ninetieth slobbery delivery of Ditzy's rubber newspaper, Spud's cloth monkey and Boomer's battered playground ball. She headed into the second bedroom, which served as her office, her canine pals trailing her, disappointed but resigned.

Her revision on a camper top manual for Thompson Manufacturing was due this week, but her column scared her, so it came first.

She turned on the desktop water feature—a miniature waterfall that spilled over three layers of rounded pebbles into a frosted glass bowl—lit two energy-boosting peppermint candles, limbered her back and arms with yoga stretches, then sat in her specially outfitted chair.

After three slow, deep breaths, she tilted her lamp minutely to be certain the glare wouldn't tire her eyes, then clicked the start button on her computer.

Her animals assumed their work posts. Spud rested his chin on her insteps, Boomer lounged to her left and

Ditzy curled up in her lap, chewing on her toy. Hopefully, its squeaker would give out before Beth went nuts from the wheezy creak.

Taking a deep breath and blowing it out, she rested her fingers on the keyboard and began her adventure.

Your "On the Town" reporter, who has faithfully detailed the latest dance clubs and restaurants, greatest wine-by-the-glass value and most intriguing after-hours venues, will now turn her attention to the rest of the evening. After all, while my date and I are savoring the saucy bouquet of our cunning cabernet, we're wondering what we'll do after the last jazz set at The Phoenician and the ginger Crème Brûlée with pumpkin seed lace at Lon's at the Hermosa Inn. Will we be intimate? And how will we decide?

Not a bad beginning, she thought, reading it over. Could she be Sara for the next part? Deciding to have sex based on whether the guy made her laugh, could dance, smelled good or, hell, wore a tie she liked?

That wasn't Beth's way. Beth waited to have sex until the relationship was solid and they were comfortable enough around each other to minimize the fumbling awkwardness of the first time.

And she did her best to make it special—perfect lighting, alluring music, erotically scented candles, something tastefully sexy to wear, wine beside the bed and an after-sex snack awaiting them in the fridge. And then she hoped for the best.

Her entertainment column was all about ambiance and turning everything, even a cup of coffee, into a celebration. Her column elevated the ordinary to the extraordinary. And now she wanted to do something like that with sex.

Sara, on the other hand, didn't care a bit about elegance. She liked sex in whatever way it came, so to speak. But couldn't sex be lovely, lyrical and hot? Surely Beth could give Sara's sexcapades Em's tasteful flare.

She looked at the calendar. She had just one week to write, revise and finalize the piece. Tight. She liked to let her columns breathe for a few days before polishing them to a gleam and sending them to Will. Her glance at the calendar brought her eye to the fan letters she'd pinned to the bulletin board. Smiling, she detached them and read the phrases she'd highlighted in each.

"Miss Em: Your words made me practically see the place," said the first. "Thanks to your recommendation, Em, our anniversary was the most romantic ever," went the second. And the third really moved her: "Oh, to have E.M. Samuels's vision. What would we do without you?"

Her readers counted on her. She would not let them down.

But when the phone rang, she was grateful for the delay. "Hello?" she said eagerly, and her mother greeted her with equal cheer.

Beth rocked back in her chair, knowing the conversation would take a while. Her mother leaned on Beth for comfort and advice, a habit that began when Beth's father had left them twenty years before, but she had to be coaxed to ask for the help she needed with practical things—repairs and finances.

It took a few minutes, but Beth finally extracted the fact that the AC unit was broken. AC was essential in Phoenix, even in April. Her brother Timmy, who lived with her mom, had patched it before heading to work, but it had wheezed its last shot of cool air shortly afterward.

The landlord, George Nichols, was insisting he'd replace it with a unit from another of his properties, but her mother didn't want that. Her rent was low because they'd stipulated in the lease that they'd handle repairs, and Tim was good at that. The offer of the AC was too much like a favor, her mother said, which it undoubtedly was. George seemed to really like her mother.

A fact her mother seemed to be ignoring. She'd dated a few men during the twenty years since Beth's father left, but the relationships never lasted long or amounted to much. George was a good guy—handsome, intelligent, kind—a little older, probably, than her mother's fifty, but he acted youthful. He'd retired from some high-tech firm and managed properties to stay busy.

Today, she wished her mother would just let the guy give them the unit, favor or not. They needed to cut costs wherever possible. Beth's work as a technical writer paid her living expenses, but the column funded the extra help her mom and brother needed. Yet more reason to make the sex column work.

She convinced her mother to let George give her the unit, without telling her about the column crisis—she didn't want her to worry—and agreed to come to dinner before hanging up.

Staring at her blinking cursor, she thought about something else her mother had mentioned—Timmy's latest invention idea. *He needs investors, Bethie, if you have any ideas.* Her stomach tightened another notch. In the past, she would have offered help from her savings. Now there were no savings. Not since Blaine. How had she been so wrong about the man?

They'd been together for nearly a year, spent most of their free time together, and Blaine had behaved as though she hung the moon, set the sun and fluffed up the clouds to boot. In truth, she'd felt a little uncomfortable because she didn't feel quite as connected to him as he'd seemed to her.

But when he'd disappeared, she'd been stunned. She'd thought she had good people instincts. Basically an optimist, she expected the best from people, and they usually delivered. Yes, toward the end, Blaine had seemed more distant, unusually preoccupied about his business. He'd mentioned some difficulty with funding for his limited partnership, and his enthusiasm about their long-planned Caribbean cruise had ebbed, but she'd never doubted that he cared for her, loved her, wanted to be with her.

Maybe his infatuation had blinded her to what was really going on. Something had, because somehow, right under her nose, he'd forged her name on a check from her money-market account and taken twenty-thousand dollars, leaving her with a balance of just two hundred.

The experience had destroyed her confidence, for sure, and it would be a long time before she got serious with a man. Or even stuck her toe in the dating pool— no matter what Sara said about getting right back on that board and diving in.

She wasn't risking another belly flop anytime soon.

Back to the column. Beth played the tape of Sara's words, closed her eyes to picture Sara, so comfortable in her body, so easy with her sexuality. If Beth could just channel Sara, she would be fine.

Four hours later, she had a draft that held enough detail to be believable and was as refined as she could manage. She'd described the specifics of the experience vividly, but tastefully. She'd been frank, not vulgar; erotic, not graphic. Pleased with the result, she shot a courtesy copy to Sara and was just about to e-mail her draft to Will—early, to make sure she was on the right track—when her phone rang.

"Tell me you haven't submitted this," Sara said without preamble.

"I'm about to. Why?"

"I'm sorry, Beth, but you can't use it."

"What?"

Sara lowered her voice. "I know it sounds ridiculous, but Rick thinks it's too personal."

"You're kidding. No way could anyone tell it's him or you."

"But we know, he says, and that's enough."

"You're kidding."

"I wish I were. Personally, I thought it was pretty hot. And, get this, now he wants us to only date each other."

"But you don't do exclusives," Beth said, her brain struggling to absorb the bad news about her column. "What about 'a pair and a spare'?" This was Sara's dating philosophy: date two guys with another one in the wings…just to keep things interesting.

"I know, I know. But it's kind of cute. He's, like, zap, all protective and sentimental. About the tongue swirly thing, can you believe it? I said I'd try it for a while and see how it goes. If he goes weird on me—possessive and jealous—I'm outta there, of course."

"I'm glad for you, Sara. I hope it works out." She sighed, trying not to think about her nixed column.

"I'm sorry to do this to you, Beth," Sara said, reading her mind. "Maybe you could modify the column a tad? Snip out the detail?"

"The magic *is* the detail. Let me see…" She clicked open the file and scanned its contents. Removing all signature elements, she was left with a measly two paragraphs. "Without you two, I've got an introductory blurb. And a week to fix it."

"You know the answer—go pick up a guy. Fresh is better than canned in more than spinach, you know."

"Can you honestly see me doing that?"

"Yeah, if you don't bring a book."

"That was one time. And it was a great novel." Sara was notoriously late and Beth had happened to have a paperback in her purse while she waited for her. *Reading in a bar.* Sara had never let her hear the end of it.

"You can do it, Beth. Wear something slinky and look friendly."

"I'll just fake the column, I guess. Fictionalize it." She sighed. "Maybe add some statistics on favorite kinds of foreplay or something."

"Statistics? Come on. Think what a great column it would make—Em *really* on the town…. Give it a try."

"Nope. Not me." When it came to picking up a man, Beth was as far from the coolly sophisticated Em as a virgin from a call girl.

She hung up and looked at her computer screen, the cursor pulsing like her own nervous heart. She pictured herself throwing on something slinky and marching into a bar, pickup radar pinging. No way. Not in a million years.

"THIS DOESN'T WORK for me, Beth," Will told her, holding the printout of her revised-to-death column. He'd asked her to come in to talk it over. Not a good sign. "It's too wooden, too cookbook. Like a kinder, gentler *Cosmo* anecdote."

"Tell me what you really think," she said glumly. The worst was, she knew he was right.

"Where's the energy? The scrumptious detail that is Em's trademark? Hell, your description of the wine is hotter than the bedroom stuff."

"I had to change it at the last minute. I can do better." Except her expertise was in reporting, observing and interpreting real experiences, not writing fiction.

Will grabbed a magazine from a pile on his desk—*Man's Man,* she saw—the California-based cross between *Esquire* and *Maxim* whose parent company was about to take over *Phoenix Rising.* He opened it to a page he'd dog-eared, tapped it and turned it to her. "*Man's Man* Gets Some" by Z. "This is what we want—our version of this Z writer."

"This is a men's magazine," she said. "*Phoenix Rising* has women readers, too." She tried to hand it back.

"Keep it for inspiration. Give me something I can work with, Em. We're leaking readers all over the place. And women like to read about sex, too."

She noticed deep worry creases in Will's forehead and sweat rings staining his shirt. Something was worse than he was saying. "What aren't you telling me?"

He sighed. "The thing is, the VP of *Man's Man* editorial will be here next week to talk about the makeover. He's going to reassign and refocus. The mantra at *MM* is edge, titillation, heat. I want to keep your column, but it's got to deliver. You have to dazzle me—and him."

"I'll do my best," she said, her stomach twisting with tension.

"I know you will," he said. "You can do it. Just, I don't know, make it more vivid, more fresh, more real."

Vivid, fresh, real? Right. Her heart heavy, Beth read over the *Man's Man* column as she headed out of the building. It was sex, sex, sex—no warmth, no class, no sensitivity.

This was lame. And gross. A bunch of phallo-centric drivel. Which was the last thing *Phoenix Rising* readers needed, no matter what the *Man's Man* hatchet man wanted.

She could do better. She had to. She couldn't fake it, though. Not and make it *vivid, fresh* and *real*. There was only one way to do what she needed to do.

On the sidewalk outside the building, she shoved the magazine under her arm and hit speed dial three on her cell.

"Hello?" Sara said.

"Tell me everything I need to know about picking up a man."

"Really?"

"No. Wait. Make that *meeting* a man. Talking, flirting, getting to know him, all that. Oh, hell, just help me, Sara."

2

ADAM RAFAEL JARVIS, AJ to friends, Rafe to the world, pushed into the hotel lobby, his work for the day done. Thank God. He ran his fingers through his hair, weary to his bones. He'd been as gentle as he could with the staff at *Phoenix Rising,* but he'd given them the reality check they needed. No point ducking facts when they came with negative dollar signs. The pub's circulation was in the toilet and the *Man's Man* formula was its only hope.

He'd done his best to minimize the pain. There would be changes—more salespeople, fewer columnists, less news, more features—but if everyone went along with what he'd laid out, no one would lose a job.

He enjoyed working with the managing editor, Will Connell, a savvy guy and seasoned editor. Still, the staff's pale faces and the tension in the air had drained him. He was getting soft in his old age. He was only thirty-five, but lately, that felt old.

He needed a drink, so he angled off to the bar for a quick Scotch to ease the tension of the day.

He sat at the end of the bar, where he could check out the clientele—an old reporter habit—and ordered a Scotch rocks.

The place was busy with conventioneers—identifiable by their plastic name badges—and locals from nearby offices, wearing business clothes, drawn by the happy-hour prices, no doubt. There were a few unattached women, he noticed—a cluster near the bar and a few in booths.

One woman in particular caught his eye. Dressed to kill in a clingy blue dress, she moved toward the restroom alcove with a determined stride, but wobbled in her heels, like a kid wearing her mother's pumps. Driven, but shaky. Hmm.

Great curves, firm-looking breasts, her hair swept up in a style that invited a man's hands, but as she passed, he saw it was held in place by a barrette in the shape of a cartoon kitty.

A hot babe with a child's heart? Interesting contradiction. And a great ass, he saw, as she disappeared from view.

He turned his attention to a guy flirting sheepishly with three women at a booth. He was either married or their boss. Rafe would love to get close enough to eavesdrop and verify his hunch. He smiled at himself. More knee-jerk reporter stuff. He was obviously bored.

He took a drink, welcoming the smoky burn. He liked travel, liked visiting the other *MM* properties, liked making his mark on the magazines they snapped up. But the rest of his job was getting predictable and he was tired of charity events, stakeholder meetings and advertising revenue reports.

Strangely enough, he found he missed journalism. He'd been thinking a lot about his days at the *Miami Tribune*, where he'd been the lead reporter on an investigative project about funeral companies. He'd dug through piles of records, coaxed reluctant bureaucrats to spill, uncovered the kernel of the crime and then helped write the series that sparked an overhaul of the industry, new legislation and a Pulitzer nomination.

The work had been rewarding, but at the time, he hadn't realized how much it meant to him. He'd been a restless guy in his twenties. A couple of feature assignments further raised his profile, and he'd gotten an offer at *Man's Man* as a feature writer. The money was great and he liked the Bay area. Before long, he'd moved into editing, a new challenge, and then into management as a vice president.

Where he now felt stuck. He'd made his choices, though. The publisher counted on him. Maybe he was just going through a restless period that would pass.

He'd spend one more day in Phoenix, during which he'd go over details with Will and talk to the last writer—E.M. Samuels, the entertainment columnist, who was coming to the magazine offices for her check and mail.

He wasn't looking forward to the meeting. The woman's work epitomized what was wrong with the pub. She reported on food, wine and clubs with a sort of *Town and Country* flavor that was passé for the target demographic—and the times. Connell, who seemed protective of her, wanted to keep her on as a feature writer because she had a flair for words and lots of talent. Rafe was willing to offer her that option, but she would have to leave the column behind.

If only she wouldn't cry. Her genteel writing made her seem the type who might. He hated making women cry. Which was why he steered clear of any female who even hinted at getting serious.

Actually, he'd steered clear of all women lately. He took another swallow of Scotch, not allowing himself to think about what that meant, focusing instead on the changes at *Phoenix Rising.*

Until Will could find someone with the right spice to take Em Samuels's place, Rafe would have the "*Man's Man* Gets Some" columnist, Zack Walker, do a few guest pieces.

In two days, he'd be back in the home office in San Francisco. Just in time for a big shareholders' meeting, followed by a charity golf tournament and a week of work on a strategic business plan. Truly tedious and deadly dull.

Unlike the woman with the kitty-cat barrette, who'd emerged from the bathroom. She caught his gaze, smiled a smile that lit her eyes, then flew past, as if afraid he might speak to her.

He felt the urge to do that—just to get the scoop on that barrette—but she lighted at a table with a morose guy. No doubt the boyfriend, though how he could look so glum with a dish like her in his grasp was a mystery to Rafe.

She said something to the guy, who answered, then grinned, stood and hurried away. Had she sent him on an errand? She smiled him off, then her shoulders slumped. She'd been faking her cheer?

She got up from the booth, seemed to hesitate, then moved toward the rest rooms again. She didn't even glance at Rafe this time—too busy fishing a phone out of her handbag. He shifted so he could watch her—and listen.

"Sara?" she said, standing in the alcove, one hand over her ear. "Except for the drinks, this was a complete bust…. What?… I did meet a guy. Yes. Except it turns out he just had a fight with his girlfriend…. Yeah. See what I mean? It's hopeless… What do you think? Of course I helped him. Plus, I suggested a gift. Roses are on sale at that shop on Central, and if he puts them in

a vase from the final clearance table at Osco's, he'll
have a sixty-dollar gift for less than thirty…. What?…
I was not sabotaging myself. The point is that I cannot
do this…. I do *too* want to get laid!"

She covered her mouth, chagrined, and looked up—not
in Rafe's direction, thankfully, because she'd have seen
him practically choke on his drink in reaction to her words.

Had her friend dared her to pick up a guy? And she'd
zeroed in on a loser on the rebound? He shook his head,
amused, and listened harder.

"I'm not the kind of woman men pick up," she continued. "I'm the kind they ask for advice about their
girlfriends. I'm going home. What else can I do?… I
know…. I know what I said. Yes, I know it will be good
for me." She chewed her lip, listened to her friend.
"Okay, okay. I'll try one more guy."

She hung up and walked slowly down the length of
the bar toward her booth.

One more guy, huh? To have sex with? Hmm. Could
it be him? The possibility gave Rafe a charge he hadn't
felt in a long time. The woman had a girl-next-door
freshness with an undercurrent of hot babe he wouldn't
mind tapping into.

How to approach her? He noticed that a ballpoint pen
lay on the floor beside her table. It was a place to start.
He eased off the bar stool and headed her way. He'd get
the story on that barrette, one way or another. And
maybe a whole lot more.

"IS THIS YOURS?" THE HUNK who had smiled at Beth on
her way back from the rest room extended a pen in her
direction.

"Uh, no. Not mine. Maybe the waitress's?" She
pointed to where the woman stood.

He smiled down at her, confident and handsome, his eyes a fierce blue. "Mind if I wait for her?" He seemed to be teasing her.

With a jolt, she realized the pen and the waitress had been a conversational ploy. He wanted to join her. "Oh. Sure. Have a seat." What luck.

He sat and reached to shake her hand. "I'm AJ."

"Beth." His grip was firm but not overwhelming, and his hand was extremely warm. That was the reason Sara'd had sex with Rick—high body temperature. So insane. *But it's just sex,* Sara would say, *not the meaning of life.*

Beth watched as her new companion sized her up in a masculine way. Unsettling, but pleasant. Flattering, really.

There was an edge to his face—he had a square jaw, a straight, strong nose and an intense, almost hard expression—but his broad mouth, easy with a smile, softened the effect.

His most dramatic features were his eyes—blue and sharp-edged as shattered glass, but there was humor and intelligence in their depths and wry crinkles at the edges.

Just as the mutual appraisal began to seem unnaturally long, the waitress breezed over. "What can I get you?" she asked AJ, smiling down at him more broadly than she had with Beth.

"What are you drinking?" he asked, indicating Beth's nearly empty martini glass.

"Tutti-Frutti Martooti," she said, the name sounding more foolish than it had when she'd selected it. She'd come to Grins for its specialty drinks for her sidebar on the top ten froufrou cocktails. Oh, and to meet a man.

"Want another one?" AJ asked, looking doubtful.

"I should try something else." She grabbed the drink

menu. "I can't decide between the Licorice Twist and the Hot Cha-Cha. Will you try one for me?"

"Sorry," he said, lifting a brow as if she'd asked a crazy question. "Scotch rocks, please," he said to the waitress as though they were old friends.

"You got it," she said, winking at him. Brother. The woman was either aiming for a big tip or an after-shift date. She made it seem effortless.

"I'll have the Licorice Twist," Beth said.

"Sure." The waitress wrote it down, then gave AJ a departing smile.

"The pen," Beth said to AJ.

"I think you dropped this," he said to the waitress, holding out the pen.

She accepted it, her fingers lingering on his. "Thanks for watching out for me." So obvious.

"My pleasure," AJ said, flirting back.

Some people could flirt as easily as breathe. Not Beth. Sara had given her tips, but they'd flown out of her brain the minute this man dropped into her lap—well, booth.

Her stomach tightened. She felt as though she was in over her head. She didn't have to actually sleep with him, or anything. They would just chat, joke around, maybe get friendly enough to kiss. Just enough to make her column sparkle. Sara, of course, would go for sex. He had warm hands, after all. What about Em? What would Em do?

She was about to find out.

"So what brings you here?" AJ asked her, leaning closer on crossed arms, his scuffed leather bomber jacket creaking deliciously.

I'm picking up a man. You interested? "Just getting out…sampling some cocktails," she said, lifting her empty Martooti glass.

"Sorry I couldn't help. Tiki drinks threaten my masculinity."

She smiled. "I can't imagine anything doing that." Not bad. Something was giving her the courage to stretch a bit—either the warmth of his expression or her determination to extract a column out of this at any cost.

"So I seem too macho to you?"

"No. Just very male." The candlelight polished his blond hair and gleamed on the leather of his jacket. Underneath, he wore a V-neck silk knit shirt in a rich brick red. The contrast of leather and silk begged to be touched. So did the muscles swelling under the shirt, pulled taut by his position.

"I think I have a feminine side in here somewhere." He pretended to pat his jacket pockets, then shrugged. "Hopefully, it'll show up when I need it."

"And when might that be?"

"When a woman wants to know what I'm feeling inside." He shuddered in pretend dismay.

"I'll try not to pry."

He wasn't really joking, she could tell. For all his friendliness, there was a guardedness about him. His piercing eyes, warm on her now, still managed to say, *Don't get close.* "So what do you do, Beth?" he asked.

"I'm a technical writer." That was one of her jobs, anyway. *Sex columnist working on her first article* would change the entire flavor of the encounter. She never revealed her identity when she reviewed venues, so why start now? With her nondescript appearance and subtle research techniques, she slipped in and out of hot spots like a ghost with taste.

"That sounds interesting."

She laughed. "You're too kind. It sounds boring, but

it's fascinating to me. I like the challenge of turning engineering jargon into something ordinary people can grasp."

"Having once assembled a stereo system, I salute you. Do you have an engineering background?"

"Not really. My degree is in English, but I took lots of math and science."

The waitress arrived with their drinks and after she left, AJ lifted his Scotch in a toast. "To tiki drinks and talking," he said, studying her over his glass.

Something hot vibrated along her nerves, connecting between her legs, which she nervously crossed. They were only discussing cocktails and technical writing, but she felt on the brink of something thrilling. And scary.

Raising her Licorice Twist in its tall glass, she said, "To getting to know each other." And more?

Only if she dared. And if he was interested, of course.

The proportions of anise and chocolate in her drink were off, and the liqueur was a cheap one, so the effect was sickeningly sweet without an alcohol bite. She mentally crossed Licorice Twist off her top ten list. That part of her column was moving along. For the rest of it, the important part, she should say something flirty, but she settled for the predictable. "And how about you? What brings you to Grins?"

"I'm staying here, in the hotel."

"Where are you from?"

"San Francisco."

"And you're here on business?" He nodded and something flickered in his eyes, some discomfort, but she asked the next question anyway. "And what work do you do?"

"I'm a transition expert. I help, uh, reorganize companies, redeploy staff, all that."

"Far more interesting than technical writing."

"It hasn't been much fun today and I actually dropped in here to stop thinking about it." He lifted his glass as proof.

"I'm sorry. I didn't mean to intrude." She'd been practically grilling the man. Any second she'd ask for his social security number so she could run his prints.

"Let's just stick with keeping each other company." He tapped his drink against her glass and studied her again. "That's what I find interesting."

"Okay. Sure." She had to look away, uncomfortable with how closely he was looking at her with those laser blues. But part of her liked it. The tingling between her legs intensified. She could see that if a woman went with certain impulses, she could end up in bed with a man like AJ with no effort at all. Some women, anyway.

"Actually, you caught my interest just walking across the room a while ago," AJ said.

"Really?" That might be a line, but there was something so direct about AJ that she was sure there was more to it. He had looked intrigued when he'd caught her gaze near the rest rooms. "How so?"

"You seemed, I don't know, contradictory."

"What do you mean?"

"You're dressed very hot, but you're unsteady in your heels and you've got a little-kid barrette in your hair."

"Oh." Her hand flew to touch the Hello Kitty clasp she'd borrowed from her neighbor's daughter to hold her hair up. "I borrowed this. And I'm just getting used to new shoes." The truth was that she never wore heels. AJ had seen right through to her inner librarian.

"Don't apologize. The contradictions suit you."

His scrutiny and flattery unnerved her, so she decided to joke away the feeling. "Excellent. I'm completely charmed. And what's my line? 'No one's ever noticed that about me before'?"

"You're catching on," he said, but a flicker in his eyes told her she'd hurt his feelings.

"I'm sorry. I guess I'm not good at this."

"At what?"

"You know. Snappy repartee, flirting, all that. I prefer to be more direct. I like people to say what they mean."

"Me, too."

"But you're good at the other. You were great with the waitress, and that dropped-pen bit with me was very fresh."

"I guess that's a compliment?"

"Absolutely. I'm just interested in how this all works."

"Why is that?"

She couldn't exactly answer that, but she could come close. And get some data on the male point of view on dating. If she wasn't going to sleep with the guy, she could at least interview him. "The thing is, I haven't dated in a while. I'm kind of, well, rusty. So, I have questions about the whole process."

"You haven't dated for a while, huh?"

"No. I was in a relationship that ended. And I've been out of, um, circulation for quite a while."

"Our loss, I would say. Speaking for men in general."

"Thanks. So, can I ask you about how all this works?"

He seemed amused by her question. "It's not like I'm an expert, but ask away."

"Great." She wiggled into her seat, feeling better wearing her reporter hat. "Here goes. How do you decide what to say first when you want to meet a woman?"

He shrugged. "It depends on the woman and the situation."

"No tired lines, right, like, 'Did it hurt much when you fell out of heaven'?"

"Hell, no. That's for amateurs." He winked, clearly teasing her. "The first line is just to break the ice. It should be funny or intriguing and certainly not sexual."

"Too offensive, right?"

"Exactly. And the first line isn't make-or-break. It's the second line that counts. By the second line, you've got a conversation on your hands."

"Oh, very true." She wished she could flip on her tape recorder, or at least take notes. "So, how do you figure out what to talk about in that conversation?"

"It varies. Say I'm at the airport and I see a woman I want to get to know. I might ask her about the book she's reading, or how she likes her laptop, whatever seems natural. Assuming I'm not intruding. You pick up the vibe if someone would rather enjoy her privacy than talk."

"I see what you mean." That would be her he was talking about—the woman giving off privacy vibes. Except even she might succumb to AJ's overtures. Something about him made her feel comfortable, as if she'd known him for years, instead of moments.

"Okay, here's something I'm curious about…" She paused, wondering if she dared ask the question flashing in her head. *Oh, what the hell.* "How often do these encounters lead to more? A date…and um…?"

"You mean sex?" He grinned again. "Depends on the chemistry, on how we both feel." His smile faded and he became thoughtful. "Lately, not often, to tell you the truth. I've been traveling a lot and just haven't been that interested."

"I can imagine." Darn. That meant tonight would be just talking. But that was good, too. She had something for her column, at least—"pickup lines and possibilities." But would that be racy enough to dazzle Will and the VP at *Man's Man?*

"Until I saw you and your kitty barrette, that is," AJ said, startling her. "You've got me very interested."

"I do? You are?" Little, fizzy sparklers began to sting her stomach. She took a big gulp of her drink to put them out. Except the drink was nastily sweet. She made a face.

"Try this." AJ handed over his Scotch.

She took a swallow, but it was too much and too strong and she choked.

He leaned across the table to pat her back. "You okay? I didn't mean to shock you."

She nodded, gasping for air. "F-fine."

"You like people to be direct, right? To say what they mean?"

"Yes."

"Okay. I want to take you to bed, Beth."

Her entire body went electric. She couldn't believe her luck. She'd not only met a hot man in a bar, but also not fifteen minutes into the conversation, he'd asked her to sleep with him. This was way easier than even Sara had said. She must have stepped into some magic wish-fulfillment time warp. The Em Zone. Maybe the universe wanted her to keep her column.

"Beth?" AJ said. "You okay?"

"Yes. Very. I'm better than okay. So, you want to…?"

"Take you to bed? Very much. So, are you interested?" His eyes flared with heat.

Even though she hadn't even dreamed she'd get this far, she'd come prepared. At Sara's suggestion, she had

a pre-pasted travel toothbrush and a selection of condoms—ribbed, flavored and ultrathin—in her handbag.

Even more amazing, she *did* want this man, with his
intense eyes and easy smile, square jaw and warm
hands. Her whole body lifted with the pleasurable possibility of being with him. It wasn't because of her sex
column or Sara's challenge, either. She just wanted him.
From somewhere deep inside, where she wasn't nervous or embarrassed or clumsy. Where she knew what
she wanted and why, and exactly how to get it.

But could she do it? It could be a disaster. Awkward
and awful. Or it could be heaven.

"If this isn't a good time, don't feel pressured," AJ
said, seeming to pick up on her doubts. "I'm just telling you that I'm available. And you should know that
you could crook your finger and get every unmarried
guy in here—and some of the married ones—into your
bed or anywhere else you wanted them."

"That's kind of you." The man had managed to read
and erase her doubts in one sentence. She wanted to kiss
him in gratitude.

"It's all true."

How could she pass up a man like this? A chance like
this? She wasn't a coward or a quitter. She was going
for it, dammit.

"Actually, AJ, I think I am interested. I would like
to, um, go to, uh, bed with you. I think." Her face
flamed.

"You sound like you just accepted a dangerous assignment." His eyes twinkled at her, inviting her to
loosen up. "As always, Mr. Phelps, should you or any
of your IM Force be caught or killed, the Secretary will
disavow any knowledge of your actions."

She laughed. "Like I said, I haven't dated in a while.

And meeting a man like this and…pursuing something so fast…well…it's just…"

"I'm out of practice, too, if that makes you feel better."

Out of practice? She'd never done it. But she wasn't about to admit that. At least not right off the bat. "So, good then. We're together on this." She bit her lip. "So I guess now we should go up to your room?"

AJ covered both her hands with his, his hot palms suffusing her with warmth, and met her gaze. "Let's finish our drinks, Beth, and talk a little more, then see what we feel like."

"But you think we'll feel like going upstairs?" She liked to have a plan.

He considered her question in mock seriousness. "Maybe we'd better be certain. So we don't waste our time."

He moved out of his seat and came to sit beside her on the banquette. He took her face in his palms and kissed her. She was stunned. Motionless with the thrill of it. His lips were gentle and he took his time, touching the seam of her lips with the tip of his tongue in a friendly coax. *I'm here with more if you want.*

She moved her tongue to barely touch his, relishing the taste and softness. Her sex began a steady pulse that made her want to squirm. A shudder passed through her body and she closed her eyes. This man understood the pleasures of a good kiss.

AJ slid his fingers into the hair at the sides of her head and turned her face at a different angle. She breathed in his cologne—something elegant that seemed natural on him.

After a delicious minute of sliding lips, touching tongues and exchanging hot breath, AJ released her.

"Well?" he asked. "Think we're going to want to go up-stairs later?"

She slowly opened her eyes. Was he kidding? She was melting like a frozen margarita on a tongue. "Uh-huh," she managed.

"Maybe we should be positive," he said and leaned in for another kiss. There was more suction this time. His lips tugged and pulled at hers, massaging them with a hypnotic, back-and-forth rhythm. He moved with care, as if he sensed her skittishness, but his breath rasped in her ears, so she knew he was as aroused as she was.

Her entire body seemed to warm and loosen, as if she'd been frozen solid and was now thawing out all over this man, dripping onto the banquette and the floor beneath them.

She moved closer, wanting to crawl into his lap, her mind hazy, but she bumped the table. The rattle of glasses reminded her that they were in a crowded bar, making a spectacle of themselves. She broke off the kiss and looked into his blue eyes, which gleamed with heat. "Let's go upstairs," she said in a rush of lust.

But he might assume too much. "For privacy, I mean. So we can do this some more." Maybe they'd go fur-ther, maybe they wouldn't. All she knew was that here was her column, her man, her moment. Em's moment.

AJ climbed out of the booth and gave her his hand to help her slide out. She wobbled a little—a combina-tion of arousal and high heels—and he pulled her tight against his body. "You okay? You're not acting faint just to make me feel manly, are you? Because of that tiki drink remark?"

"It's just the heels," she said, not wanting to let on how weak-kneed he'd made her. She felt safe with him.

She trusted her instincts on that, though her self-defense training gave her extra confidence if those instincts proved off-kilter.

She knew her only danger was from her own nerves. Sara did this kind of thing all the time. So could Em.

They walked across the lobby and in seconds were riding the elevator to his room. Hotel bars were the perfect place to meet men if you tended to jitter, she realized. Just say the word and you were in their room. No time for second thoughts.

They swooshed upward, alone in the elevator, AJ's eyes hot on her body. His hands slid up and down her sides, bunching up her dress, exposing her thigh to the air. Everywhere he touched went liquid with heat. Out of the elevator, she Jell-O-walked her way to his room, grateful for his arm around her waist keeping her upright.

He key-carded the door and guided her inside. The room was impersonally elegant. Cherry wood faux antiques and naturalist watercolors surrounded the centerpiece of the room—a huge, pillow-top sleigh bed, where they would soon be engaged in, gulp, intimacy. No, sex. *Beth* got intimate. Em had sex.

AJ led her to the bed in question, where she sat, nervously running her fingers across its quilted expanse. He went to turn on the stand-up lamp, then flung open the night blind and sheers to reveal a sparkling view of the city. He tossed off his jacket, then returned to help her to her feet and into his arms, pleasurable anticipation on his face.

Her courage failed her for a second. What if he expected her to be good? Her purse had gotten trapped between their chests, and that reminded her of what it held. "I, um, have protection. Three kinds, depending on your preference—ultrathin, ribbed or flavored."

His eyes twinkled. "Let's make that lady's choice."

"Oh. Right. Okay." She'd decided to do this in a haze of lust, but now she'd have to face the awkward newness, the fact they were strangers. All she knew was that he kissed well.

"I'm glad you're prepared," AJ said, clearly trying to calm her. "The use-by date is long expired on whatever I have in my toiletry kit." He studied her face. "It's just us here, Beth. We can stop anytime. You're in charge."

"Right. Good," she said, releasing a shuddery breath. "I have to use the bathroom."

Mostly, she needed to calm down, figure out how she'd gone from barely being able to listen to Sara describe an orgasm to waltzing into a stranger's hotel room ready to leap into the sack with him.

Had her column made her bold? Or was it something about AJ? Or was Em just ready to step out? Em might be ready, but the woman who'd just ducked into the hotel bathroom was Beth all the way.

3

You CAN DO THIS, Beth told herself, sitting on the edge of the bathtub. *You have to, if you want to keep your column.* The situation couldn't be more ideal, really. AJ was the perfect guy for her first adventure in the wild world of easy sex—confident and comfortable with himself, he'd sensed her uncertainty and knew how to reassure her. Plus, he was from out of town, so he wouldn't ever see the magazine and figure out he was in it. She would disguise him, of course, but some guys got funny about even anonymous exposure, judging from Rick's reaction.

AJ was perfect. She was the problem. She just had to turn herself into Em for the next couple of hours. To gear up, she took her notepad from her purse and jotted a few Em-worthy observations.

Broad shoulders...smile as spicy as a crantini...fresh pickup line: Is this your pen? What did he say about the second line being more important than the first? Note: Hotel bars ease transition to intimacy. Just an elevator ride to ecstasy...

Except, now here she was, hiding in the bathroom, shivering on the edge of the bathtub.

She took a deep, cleansing breath and blew it out slowly. *It's just us here, Beth. You're in charge.* Maybe they would just make out for a while and call it a night, and she could write about hot first kisses.

She had to get moving. She'd been in here long enough to shower and put on makeup. Or at least undress. Lord. What if he thought she was taking off her clothes? Would he be naked when she got out?

She had the urge to call Sara for advice, but stopped herself. In the mirror, she looked into the pale face and shiny eyes of a nervous woman. How had she gotten into this mess?

"Beth…you okay?" AJ called to her from outside the door.

That was how. AJ's voice made her melt, despite her fears. "F-fine," she said. *You can do this. Be the sensualist you truly are.* She slid her purse strap over her shoulder, took a determined breath, faked a smile and opened the door.

AJ still had his clothes on, thank God, though he'd slipped off his shoes and socks. Jeez, he even had sexy feet. He peeled her purse strap off her shoulder and tossed her bag onto a nearby chair so he could pull her into his arms. His warmth worked through her nervous chill like a hot bath.

"I guess I'm a little jumpy," she said.

"It's all right," he said. "You seem to be pushing yourself into this. We can go slow. Or just kiss. Whatever you want. No pressure." He kissed her again, as slowly as he'd said, and she got that melting margarita feeling again.

He was so easy to be with. If she forgot herself for a second, she could just move into this moment and really enjoy it. She spread her fingers against his back, loving how broad and sturdy he seemed. Their tongues tangled, danced, traded places, explored, rocking with the same rhythm as before. This was familiar. This worked. If they stuck with this she'd be just fine.

Then he reached down and cupped her bottom with both hands, hugging her against his hardness, sending shock waves throughout her lower body. Okay, maybe they should try more than kissing.

He broke away from her mouth, still holding her snugly against him. "Are you okay?" he asked, his gaze hazy with arousal.

"Okay? Oh, yeah," she said. She was more than okay. She loved feeling his need against her stomach. With Blaine, an erection had meant, *I'm ready*. With AJ, it said, *Look what you do to me*.

He lowered his mouth to hers again, his tongue more insistent this time. She opened wider, the way she wanted to open her body to him. He tasted of smoky liquor and sweet flesh, and smelled of his elegant cologne. She wondered how his skin would feel, how his chest would look. And down there…how would that be?

Kissing like this, holding AJ and being held by him, made the impersonal room seem intimate. She felt safe and desirable and right. Even better, the embrace seemed to erase the bad memories of Blaine, like an Etch A Sketch shaken clear of a bad drawing.

She would make sure her column captured this—the magic of a first time with the right man.

AJ's hands slid upward from her butt, lifting her dress, exposing her thighs all the way to the tops of the lacy bands of the thigh-high nylons she'd worn. Then he moved his hands to the front of her dress. The bottom half dropped down, warm against her thighs, just as he cupped her breasts through her bodice.

Hot lust shot through her so swiftly she had to catch her breath. She broke off the kiss.

"Too fast?" he asked, searching her face as if she

were some fragile creature who might run, or faint. She didn't want to be fragile. She wanted to be bold.

"No. You're perfect. Keep it up. Please."

He smiled, then brushed her nipples softly. They tightened in response, sending electricity through her. She had to touch him, too, she realized, to give him the kind of pleasure he was giving her. As best she could, she grasped him through his pants.

He felt thick and long, and she had a fleeting thought that he would be too much for her. But he would be careful, she knew already because of how sensitive he seemed to be to her reactions. He would take it slow, make sure she was comfortable.

Then he surprised her by sliding his hand down her body and putting one finger gently against her cleft. He was right on target, and it took her breath away. Her parts seemed to loosen and swell, ache and dissolve, all at the same time. Her legs trembled and she thought she might swoon like some Victorian virgin in whalebone. "Let's get…in…bed," she managed to say.

If only they could whisk themselves there and clothes would disappear without any jiggling or tangling or hip-hopping out of panties.

AJ stopped touching her and held her gaze. "You sure?"

She nodded. "Just close your eyes while I change." She was too modest to strip with him watching her.

"Don't ever change," he joked, but he closed his eyes.

That gave her a second to look at his face again— the strong brows and cheekbones, deep tan, the golden bristle emerging from his skin, his lush mouth with its knowing smile. Wow. And he was about to make love to her.

"No peeking now," she said.

"You're beautiful, Beth."

"Humor me," she said, and wobbled over to turn off the lamp, then punch off the entry light. She would definitely skip this part in her column—this dashing around, ripping off clothes while he hid his eyes, like some demented game of hide-and-seek.

She shook off her shoes, unzipped her dress and shoved it down, rolling her panties and the tops of her hose down along with the dress. Last, she unclipped her bra and took it off.

"Ready or not?" he teased.

"Not." She shot a glance at him, crossing her arms over her naked breasts. His eyes remained closed, though he was grinning.

Wrapping her underthings into her dress, Beth placed the bundle neatly on her purse, her shoes beneath the chair, just as she did for a gyno exam, then started for the bed. Halfway there, she remembered the condoms in her purse. *Note to self: Before things get too hot, extract condoms from purse and discreetly place on nightstand.*

Beth rushed back for the squares of protection, deposited them on the nightstand, then whipped back the bedspread and slid between the sheets, pulling them up to her chin. The pillowtop was deeply soft and she seemed to sink for miles into its luxuriance. She turned the bedside lamp to the lowest glow—just enough light for AJ to see the condoms, but not enough to reveal too many of her physical flaws. Then she rested her arms along her body, over the sheet. "Now you can look."

AJ opened his eyes. "But I missed the good part." He walked to the bed, looking at her. He seemed to see right through the thick-ply fabric to where she trembled, her nipples taut, her sex tight.

"There are plenty of other good parts."

"Sure, but a chance to see you naked—a little at a time—now that's not to be missed." Still watching her, he lifted his shirt over his head, then tossed it over the chair, where it wafted over her dress like a caress.

He opened his belt, undid his zipper and slid off his pants and boxers with quick grace. His arousal looked natural against his abdomen, which was flat with light muscle. His thighs bulged from what must be regular exercise, and his chest bore a feathering of golden hair.

She sighed and he slid under the sheets and enveloped her in his arms, radiating heat like a human furnace. Maybe Sara had a point about warmth. She spread her fingers against his back, reveling in the ripple of muscle, the pressure of his chest against her breasts, his penis and belly against her stomach, his thighs against hers.

"You feel so good," he said, sliding his lips down her neck. He nipped, then sucked at a spot below her ear. "I want to look at you," he said, and before she could object, he'd pushed the sheet down to her waist.

Feeling exposed, even in the dim light, she had the impulse to snatch the covers up to her chin, except AJ's worshipful expression quelled that urge. He ran his hand over her breast, looking at it in wonder, like a geographer mapping beloved terrain, relishing each millimeter he skimmed and studied. "I wanted to touch you the minute I saw you in the bar."

"You did?" she said.

"Oh, yeah." He pushed the sheet farther down, making it rustle, exposing her pubic area and thighs to the brush of cool air, then his warm fingers. She tightened her tummy, to reduce the slight pooch, but he cupped it with affection. "Your body is amazing." No man had looked at her with such frank appreciation, as if her flaws were part of her charm.

He traced the edge of her ear with his tongue while his fingers brushed lightly back and forth across her stomach, then breezed over her pubic hair.

"Oh, oh, wow," she said, loving his teasing tongue, the surprise and grace of his skimming fingers. Her nerve endings were on fire in places that had never been ignited before. Was it possible to melt any more? Somehow she seemed to manage it. Waves of tingles washed down her arms and legs and pooled in that spot between her legs, which grew hotter, tighter and more hungry every second.

Pushed by need, she reached for AJ and curled her fingers around his shaft—velvet on the outside, sturdy underneath. She slid her hand up, stalling at his crown. He closed his eyes and pushed into her grip.

They would get serious now, and here was where her performance got iffy. "I should warn you that sometimes, when I'm nervous, I can't…get *there*, you know…so don't wait for me. Just go for it. It'll still be great for me."

"This isn't a race, Beth," he said, his eyes twinkling.

"I know, but I just don't want you to be disappointed."

"Don't worry. I'm enjoying every second of this. How about you?" He slid his finger into her cleft and gently pressed the spot above her clitoris, sending a wave of heat surging through her. "Are you disappointed?"

"N-n-no," she managed.

"Doesn't seem like it. You're wet and swollen," he said, exploring her gently, "and…so soft…. Are you nervous?"

"Uh-uh," she said, so swept away by his touch, she sounded like a slack-jawed idiot. "Sometimes, I just get…oh, never mind…." She didn't care about past history, about explaining herself, about anything but what his finger was doing to her flesh.

AJ gave a slow smile. While still stroking her sex, he kissed her neck with gentle suction. He kissed his way down to the swell of her breast and then took her nipple into his mouth.

She arched into the electric tug, feeling as if her very being was being sucked into his mouth. "Oh, oh, oh," she said. Instinctively, she opened her legs wider and AJ took the hint, and moved his finger more rhythmically over and alongside the flesh that covered her clitoris—now a tight knot of need.

She wanted to reach for his penis, connect with his body, too, but she was riveted by the energy pulsing through her.

AJ released her breast and slowly shifted his body downward until his hands were on her hips and, oh, dear heaven, his mouth was *there*. Right *there*.

"Oh, my…oh, oh, oh." What was she saying? And did she even care?

He huffed hot breath onto her, starting up bottle rockets and sparklers in her most sensitive flesh. His tongue reached her clitoris, now swollen enough to welcome direct contact. He licked gently, then sucked and teased. She rocked against his mouth, wantonly pushing at his tongue, greedy for more, not quite sure where she was, feeling lifted off the bed, even while his hands held her bottom securely in place.

He seemed to enjoy what he was doing. No way was he going through the motions because he thought it was what she wanted. He kissed and sucked and stroked as if he were in her head, understanding exactly what she needed, and wanting above all else to give it to her.

She thought she should stop him, do something for him, but she was pinned in place by his mouth, held in his hot hands, and she felt treasured and lusted after—pure and wanton at the same time.

The feeling grew stronger and more irresistible—a wave she had no choice but to ride. She called out his name and other words, possibly in a foreign language, and AJ intensified his movements.

With no effort or anxiety or doubt, her climax tightened like a fist clenching, natural and fierce and unstoppable, and punched her through to glorious release.

She bucked up against his mouth and cried out loudly—too loudly for a hotel room, but she was beyond control. The waves rolled and rolled through her, so that she felt like one of those multi-orgasmic women she'd read about. Except this was just one great, endless release.

AJ held her tight, his tongue not moving, just resting on her, until she quivered to a stop. Then he slid slowly up her body, kissing her as he rose.

"That was amazing," she gasped, trying to blink away the gray her vision had faded to, trying to catch her breath. "That was…incredible… That was…"

"Fun," he said, reaching her face. "And you taste great." His hair was tousled, but he looked so handsome and so pleased with himself. "I thought you said you had trouble getting *there*."

"I do…when I'm nervous. But, wow, for a while there I didn't know my own name."

"You got mine right, I was pleased to hear."

"After what you just did, I'd better."

"I had a good time, too." He chuckled lightly and kissed her. She tasted herself on his lips—clean and muskily female. His eyes shone with unquenched arousal. She had to fix that—do something as wonderful as what he'd just done for her—but she wasn't great at oral sex. At least, she didn't think she was great at it. She'd never gotten any real feedback.

What could she do that she'd do well? She'd read that men liked the woman to be on top. She could do that. She rolled over and pushed AJ onto his back, straddling him. "Your turn," she said.

"Oh, if you insist," he said with mock reluctance.

She reached across him to the nightstand for a condom packet, but when she tried to tear it, it slipped out of her fingers and to the mattress.

"Allow me." AJ grabbed it, opened it and rolled it onto himself in one smooth motion. She took over when he'd finished, rubbing his latex-encased erection with more pressure to make up for the barrier, though this was a very transparent condom. "Ultrathin for maximum sensitivity," she breathed.

"I love it when you talk dirty," he teased, lying back, relaxing into her touch.

"I hope you'll love this even more." She moved so his tip pushed against her opening. She was so wet that he immediately slid into her, thick and long, and the sudden fullness made her gasp.

"Oh, yeah," he said. "I love this even more." He reached deep, providing a sweet ache that made her throw back her head with the pleasure of it. That pressed her clitoris against his shaft. So, so good. This had to be instinctual behavior.

AJ dug his fingers into her hips. "You're good."

She raised and lowered herself experimentally. She

felt awkward, jiggling above him like that, until AJ released her hips and grasped her breasts with both big hands.

She arched into his palms, stretching her breasts until the skin was taut and her nipples ached for action.

Which AJ gave her, pinching the tips with just enough pressure to send arousal beelining along her nerves, straight to her core.

She began to ride him, slowly at first, sliding against his shaft, dropping the weight of her breasts into his palms.

"Beth," he said, thrusting upward, reaching deeper.

She went faster, feeling his urgency, wanting to quench his need. She looked into his eyes, which told her with every flicker and flash of light that she was pleasing him.

He was close, she could tell, and she matched the force of his upward thrusts with her downward pushes. Then he stilled for a second and, looking into her eyes, placed the pad of his thumb directly on her clitoris. She'd been so intent on pleasing him, she'd forgotten about her own climax, which had been moving happily closer all along. This just-right pressure brought her instantly to the brink. Her climax surged and she rocked mindlessly on him, pivots and circles and trembling jerks.

When she was nearly finished, he exploded inside her.

She collapsed onto his chest, panting, sweat making their bodies slide and squeak, but the sound didn't embarrass her.

"That was great," he said, his voice rumbling against her ear.

She rose up and looked down at him. "I know," she

said, feeling positively triumphant. She'd just had two orgasms in the space of a few minutes with a man she'd barely met. Talk about Em on the town.

"Got any more things you're not good at?" he said.

"Oh, lots," she said, gratified that this incredibly hot man seemed to think she was good in bed.

"Can't wait for you to show me," he said. "If you don't kill me first."

She rested her cheek on his chest and he held her snugly on him. They rested like that for a few silent moments, hearts beating as one, and then he slowly pulled out and headed to the bathroom.

She lay on her side, propped on an elbow, waiting for him, completely thrilled. She was so glad she'd been bold enough to take a chance. Not only did she have tons of material for her column—practically writing itself in her mind—but her sexual self-confidence had gotten a major boost.

AJ slid between the sheets again and she opened her arms to him, twined her legs with his. She wanted to thank him somehow. "That was really special. I have to tell you that I've never even slept with a man on the first date before, let alone picked one up in a bar."

"You're kidding!" he said, in mock amazement.

"Was it that obvious?"

"You did lock yourself in the bathroom, babble about condom selection and issue a disclaimer about how I should forget about your climax and go for mine."

"That tipped you off, huh?"

He chuckled softly, tucked her hair behind her ear, then stroked her cheek with the backs of his fingers. "You're a very sexual woman, Beth. If some man made you feel differently, he was an idiot."

Or not as skilled as AJ. Sara was right about one

thing—*okay* and *sex* shouldn't be in the same language, let alone sentence.

"Though I wouldn't brag about picking me up," he said with a wink. "Technically, I picked you up."

"No, sir," she said in mock outrage. "I invited you to my table. All you picked up was a pen."

"But I insisted," he said, pushing her onto her back on the pillowy mattress and pinning her by the wrists, which made her feel very sexy.

"So, am I threatening your masculinity?" she teased.

"Nope. You make me glad I have it." He kissed her softly, then released her wrists.

"I'm serious, though," she said. "I was nervous and you made it so easy. Like I said, I've been out of circulation…and you helped me get my feet wet."

"Your feet?" he asked, sliding his hand to where she was still slippery. "I'd say something way more fun than your feet got wet."

"Oh, yeah. Very true." Wow. She'd never felt like this before—in or out of circulation. The three men she'd slept with hadn't been much interested in sex, now that she thought about it. Dan, in college, had been a virgin, too, she'd been sure. She'd gotten a book to help them, but he'd been embarrassed to admit his inexperience, so sex was always fumbly.

Mark had been a philosophy professor—very cerebral—and sex had been a low priority. And then there was Blaine. Blaine had been haphazard about sex, sometimes rushed and often preoccupied. Had she subconsciously chosen men who didn't enjoy sex? Or maybe she hadn't rocked their worlds. She could have made more of an effort, she guessed, but the awkwardness of the topic had intimidated her.

What a mistake, she realized now. There was way

more to sex than she'd thought. And what a perfect time to find out—when she had a column where she could share all her insights. She had the tiniest impulse to slip into the bathroom and take notes, but then AJ touched her and her thoughts flew away like dandelion fluff.

Her notes could wait until AJ was finished with her. And she was finished with him. Who knew how long that would take?

A FEW HOURS LATER, Beth rested her cheek on AJ's sweat-damp chest and listened to his heart thud steadily against her ear. He was dozing now. He'd earned a rest, having given her another amazing series of orgasms. Even in sleep, he held her close. She breathed in his wonderful smell and sampled his salty skin with her tongue. Mmm.

She would love to spend the night here, tangled up in sheets and man, but she didn't dare. She had to let her dogs out to pee, and she itched to start her column. Plus, she didn't want to spoil the moment with talk. AJ might have annoying opinions and she wanted to preserve the magic at all costs. For her column. And for herself.

Moving carefully so she wouldn't wake him, Beth untangled her limbs from AJ's, rolled over and slid out of the bed.

"Don't go." His sleep-fogged voice floated to her in the dark.

"I have to," she said, grinning madly at the desire she heard beneath his slurred words.

"I'll be back in two weeks," he muttered so faintly he might have been talking in his sleep.

She grabbed her clothes bundle and ducked into the

bathroom to dress. Her reflection in the mirror stopped her. Her face was soft, her lips swollen and her eyes gleamed. *Freshly laid.* That was how she looked. She'd had no idea sex could be so easy and so fun.

Dressed, she tiptoed out of the bathroom, then stood watching AJ sleep for a moment. He was a big man, a bundle of male power curved under the sheets, his muscular arm and chest slightly revealed, dark against the white sheets in the dim room. He didn't want her to leave.

For a moment, she was tempted to crawl back in and go for more. Maybe she'd turn out to be good at oral sex, too.

No. She had to go. Her pets and her column were waiting.

I'll be back in two weeks, he'd said. That was a lovely thought. She smiled to herself as she went to the desk and wrote, "Call me when you're back in town," on the hotel notepad. She left her number and signed it simply "Beth." Easy-breezy.

Then she left, walking as silently as she could down the hall, in deference to the hotel's sleeping guests. She was leaving a man's room in the middle of the night like the "Sex on the Town" columnist would do, casually scribbling her number for next time. She tossed her hair, loose now, and waltzed to the elevator. In the lobby, she gave the sleepy desk clerk a jaunty wave, then bounded out to the late spring night.

The barest hint of dawn lightened the horizon, she noticed as she drove. She liked how few cars there were on the streets. She felt part of the secret society of middle-of-the-night lovers. Her skin felt so silky, her muscles were tired and she could still smell AJ's cologne on her skin, hear his voice in her ear telling her how good she felt and sounded and tasted.

At home, she took her guys out back to do their business, then went straight to her computer. Four in the morning or not, she was wide awake, alive with sense memory. She would write about the sex she'd just had with the same confident verve she used in her entertainment column—leaving out the bathroom jitters and her orgasm disclaimer, of course. Otherwise, she'd be Em all the way.

Her animals sensed her excitement and jostled for position around her in her office. Ditzy curled up on her lap to sleep and Beth began to type.

Along with hot new drinks, your "Sex On the Town" reporter decided to sample a hot new man. I scoped out a popular watering hole known for its trendy drinks—two birds with one bar, after all—for likely bed buddies. My first choice was nursing a heartbreak along with his microbrew. (Check out the mouthwatering Raspberry Wheat Cream from Copper Springs Brewery, by the way.) After a quick pep talk, I sent him back to make nice with the girl he'd gone emotionally AWOL on, along with an appropriate gift idea. Your ever-helpful Em.

Then I set my sights on Mr. Broad Shoulders, Lazy Grin, whom I'd spied as I was returning from the ladies' room. Note: Before deciding your perch in a bar, girls, take a trip to the powder room to assess the best seats for ogling the playmate buffet.

Oh, and note to fellow fashionistas: Hello Kitty barrettes can be man-magnets.

After exchanging a few conversational bon mots with Mr. Broad Shoulders, hereafter to be known as Mr. Perfect Timing, the steam rose and so did we—up the elevator to his room.

Note to the nervous: Hotel bars ease the transition to intimacy. One quick lift and you're bedbound....

The words flew and soon Beth was reading over her first draft, smiling so broadly it hurt. She'd described first-time sex with a sensual man in luscious detail, without being explicit, and ended with her meditative drive home enjoying the intimacy of empty streets in the pre-dawn light.

She had to know what Will thought of this right away, so she slapped the column into an e-mail and shot it through cyberspace. By the time she got to the *Phoenix Rising* office at ten, Will would be ready to sing her praises.

Her lavender-sprayed sheets welcomed her, but she wished they didn't carry a scent, so she could keep smelling AJ. Maybe he would call before he left town, just to say goodbye. She couldn't stop thinking about how he'd looked at her with such appreciation, as if her body, with all its flaws and flab, was gorgeous, as if his whole purpose was to make her feel good.

He was a special man. Or maybe he was just the first of a breed she'd be on the lookout for from now on. Beth had fought the new column tooth and nibbled nail, but she realized now that it was a gift to herself and, she hoped, to her readers.

4

RAFE WOKE AND STRETCHED across the spongy hotel bed, reveling in the open space. Except something was missing. Beth. He usually liked sleeping alone, not having to worry about disturbing a woman when he rolled around or punched the pillows. But this morning he missed Beth.

Sure, he'd been celibate for a while, and hunger made the best sauce, but something about Beth's wide-eyed pleasure and eager interest had superheated the experience. She'd challenged herself into circulation, evidently—made a bet or accepted a dare from her friend—and he'd been in the right place at the right time to enjoy her win.

The sex had been remarkable. She'd been so focused on every nuance, every movement, as if it were completely new to her. *Does this feel good? Do you do this with other women? Why like this and not this?* Almost like she was taking notes. She was a technical writer, so of course she'd be detail-oriented. That made him smile.

He wasn't sure why he'd been ducking sex lately. It was a fine pastime. But the pleasure hadn't seemed worth the hassle for the last year or so—roughly coinciding with his restlessness at work.

When he had gotten involved, it was never serious.

He made certain of that. His parents' marriage had failed, largely due to his father's lack of emotional staying power—a lack Rafe believed he shared. So he kept things light with women.

Being a journalist led to a certain dispassion—a neutrality that kept him from really putting his weight down in one place or with one person. Forever was a hell of a long time.

Meeting Beth had been a splash of ice water in the face—fresh and bracing and impossible to ignore—reminding him that not only had he spent too much time alone, but he hadn't been paying much attention to the little joys of life.

Beth had reacted to sex with the wonder of a child getting her first taste of ice cream, and that was damned erotic. She was sweet and smart and surprisingly innocent. An uncertain sex goddess.

But a hell of a quick learner.

He'd like more, but she was gone. Hell, he didn't even know her last name. Probably just as well. For all of her one-night-stand enthusiasm, she struck him as a woman who cared a lot about everything. So if last night had been enough for her, that was okay by him.

He was glad he hadn't told her he'd overheard her phone conversation. The last thing she'd want in her sexual triumph was to think that he'd felt sorry for her in her little-kitty hair thing and shaky heels.

Hungry, he climbed out of bed to locate the room-service menu. He would eat before he headed across the street to the *Phoenix Rising* office.

He pressed the digits for room service, then noticed words on the pad next to the phone. *Call me when you're back in town.* Beth had written him a note. Had he told her he'd be back?

He studied the number. Different area code from the office. How far away did she live? Maybe he'd pop over there before his flight this evening. Nah. Too eager. Out of character for him. And she might read too much into it.

He remembered her fingers on him, how smooth her skin had been, her cries at climax. He loved how her breasts had felt in his hands—soft, but solid. Like the woman. Her green eyes held depth, sensitivity and some pain. Someone she'd been with had made her doubt herself sexually. He hoped he'd helped with that at least.

Truth was, he was better off not calling her. Keep it simple. Still, he tucked the note into his wallet.

Just in case.

THE RECEPTIONIST AT *Phoenix Rising*, Heather, took her sweet time letting Will know that Rafe had arrived, making small talk and flirting with him. She was pretty and funny, with a great mouth and a way with quips— the kind of woman he used to be happy to sleep with— but the possibility made him feel tired. Maybe that was because of last night with Beth.

He gave up on getting Heather to call into Will's office and headed there on his own. They were to go over the new organizational chart and editorial calendar before he met with the entertainment writer to take her column away from her—his last unpleasant task before heading home.

He and Will concluded their business quickly and exchanged small talk until all that remained was meeting with the columnist. Will turned back to his computer and Rafe opened E.M. Samuels's employment folder to her résumé, looking for something to comment on when they began talking.

"Well, I'll be damned," Will said, spinning away from his screen to face Rafe, who looked up from the paper. "You've got to read this." A sheet of paper hummed off the printer and Will handed it to Rafe. "It's Em's new column."

It was entitled "Sex on the Town: Hot New Drinks and Hot New Men." Rafe read a few lines of the breezy text, then phrases began to jump up and smack him in the face. *Tutti-Frutti Martooti…our waitress's pen…the steam rose and so did we—up the elevator to his room.*

Omigod. The uncertain sex goddess he'd made love to last night was none other than E.M. Samuels herself. He looked at the heading of the résumé staring up at him from the folder—Elizabeth Mary Samuels. And *Beth* was a nickname for *Elizabeth*. He recognized her area code as the same one she'd written on the note he'd folded into his wallet. Beth was Em Samuels.

"You okay?" Will asked.

"Sure. Just checking." He looked at the résumé. Technical writing was listed as a current job. So, she hadn't lied when she'd told him what she did, but she sure hadn't told him the whole story. Ruefully, he remembered her words: *Mind if I ask you a few questions? I've been out of circulation for a while.* Lord. The whole time they'd been in bed together, she'd been working on her column.

"So, what do you think?" Will said, calling him back to the present moment. "I think she's got what you want."

No kidding. "She has potential," he managed to say.

"I had no idea she had this in her," Will mused. "She's pretty shy and reserved—the cat-lady type, except she has a bunch of dogs, too."

A cat lady with a sex-kitten side, Rafe knew. While

Will raved about the column, the reality of what he'd done thundered through him. He'd slept with one of his writers. One he was about to fire…well, redeploy. He couldn't possibly have known what she looked like— no picture ran with her column—and she didn't know him.

He'd introduced himself to her as AJ, as his friends knew him, though he went by Rafe at work—even thought of himself as Rafe—and told her he was a "transition expert." He hated talking about *Man's Man* and magazine takeovers, so he tended to skim over the work details. And they hadn't exchanged last names.

His mind raced. She'd be here any minute. They didn't have an appointment, so she didn't know she'd be meeting with him. Will hadn't wanted to alarm her.

Would she believe he hadn't known who she was? The fact that he'd avoided talking about work probably made him seem elusive. Would she think he'd deliberately tricked her? To get her into bed?

"Rafe? You okay?"

"Sure. I'm just considering the piece." He looked down at the paper, the words blurring.

"How about giving her a chance to keep the column?" Will said.

"Possible. Let me make a quick call." He flipped open his cell phone and headed out the door, as if for privacy, needing time to think.

From the hall, he could hear the husky alto that had called his name in ecstasy just a few hours ago. Beth stood at the front desk talking to Heather. He didn't want to run into her until he'd decided what to say, so he headed for the back fire exit and took the stairs down sixteen floors.

He called up to Will from his rental car, explained that he'd been called away and asked him to forward

Em's column to him at *Man's Man*, where he'd consider letting her keep it.

The column was good, so that much wasn't a lie. But he would avoid meeting the woman—e-mail her his decision. She rarely came into the magazine, according to Will, and Rafe would only be back in Phoenix once or twice more.

Any explanation would invite doubt. She could accuse him of sexual harassment or God knows what. If it got out to others at *Phoenix Rising*, it would intensify the friction between him and the staff and destroy whatever respect they had for him.

Beth struck him as a sensible woman, though. Maybe he could tell her. It was an honest mistake. He'd overheard her phone call about wanting to have sex and had been intrigued.

Yeah, right. His being from *Man's Man* would be all too coincidental for anyone with a dab of skepticism in her soul. Even Beth, sweet and innocent as she seemed, wouldn't buy that.

On the plane, he read her column more carefully.

Nothing quite caps a perfect evening like a man who knows his way around the female body. Note to men: Taking your time reaps intimate rewards and swooning bedmates.

He looked up, embarrassed to be reading about himself in the sack. He was like a voyeur to his own performance. He cleared his throat, shifted his position and kept reading.

A man who cups a jiggly abdomen as though it's beautiful, who kisses you as if he'd love nothing

better than to lock lips all night, well, that's better than the finest wine to this "On the Town"
girl.

Looking at it from an objective perspective, she'd
done a good job of capturing the essence of their night,
though she'd left out her nervousness, the bathroom
panic and the "don't look" dash to undress. Her writing persona—Em—was far more confident than Beth.

The fact that she'd hidden her intentions for the evening made him feel a little less guilty about misleading
her.

On the other hand, what was she supposed to say?
*Oh, um, AJ, just so you know, I'll be writing about this
for a magazine with a circulation of fifteen thousand.*

He smiled. Being in the column didn't bother him.
He was anonymous—she'd called him *Mr. Perfect Timing*—and everything she'd said had been flattering.

Putting on his executive editor hat, he had to say that
the column bore an enthusiastic freshness that was appealing…and sexy. Phoenix was not as jaded as New
York, L.A. or San Francisco, so maybe her tone fit the
new *Phoenix Rising*. Will was right. She deserved a
chance.

This had been a bold step for her, judging from what
Will had said and her own words: *I've never even slept
with a man on the first date before, let alone picked one
up in a bar.* She'd done it to keep her column, he was
sure, which impressed him even more.

He would send the column around *Man's Man* to be
sure that sleeping with its author hadn't clouded his
judgment, then e-mail her his decision, keeping his true
identity a secret.

He couldn't sleep with her again, though. That was

certain. A case of mistaken identity was one thing, but
deliberately pretending he was someone else—AJ the
transition expert—was another thing entirely. Disappointment coursed through him like the hot wash of
Scotch after a bad day.

TWO DAYS LATER, RAFE read over the e-mail he'd carefully composed.

Dear Ms. Samuels:
Rafe Jarvis here, from Man's Man. *Will forwarded me
your take on the new singles column. You offer a fresh
perspective that we agree* Phoenix *readers will value.
We'd like to assign you three more columns. If we like
what you do and reader response is positive, we'll ex-
tend your assignment into the future.*
   *Let me congratulate you on your willingness to adapt
to the change in the magazine's focus. I admire your determination and your versatility. If you have further
questions, I'm accessible by e-mail.*
Sincerely yours,
Rafe Jarvis

He couldn't resist one last, more personal observation.

*P.S. Like a gifted artist, you have the capacity to give
ordinary things fresh appeal. Thank you for sharing
your vision with* Phoenix Rising *readers. And with me.*

That seemed safe. His own private thank-you for the
privilege of having tasted and touched her and felt her
tremble under his fingertips.
   When he checked his e-mail an hour later and saw

Samuels in the "From" header, he felt a shot below the waist. He opened the message.

Mr. Jarvis:
I'm so glad you enjoyed my column. And, yes, I feel like I captured an authentic experience. It was a challenge, but I had willing help from Mr. Perfect Timing, as you could probably tell. I only hope I can continue to create a column that informs, warms and intrigues my readers, who, I should add, were quite loyal to my entertainment column. I hope to effectively meld the two elements—entertainment and intimacy—in a satisfying message each month. Thank you for affording me this opportunity. I won't let you down.
Best,
Em Samuels
P.S. And may I say, your personal observation means a great deal to me. The male perspective is invaluable in my work.

He smiled at her dig about how much readers valued her old column. She was a pro, for sure. What would she say if she knew she was writing to Mr. Perfect Timing himself?

Before he stopped to think, he found himself writing back.

Em:
Glad to assist you. If I can be a resource—offer the male perspective, as you said, for other columns—I'd be more than happy to do so. If there's something we know about at Man's Man, *it's the male perspective.*

He'd helped her with her first column, why not the

next? That was something her editor might do. As a professional courtesy. Not just because he happened to
know how great she was in bed. Lord. He was an idiot.

BETH COULD NOT BELIEVE how warmly the hatchet man
from *Man's Man* had reacted to her column. In his
e-mail, he'd seemed genial, supportive and helpful—
even offered to be a source for her. He didn't seem a bit
like the terse, no-mercy guy the other staffers had described to her. Only Heather had said he had a soft side.
But she had a weakness for tough guys.

    Best of all, he'd given her three columns to prove
herself. She felt up to the challenge—out-and-out hungry for it. Though that might be because AJ would be
back in town in two weeks to give her the material she
needed. She already had the column title in mind: Second Dates: Better And Better? or Let's Call The Whole
Thing Off?

    He might not call…

    After the night they'd shared? No man would pass
up another round of great no-strings sex. He'd even
asked her not to leave that morning. And the one thing
she knew for certain about AJ, beyond how good he was
as a lover, was that he said right out what he wanted.
And he'd wanted her.

    Maybe starting with sex allowed her to really con-
nect with the person, instead of being misled by intellectual appeal or shared interests, as she had with
Blaine. He had cared for her, she'd been sure, but he'd
left anyway.

    It had to be because of the money. Why had he
taken it? He'd never even asked her to invest in his
project—some kind of singles time-share. She might
even have wanted to buy into it—more modestly than

twenty-thousand dollars, of course—but when she'd asked him about it, he'd insisted he wanted to keep her out of his business. Thinking of the mess made her stomach ache. She'd been misled somehow, her instincts thrown off.

But her instincts were right on with AJ, she was certain. They'd had great sex and would have more of it when he returned.

Her thoughts returned to her next column. Besides seeing AJ again, she'd interview women about the significance of date number two and get recommendations on second-date activities—inside the bedroom and out.

And if AJ didn't call, she'd just march into a likely bar—Grins again or T-Three, which she had written up as a top pickup bar—and go for a repeat performance.

Maybe not an exact repeat. She still couldn't see herself taking a stranger to bed after sharing just a Martooti or two. AJ had been special. He'd seemed to know her doubts and set out to help her overcome them. She couldn't expect to get that lucky twice.

"YOU HAVE TO GO OUT WITH ME," Beth said desperately, sitting cross-legged on her couch, two weeks after she'd made her second-date plans.

"You don't want me," Sara answered, lifting a red licorice whip from the silver tray where Beth had created a sun design—the whips like rays around a mound of M&M's. She could turn even the simple candy Sara brought into a visual feast.

"Yes, I do. I have a column due and no man to do it with." AJ had not called after all, which left her chagrined and uncertain about her instincts. Again.

She'd wasted all that research on second-date dynamics and now had just one week to finish her column, which had to be at least as good as the first. Better, really. "Come on. It's dancing at that new place—Zoot Suit—and they've got a swing group from L.A. Bring Rick if you want."

"Come as a couple? Have I taught you nothing, Grasshopper? You can't pick up a guy when you're with a group."

"See? That's why I need you—to steer me right."

"Dance clubs are easy. Just smile, make eye contact and move like you're dying to dance, and men will ask you."

"I can try that…I guess."

"Of course you can. First time out of the chute you got AJ. You're cooking. You were meant to do this."

"Maybe Em is, but not Beth. Beth was meant to stay home and watch Doris Day tease Rock Hudson."

"Bull." Sara bit off both ends of a whip and blew cherry-flavored air through the red tube into Beth's face.

Beth breathed in the sweet scent of childhood pleasures. She'd like to find a candle with that smell. "How could it be as perfect as it was with AJ?"

"So it's lousy. Compare and contrast in your piece."

"I was positive he'd call again."

"Sometimes they don't. Maybe his trip got canceled."

"Maybe he lost my number."

"Maybe he was one of those guys who say what sounds good at the time. They did that to their mothers, too, I'll bet. 'Sure I'll clean out the garage, Mom.' 'No, I would never drink and drive.' They mean it when they say it, but men don't think past the moment. It doesn't dawn on them that we'd actually expect them to call and be hurt when they don't. They figure if their plans changed, so did yours. Don't take it personally."

"I'm not. And nothing says I can't meet another AJ, right?"

"Exactly. You are woman, watch you come."

She groaned at the bad joke. Maybe the next guy wouldn't be as perfect as AJ, but surely he could teach her something she could share with her readers. She'd have to get to know him before she slept with him, though—she was pretty sure she didn't have another one-night stand in her—and that would take time. She had just one week and she'd wasted all that research.

"Maybe I should write about second-date busts. I could interview women about how they handle it when the guy says he'll call, but doesn't."

"You mean like eat licorice whips and raw cookie dough?" Sara tilted the cookie dough tube in her direction.

Beth shuddered at the hunk of uncooked goo. "Next time, I'm in charge of the food and you do drinks. It would have taken ten minutes to bake the cookies."

"Raw is more wicked," Sara said, licking a blob of the tan paste from her index finger.

Wicked was how Sara liked sex, too. And raw. Beth preferred refined and careful, with maybe a little wildness thrown in. Her first date with AJ had involved no preparation beyond condoms in her purse, but she was sure he would have enjoyed all the special touches she'd planned for date two—snacks, wine, candles and music. Now she'd have to save them for the next guy she found. *If* she found him…and liked him enough for a second date.

She gathered a fistful of M&M's, mindful of Ditzy, who had a sweet tooth, and was watching her every move. "What else do women do when a guy flakes on date two? Besides eat cookie batter?"

"The first thing I do is leave a cheerful phone message. 'Had a nice time, give me a buzz when you've got a sec.' E-mail works, too."

"Good suggestions. Any no-nos?"

"The worst is drunken dialing. You cannot take back those messages…unless you learn the guy's message-retrieval code, of course. Then you can risk it."

"You can do that? Get their retrieval codes?"

"Beth, you are such an innocent. The best thing to do about a no-show is to forget Flaky Guy and move on to New Prospect Man. So go to Zoot Suit and meet someone new."

"I guess I'll have to. I want my column. Readers like it. I got this great e-mail." She jumped up and fetched it from her bulletin board to read to Sara.

Dear Em,
Your new column showed me that being shy is not the kiss of death in dating. There are nice men out there. You and Mr. Perfect Timing gave me hope. Thank you, thank you.
Signed,
Like a Virgin in West Phoenix

"There you go," Sara said. "You get out there and get laid for all the virgins in West Phoenix and beyond."

"Oh, stop it." She whapped her friend with a licorice whip, then chewed thoughtfully on it. "So you say just look interested in the music?"

"Yeah. I've got a great skirt you can use. Jagged, wispy hemline, and it swirls great—shows a little thigh, but not enough to make you look like a slut."

"Right. I don't want to look like a slut, I just want to act like one."

"You have the right to get laid just like any man. Just because there's no girl word for *stud*, doesn't mean you can't be one. Just use discretion, taste, good judgment and safe sex."

Before Sara could give her any more pickup tips, the phone rang. Sara, who was closer, picked it up, said hello, then rolled her eyes. "Your brother," she said and extended the handset.

"Hi, Timmy," she said, releasing the last whisper of hope that AJ was calling, back in town after all.

"Just wondered if you'd talked to that client of yours at Thompson Manufacturing about the pet-door opener idea."

"I did." She sighed. "He said you'd need a prototype. And it's a long shot, so don't get your hopes up."

Timmy had great ideas, like this electronically controlled pet-door opener operated by a device on the dog's collar, but he tended to get obsessive and skip the practical steps. Meanwhile, he worked numerous part-time jobs and spent too much time helping friends with their jobs and projects.

"I figured that," he said gloomily. "I need cash to get materials and Julio can't pay me this month."

"Quit working for Julio until he *can* pay you," she said, exasperated. Her brother was a pushover with employers.

"He's turning it around. He's got some parties to cater coming up. It'll be cool, not to worry."

The whoosh of traffic was loud from wherever Tim was calling. A siren blared. "Where are you?" she asked.

"At a pay phone at Sal's Auto Repair. The van, um, kinda broke down, and I'm waiting for them to put in a new alternator."

"I thought you replaced the alternator." In fact, she'd given him the money to do it. She caught Sara's eye roll. Sara thought Timmy was a flake. He was only twenty-two, though, and their father's disappearance had left him with no male role model. She consoled herself with the fact that their grandfather, also a dreamer, had hit it big late in life with his own invention—a lightweight motor element now used in wheelchairs all over the world. One day, she hoped, Timmy would nail something as well.

"Sal said I could nurse the old one longer. James's hedge trimmer broke down, so I loaned him the cash."

"Who's James?"

"You know, my friend who started that yard business? I helped him with that resort job?"

For which he'd gotten paid less than minimum wage. "I remember. Look, you don't have to rescue everybody you know."

"He's paying me back, don't worry."

She blew out an exasperated breath. Now that she was worried about losing her column and the money that went with it, her brother's financial ineptitude bothered her more than ever.

"So, listen, I hate to ask this, but could I, like, borrow your car for a couple hours? I was in the middle of some deliveries for the deli. It's all in sacks. We can get it in the trunk and back seat, I think."

"All right," she said, catching another eye roll from Sara.

"I hate to ask, because you're always bailing me out. I'll replace the gas and pay you back. You know I will."

Since Blaine had left, Timmy had been fierce about promising to repay her for her help. He'd taken Blaine's disappearance hard, too, since the pair had become friends.

"You'll pay me when you can," she said. "Just try to think ahead." She finished the conversation and hung up, then held up a hand before Sara could start criticizing him. "He's trying. He gets in over his head."

"Cut the cord, Beth. That's all I'm saying."

"He's my brother, Sara." She'd help him until he didn't need her help anymore. She just hoped that would be in her lifetime.

5

IN THE END, BETH HELPED Timmy with the deliveries, then drove them both home for the dinner her mother had invited her to. They arrived to find the landlord on a ladder tightening the screws that held the air vent in place. The rich aroma of her mother's famous meatloaf—blended with sausage and layered with sharp cheddar—filled the air.

George climbed down the ladder, brushed his hands on his jeans and shook first Beth's, then Timmy's, hands, though they'd all met before. He was silver-haired and distinguished, wearing fashionable eyeglasses and a designer golf shirt and jeans on his lean frame.

"Beth, honey." Her mother came to her for a hug. Beth breathed in the familiar Chanel No. 5 scent, then smiled at her mother. Young-looking for fifty, her mother was petite with a pretty, heart-shaped face and a decent figure.

"Mr. Nichols insisted on changing the air filter, and he won't let me pay for the AC unit."

"It was a spare and I'm your landlord. And call me George, Helen."

"We agreed to handle all repairs. And certainly we can afford air filters." Her mother's cheeks were pink from blushing, and she ducked George's gaze.

"It was no trouble. I'm glad to help." George smiled at her.

"Meatloaf smells done," Tim said.

"Just about," Beth's mother said.

"Would you like to stay for supper, George?" Beth asked, pleased at the idea.

"Yeah, stay," Timmy added. He, too, encouraged their mother to be social.

"I'm sure George has other plans." Her mother shot her and Tim a look.

George smiled. "As a matter of fact, I—" Something on Helen's face made him change his answer. "Maybe another night. You probably have things to talk over."

"Sure," her mother said. "Another time." Her relief was embarrassingly evident. She grabbed his toolbox and went to open the door for him. "Thanks again for all you did."

George joined her in the doorway, accepting his tools. "Let me know if anything else gives you trouble."

"We'll be fine. Timmy can fix almost anything."

When her mother had closed the door behind the man, Beth said, "What are you doing? He could stay for dinner."

"It's just meatloaf. And he makes me nervous."

"Your meatloaf is the best," Timmy said.

"He likes you," Beth said. "And you rushed him out of here like he had an infectious disease." She noticed a crescent wrench still rested on the table. She grabbed it and rushed out the door, catching George heading back up the walk.

"You beat me to it," he said, taking the wrench from her.

"I don't know what's up with my mother," she said. "She's usually very gracious."

"I make her nervous, I guess," George said.

"Don't give up on her. And thanks for helping out."

"Frankly, if your mother needed a jar lid opened, I'd cross town barefoot to do it. Put in a good word for me, would you?"

"Of course." She liked George. So did her mother, judging from how flushed she'd been. If only she would give the guy a chance to get close to her. Beth fleetingly considered taking a hammer to the water heater or something.

When she reentered the house, her mother was in the kitchen, sliding the sizzling meatloaf out of the oven, flooding the room with warmth and the scent of beef and garlic.

"Give the man a break, Mom. Get to know him."

"When I get home, I want time to myself, not social hour. Mash the potatoes, would you?"

"He's a nice guy." But that didn't help. Her mother was always cautious with men. Since her father had left, of course. He'd gone to California on a sales call—he sold hardware—and had never returned. Or written. Or called. When it was clear he'd abandoned them, her mother had gone to bed for what seemed like forever, but was probably just a few weeks.

Beth, at age seven, took over household duties and most of the care of two-year-old Timmy—feeding them all sandwiches or soup, getting instructions from her sadly quiet mother.

The neighbor lady watched Timmy while Beth was at school, and tried to cheer her mother up. Eventually, her mother eased out of her slump, but there was something fearful in her eyes after that. She'd stayed close to home and leaned on Beth.

Her mother worked part-time as a secretary at the

nearby elementary school and with her salary and a modest trust fund from Beth's grandfather's invention, she managed fine. Beth helped out with emergencies, repairs and extras. Timmy did what he could—when he got paid.

"There's no point in it," her mother said now. "I don't need a man to be complete. I can ride my own bicycle, fish or no fish."

"I don't know about bicycles," Timmy said, taking glasses from the cupboard, "but George has a fishing boat. You like to fish, Mom. Plus, it can pull water skis."

"I'm not dating a man to use his boat, Tim. Let's talk about something else."

"He's bored, you can tell," Tim said. "Looking for any excuse to hang out here. He's only a landlord to kill time."

"How do you know that?" she asked.

"We talk. He knows a patent attorney he's going to hook me up with."

"I'm not interested in dating right now," she said.

"You haven't dated in forever," Beth said, picking up the argument. Taking a break from men was fine—Beth was doing that herself—but she was afraid her mother had shut herself off for good.

"Subject closed," her mother said. "Let's talk about you and your new column. I am so proud of you." She hugged her shoulders. "You seem so on top of the, um, dating issues."

She meant sex. Her mother wouldn't say the word, but she wasn't scandalized by the idea or by Beth's column. From her teen years on, Beth and her mother had been like girlfriends.

"I'm just happy you're coming out of your shell again."

"Blaine was a bastard," Timmy muttered, banging the plates on the table.

"Could we not bash Blaine tonight?" Beth said. Rehashing it all never helped, and she hated that Blaine's departure had reinforced her mother's general distrust of men. "After dinner, I want to see what you've done on the pet door."

"It's coming together great," her mom said. "I think this one will make it. I'd like to dip into the house fund to get him started on the prototype, Beth. Don't you think?"

"You can't, Mom," Timmy said. "That's your savings. I'm not taking your savings. As soon as Julio pays me, I'll have some money for parts. No sweat."

If Julio ever paid him. If Tim would ever demand it.

If she kept her column, she could help out with materials. That meant she needed a dynamite test column…which meant she needed a dynamite night to write about. She'd get one. She'd get out there with Sara's dance-worthy skirt and her travel toothbrush and condom pack, and make it happen.

FRIDAY MORNING, BETH was supposed to be finishing the instruction manual for a portable shed, but she couldn't stop thinking about the next night's adventure at the new club. To jolt herself to life, she clicked over to e-mail, where she found that Will had forwarded some complimentary fan mail and Rafe Jarvis had written to her. She clicked open his message, her heart thudding in her chest.

Em: Excitement high here about your next column. How's it coming?

Hard to say. But she'd never tell Rafe Jarvis that. For him, she was woman-of-the-world Em, not wallflower Beth shaking in her dance shoes about meeting a new man. She typed back. *Hot new swing band in town. A shame Mr. Perfect Timing didn't return. Oh, well. Can't wait to meet ab-fab new man who knows how to move. Wish me luck!*

Light, casual, confident. Exactly how she didn't feel. She'd fake it, though, to impress her editor. She took a deep breath and hit Send.

Sounds fun, he wrote back. *Something must have happened to Mr. P.T. for him to no-show.*

Her editor felt sorry for her? She decided to joke. *Oh, so that's how it goes. You're defending him. Is this a male solidarity thing?*

You got me, he wrote back immediately. *How about switching to Instant Messenger?*

That was nice. He wanted to chitchat. In a few seconds, they'd moved to the swifter e-mail mode. *I figure his plans changed*, she typed, then realized she could get useful insights on men's attitudes from Rafe while she had him online. *Since you're an Official Male Source, here's a question: Don't men *always* want a second time?*

The normal ones. LOL, he wrote back. Beth smiled at the LOL—laughing out loud—before reading on. *If you had a good time, so did Mr. P.T. I can guarantee that.*

You flatter me.

Not at all. Don't forget I read your column. And I'd swear on my Y chromosome that if Mr. P.T. could be there Saturday night, he would be.

Thank you. Wow. She couldn't be sure, but she thought maybe Rafe was flirting with her. Maybe reading her sex column made him feel as if he knew her. She thought about him poised over his computer, typing away, pausing to drink a smoky port, wearing a tweed jacket with leather patches. Where did she get that idea?

He was mid-thirties and hot, according to Heather, in a "hard, chiseled, don't-screw-with-me way." Beth had run into Heather—almost literally—while walking her dogs, and got the skinny on Rafe. Heather, who lived in an apartment building just two blocks away, had whipped around a corner, jogging, and thumped into Boomer.

She'd told Beth all about Rafe's visit to the magazine, the way everyone scurried around trying to look busy and important. Heather insisted Rafe had a soft side.

Beth sure seemed to be seeing it. She leaned forward, bumping Ditzy who yelped and rose up, causing her to accidentally send a blank message. *Sorry*, she typed quickly. *One of my dogs bumped me.*

Dogs, huh? Em doesn't strike me as a pet person.

Em has a homebody side, she wrote.

Means you're well-rounded.

Thank you. She didn't want Rafe to feel obligated to keep up the small talk, so she added, *I should let you get back to work.*

Please don't. I'm enjoying this far more than the meeting I'm supposed to be at.

That was nice to hear. *I'm avoiding work myself. Writing instructions for a shed. My other job.*

Quite a change from your column.

Not as emotionally rewarding, she replied, *but still satisfying. Calls for the same attention to detail, but requires strict logic and careful order.*

So, you're a well-rounded writer, too. You're lucky you enjoy your job.

Don't you enjoy yours? There was a long pause, during which she feared she'd overstepped their professional relationship.

It's gotten routine, I guess, he wrote, so she knew the delay meant he'd been thinking, not offended.

Seems like it would be challenging.

Meetings, reports, receptions, strategy sessions, then more meetings, reports, receptions. It gets mundane.

What would you rather be doing?

I used to be a reporter. Investigative work, believe it or not. I miss that.

She paused, thinking about what he'd written. The answer seemed obvious. *Can't you write a story for one of your magazines?*

Not as simple as it sounds, he answered. *I'd leave people in the lurch. Story budgets are set months in advance. An exec editor jumping in the middle? That's complicated. And politically delicate.*

So, write a freelance piece on spec, she replied. *I pay my bills as a technical writer. I write my column because I love it.*

Possible. When things slow down. I'm heading to Denver soon to work on another makeover. That will be interesting.

My guess is the Denver staff will be riveted. She couldn't resist the jab.

Don't mean to sound cavalier, he replied. *I do my best to save jobs and keep the voice of the pub intact.*

I can't complain, she quickly responded. *You gave me a chance at my column. I appreciate that a lot.*

You do good work, Em.

The compliment made her smile and gave her hope about winning her column for good. *You do, too, or you wouldn't be where you are.*

Don't know about that. Sorry to be spilling my guts to you. I usually don't get into that stuff.

Then I'm honored. And a bit uncomfortable to be writing so long and so personally to a man who was, in effect, her boss. The exchanges had flown, though, quick as thought, as if they were longtime friends, not barely colleagues. *My shed manual beckons and you'd better get to your meeting.*

You're right, but let me say this… I would bet Mr. Perfect Timing is kicking himself right now that he can't be with you, Em.

I'm flattered. He *was* flirting with her. Definitely.

Reading your column, I feel I know you.

Writers aren't always how they seem in print. That was as close as she cared to come to admitting that Em was a librarian in a miniskirt.

I still think I'm right.

You're stubborn, I see. Probably how you got where you are.

A trait I'm sure we share.

I'll never tell. Ciao for now. A very Em-like good-bye. Online, Em was good. This was probably how she should try to meet men. Maybe she could write a column about that. Something on cybersex. Hmm.

Leaning back in her chair, she smiled in satisfaction. She'd just flirted with her boss—the man who controlled her future at *Phoenix Rising.* This, on top of her boldness with AJ, was way out of character. For Beth, of course. Not Em. It was very Em.

THE PHONE WOKE BETH early Saturday morning. "Hello," she managed groggily, clearing her throat and squinting at the clock. Six-thirty. Her three dogs lifted their heads—Ditzy from her pillow, Spud from atop her legs, Boomer from the floor beside her—and tuned in to what had caused this disturbance in their sleep cycles.

"Did I wake you?" The caller's phone faded, then cleared enough for her to hear, "It's AJ."

"AJ?" She sat up. "No, no. I'm awake." She was now.

"Listen, I'm in town again and wondered if you were free tonight. I know it's short notice, but I had such a great time the other night."

"Me, too," she said quickly, hopping out of bed. She didn't even pretend to consider her plans. "How's your jitterbug? I'm checking out a new swing club tonight and could use a partner." She held her breath and crossed her fingers. What if he didn't dance?

"I'm a decent dancer. My mother strong-armed me into dance lessons when I was in junior high. She told me the girls would love it."

"She was right."

"I've come to realize that." He chuckled, a low, husky sound that vibrated in her ear and made her feel soft inside. "Shall I pick you up at seven-thirty?"

"Perfect," she said. She explained how to get to her house, pacing as she talked to release the tight coil of excitement building in her. She couldn't wait to see AJ again, to be in his arms, to test the magic once more.

Her dogs galloped beside her, thinking it was a game. The ever-hopeful Ditzy fetched her leash.

"See you tonight then," AJ said when she'd finished with the directions. He paused and then his voice got serious. "I'm sorry I didn't call when my plans changed, Beth."

"You're calling now," she said, glad to show him how casual she could be. "We had a great time the other night and we'll have more fun tonight. No apology needed."

"Right," he said, exhaling heavily in what had to be relief. "I can't wait to see you," he added, his voice husky. She could almost feel his lips against her ear.

"Me, too," she said, shivering with pleasure. "Me, too."

He'd called in the nick of time. Almost as if he'd read her mind—or her e-mail to Rafe. Tonight she'd have the comfort of being with a man she knew, and could use her second-date research, too. She was getting One-Night Stand—The Sequel after all. Yippee.

CLICKING OFF HIS CELL phone at the car rental area in the Phoenix airport baggage claim, Rafe rubbed eyes that burned as though he'd been in a sandstorm. He'd had to cancel his weekend plans—crap out on a charity auction and a golf game with *Man's Man* top management, both bad moves—to book a crack-of-dawn flight to Phoenix, but it was worth it to see Beth again.

Why was he doing this? He'd read between the lines on her breezy e-mail and knew Mr. Perfect Timing's no-show had rattled her. The idea of trying to meet a new guy had made her nervous, he was sure. So, he'd come to help her.

Yeah, right. He just wanted to see her again. He wasn't going to examine his motives any further than that. The too-friendly e-mails had been inappropriate, but, hell, it had been fun. Maybe because he could see her in his mind's eye, imagine her fingers flying over the keyboard. Online, she was the confident columnist Em, but he knew shy, nervous Beth, too. He'd slept with her, made her cry out, brought her to climax.

That started an ache below the belt. He couldn't wait

to see her. So he'd flirted online a little. Where was the harm? Sexual innuendo hummed among the staff at *Man's Man* like a fluorescent light buzz. Except Em was not at the home office but at a new acquisition, where it was more important to establish a level of professionalism. Not smart.

And coming to see her was even worse. He just wanted one more chance to get lost in those green eyes, expectant and intense, charting every detail with total focus. He wanted one more night of startling sex and then he'd fly off into the sunset. He'd tell her business was taking him cross-country, and that would end it. Nice and neat. Goodbye for good.

But what if he told her the whole story? Could they laugh about it and be friends? Or lovers?

No. Not when she was so delicately positioned job-wise. Or so serious a person. He slept with women who didn't expect more from him than he could give—his attention, his body and a good time. Beth would want more. It was how she was built.

But one more night wouldn't hurt anybody. It would reassure her how attractive she was, give her another column, he hoped, and allow a clean, honest farewell. He'd be back to Phoenix a couple more times because of the magazine. But if the changeover continued to go smoothly, he'd soon be gone, making his departure story to Beth almost true.

6

BETH BURNED OFF HER pre-date jitters with housework.
She dusted, vacuumed, scrubbed, shifted the sofa's position, cut new flowers, set out a more erotic candle
cluster of rose, cinnamon and vanilla and washed the
windows and all three dogs.

The extra effort seemed silly. The dogs sure thought
so—they moped around, soggy tails sagging, accusa-
tion in their doggie faces—but she had to keep busy.

She'd consulted with Sara, who'd advised her to be
warm, but not overly eager, friendly, but not too cozy,
and above all, to keep things simple. *Complications
scare guys.* By that, Sara meant don't fuss. But Beth was
still Beth.

In the afternoon, she bought a tailored white blouse
to go with the gauzy skirt Sara had loaned her and
splurged on a little fake fall of curls and an adult barrette, so she could return the Hello Kitty one to her
neighbor.

Then she headed to the gourmet grocery store for
the right wine to match the medley of Greek hors
d'oeuvres she'd bought with the help of the deli man-
ager, who shared her obsession for perfect taste com-
binations.

By seven-fifteen, everything was ready. The air was
filled with the romantic light and scent of candles mixed

with the lemon/garlic/herb aroma of the Greek snacks she'd artfully arranged and accented with silver tapers, their holders trimmed with fresh rosemary sprigs. Underlying these more obvious smells was the natural perfume of the new flowers she'd cut and arranged throughout the house. For music, she'd chosen acoustic jazz from a new CD well-reviewed by *Phoenix Rising*'s music critic.

She'd outdone herself in the bedroom, too, with extra candles, pink satin sheets, wine at the ready and a cute little overlapping circle of condoms on a candy dish on the nightstand.

Regarding sex, Sara had advised her to tempt and titillate. *Sex once does not guarantee sex twice. Men are romantic when they have to work for it. A sure thing is bo-ring.*

About that, Beth would have to see. Waiting for AJ to arrive, she was so jumpy and eager that she imagined herself knocking him to the Oriental rug and ripping his clothes off. That surprised the hell out of her. She wanted *sex*. Forget euphemisms like *intimacy*. This new feeling was raw and wild—well, with a few dashes of taste and care. She finally understood what all the fuss was about.

When the doorbell rang, all three dogs barked and galloped for the entryway. They'd picked up on her excitement and she could hardly make it to the door for their swirls, lunges and jumps.

"Settle down," she said to them, then opened the door to AJ, who looked devastating in a silky forties-style bowling shirt in a pattern of diamonds in brown, burgundy and olive. His black pants hugged his hips, reminding her how he looked naked.

"You look great," he said, his thorough survey of her

body making her weak in the knees. The two bigger dogs circled him and Ditzy wove a figure eight between his legs, but AJ seemed to only have eyes for her.

"You, too," she said.

He held a gift sack, from which a bottle of red wine peeked. Should she hug him? He decided for her, pulling her into a one-armed embrace and a soft, slow kiss that felt so familiar and yet so new, she forgot all about second-time sex not being a sure thing. They'd be in bed together tonight without fail. This minute, if this kiss went on much longer.

AJ broke it off and handed her his gift.

"You didn't need to bring me anything," she said, looking into the sack which held more than wine. AJ took the bottle out and she pulled out a CD and a cellophane packet that held biscuits from a gourmet pet store. "How did you know I had dogs?" She blinked at him, puzzled.

His face paled for an instant—was he embarrassed by his thoughtfulness? "I, um, heard them in the background when we talked on the phone." He rushed on. "The music is Dan Hicks and His Hot Licks, a classic swing group. I thought we could practice before we head out…if you're up for it."

"I'd love to," she said. "And the gifts are sweet. You didn't need to bring anything but yourself." She'd have to include something in her column about unique date gifts.

"It was my pleasure," he said, putting the wine on the table. He took the dog treats from her and crouched to eye level with the dogs. "So, who's who?" he asked, opening the crackling cellophane.

She caught Boomer by the collar before he made a slobbery pass at AJ's face. "Sit!" Boomer sagged resignedly to his haunches. "This is Boomer."

AJ patted him, gave him a treat, then let Spud sniff the back of his hand. Very pet-savvy. Another star on his chart. "Unusual dog," he said, extending a pretzel-shaped biscuit to Spud.

"Don't you mean the ugliest dog you've ever seen? That's what most people think. He's a Chinese Crested hairless." Bald except for the bristle at the top of his head, barrel-bodied with black skin and bulging eyes, Spud looked like a Chihuahua on steroids that had been left too long on the hibachi.

"But he's got a great personality, right?" AJ said, roughing up his topknot. Spud closed his eyes in ecstasy, completely charmed.

"He got left with my vet, and no one wanted a dog so…unique."

"So you took him?"

"How could I not? His self-esteem was in the toilet." She noticed that Ditzy was doing her spinning stunt. "Would you please clap for Ditzy? She'll keep going until she gets sick and vomits."

AJ raised his brows, then gave quick applause. Ditzy dropped onto all fours with relief and he gave her a treat just her size.

"Ditzy's a circus refugee," she said.

"So, you're running a home for wayward animals?"

"Pretty much." She nodded up at the cats lounging on the archway. They indicated their displeasure at being ignored by snapping their tails in a we-are-not-pleased motion. "A friend was moving to Europe and asked me to keep Frick and Frack."

"Don't have anything for them. Sorry. I didn't, um, hear them on the phone." Something about that clearly bothered him, but before she could ponder further, he stood and glued his gaze to hers. "You look great…like I said."

"My friend loaned me the skirt—it's good for dancing."

"Good for touching, too." He slid his hand up and down her hip, a gesture of possession that warmed her to her toes. Then he led her closer so he could thread the fingers of his other hand into the hair at the side of her head, making her scalp prickle deliciously. His fingertips tapped the hairpiece. "Where's my kitty barrette?"

"I thought this was more dramatic."

"The kitty's more you. I do, however, like being able to get at your neck." He kissed the curve of her throat, sending heat cascading down her body, then moved to her mouth. The kiss was long and lovely and if she didn't have a new bar to review and a new column to write, she'd have given up and led him to bed.

"I have food," she said, reluctantly easing away. "Come and taste."

"I'm already tasting what I want. Come back here," he said.

She laughed, but kept moving toward the dining room.

He followed and stood behind her, kissing her neck until her knees wobbled, while she shakily loaded their plates. She'd prepared all this, darn it, and they were going to enjoy it. "Here." She thrust a plate between them.

"Okay." He shook his head, then settled into a chair at the table. He looked around the room and beyond. "Nice digs, Beth."

"Thank you." She followed her gaze, pleased with the warm, appealing room laid out before them.

"It's very you." He smiled at her.

"What's your place like?" she asked.

"I have a condo in the Marina. It's simple. Big windows and a great view."

"San Francisco is a wonderful city."

"Yeah. I haven't seen much of it lately. I've been traveling a lot."

"That's a shame. How's your work going here, by the way?"

"As well as can be expected." His amusement turned to wariness and he took a quick bite of a stuffed grape leaf. "Did you make this? It's delicious." He was clearly changing the subject.

"No, I bought it. Try this, too." She picked up a flaky triangle of spanakopita and held it to his mouth. He cupped her hand in his warm palm and bit with slow care, his lips and tongue lazy on the food and her fingers, from which he licked the oil and crumbs, holding her gaze the entire time.

Her eyes closed with the sensation of warm, wet tongue on her skin. She couldn't help thinking where else his tongue might go on her body tonight and squirmed in her chair.

He released her hand and she opened her eyes to see him smile a slow smile. "There's a Middle Eastern deli where I get takeout. From now on, when I order from there, I'll think of you."

"That's sweet. So you eat takeout? Do you cook at all?"

"Now and then. When I have company."

When he had a woman over, no doubt. But she didn't want to think about the other women in his life. She preferred to picture him all alone, nibbling on a pita, looking out over the lights of San Francisco and thinking of her.

The rattle of collars made them turn their heads. The

three dogs were lined up, alert to every movement she and AJ made.

"Can I give them something?" AJ asked.

When she nodded, he broke a spinach pastry into three parts and gave each dog a share.

"Do you have any pets?" she asked, pleased by the attention he was giving her animals.

"I had a Lab when I was a kid. Having a dog now wouldn't be fair to the animal. I'm away a lot."

"A pet makes good company. Maybe a friend or neighbor could take care of it while you're gone."

"I only know my neighbors in passing."

"That's too bad." She felt sorry for him, all alone, not even knowing his neighbors.

He shrugged. "I'm comfortable. My life is good."

"You probably have buddies you get together with, right?"

"Sure. We play squash. Take in a ball game. Grab a beer after work. Are you trying to worry about me? Don't. Please. I'm fine." His face tightened just a little. *Don't get too close.* The warning she'd seen the night they met. AJ was friendly, but he held people at arm's length. Maybe traveling made him emotionally guarded. Or maybe being emotionally guarded made him want to travel. She found she wanted to figure that out. If only there was time.

"Hey, we're getting too serious here," AJ said. "How about we bust some moves to that CD? See if I'm good enough for you to take to the club." He stood, pulled her to her feet and kissed her softly. He tasted of mint and lemon and allspice, and the kiss was lovely, but it didn't erase her awareness that he was a lonely man.

Evidently sensing her hesitation, he leaned back and looked at her. "I'm fine, Beth. I don't need a dog or a best buddy or neighbors to borrow a cup of sugar from. That's you, not me. Tonight's about having a good time together, remember?"

"Sure. Of course." Her questions made him uneasy—exactly the kind of thing Sara had warned her against. *Men hate complications*. She would try to behave. "Why don't you put on the music and I'll put the food away," she said and hurried off.

RAFE UNWRAPPED THE CD while he watched Beth transfer the elaborate spread from the dining room to the kitchen, loving the curve and wiggle of her backside, her quick movements, her wound-tight energy.

She'd been trying to fix him, asking about his home, whether he cooked, if he was lonely. He found that charming, but also disturbing. She was trying to get to know him—a pointless activity, considering the limits to their relationship.

He'd contributed to the illusion that there was more going on, he realized now, by coming to her cozy house bearing gifts, acting like a true date—someone who could offer her far more than he ever could. He should have met her at his hotel again. Much simpler, clear-cut, more neutral.

Still, he wasn't sorry to see her in her own milieu. She was much more relaxed here. He enjoyed the way she glided from room to room, her hips swaying in a seductive way that she seemed oblivious to. Beth was all sweet innocence and matter-of-fact efficiency. Kind of like Mary Ann from *Gilligan's Island*—the pigtailed star of his pubescent fantasies.

He replaced the jazz CD she had on her player with the quick swing of Dan Hicks and watched as she came toward him, a tentative smile on her face.

Ah, hell. He was so glad to see her, he wasn't going to worry about the fallout right now. He laced his fingers with hers, then led her in a quick side-to-side, back-rock step. She responded perfectly, as good a partner in dance as in sex. No surprise.

Neither was the way she concentrated, her brow furrowed, trying not to make a mistake. "You're doing fine. Just relax," he said. He rocked her close to his chest, lifted both her arms to spin her beneath their twined hands, then pulled her close and away.

She laughed and that made him happy, so he showed off a few more steps, dipping her at the end of the song, loving the wide-eyed surprise on her face.

The next song was slow, so he pulled her close and kissed her neck, loving the taste of salt on her skin, the warm perfume she wore. Sweet and spicy, like the woman she was.

"May I say your mother's money was not wasted on those lessons," she said. "Please thank her for me."

"I'll do that," he said, feeling a twinge at the thought.

"Did I say something wrong?" She'd caught his tension. She didn't miss anything—a fact that both touched and unsettled him.

"No. It's just that we're not much for conversation, my mom and I." He rocked her back and forth, enjoying the weight of her hand in his, the brush of her swaying body.

"Really? How about your dad? Do you talk to him?"

"Less. My parents are divorced."

"I'm sorry. Was it recent? The breakup?"

"God, no. It happened when I was in college—what, fifteen years ago."

"Still, that must have been hard." They danced in silence for a few seconds.

"It was a long time coming. They were miserable when I was growing up." He wanted off this unpleasant subject. The concern in Beth's eyes made him uncomfortable. "How about your parents? Happily married?"

"No." The look on her face made him regret the question. "My father left us twenty years ago, when I was seven."

"Now that would be hard," he said, stopping long enough to kiss her forehead. "Sorry to bring it up."

"It's okay. We've adjusted." She smiled at him, easier about her family history than he was about his own. "I used to hope he'd just show up one day with presents and a story about being kidnapped or spending years on a merchant ship, but nope. My mother thinks he felt too guilty. She says he was…limited."

"My dad shouldn't have married. He wasn't equipped for it. A castle with no bridge over the moat, my mother claimed. Of course, his story was that she expected too much from him. Everybody has a point of view."

"That's true. I just wish I'd known my dad's."

"That would be tough—having to guess about it."

"One good thing is that my brother was only two when he left, so he doesn't miss him really. Do you see your parents often?"

"Occasional holidays. Mom's in Chicago, Dad's in New York." His childhood had been heavy with withheld emotion and angry strain. He'd spent as much time as he could away from home—hanging with friends or at the gym. The avoidance hadn't changed over the years, though this was the first time he'd actually thought about it.

"I'm sorry to hear that. My mother and brother and

I are very close." Her eyes were luminous with sympathy. The woman had grown up fatherless, but she seemed more troubled by his estrangement from his parents than her own loss. Sweet, really, except she was making him feel closed in and tight in the throat.

"Your brother lives at home?" he asked, to shift attention away from him, changing the direction of their slow dance.

"He's only twenty-two and he's good company for Mom, who's a little uncertain of herself."

"What's he do for a living?"

"Now that's an interesting question. He's an inventor, actually, but he's working low-paying jobs until he sells something. He's got some great ideas." She smiled, but there was hesitation in her voice.

"You don't sound so sure."

"He's a good guy, generous with friends, but a little hazy about the details. What can I say? He's my brother."

"Sure," he said. "It's nice that you're close with your family." He and Beth shared screwed-up family histories, but had reacted in opposite ways. She'd held on tighter; he'd learned to let go.

He imagined her as a seven-year-old, hoping every car that approached would be her dad's, her mother crying in the background, both of them poised for each phone call to be a reprieve from abandonment.

Emotion filled him, made him hold her tighter, wanting to comfort her somehow, even though she hadn't asked for it and probably didn't need it. The sudden emotional intensity felt peculiar, so he forced himself to notice her body, focus on the sexual heat between them. He squeezed her backside, pressing himself closer to her so she could feel her effect on him. "Sure you don't want to skip the dancing?" She needed to check out the bar for her column, he knew, but all he wanted right now was her. Naked.

She responded to his words with a gratifying sexual shudder. She was so responsive. Every move or word elicited something—a sigh, a gasp, a shiver, a moan.

"So tempting," she said, looking up at him with lust-glazed eyes, "but we can't waste all those dance lessons."

"Okay, but the walk to the car's gonna hurt," he said, leaning forward as if in pain from his erection.

"I'm so sorry," she said, not sounding sorry at all. "I'll go get my purse. Shall I bring back ice water?"

"No, no. I'll manage somehow." He watched her sashay off, knowing this date was probably a terrible idea. But when she headed his way, purse over her arm, fresh lipstick on her pretty mouth, her eyes shiny with excitement, his doubts disappeared like shade conquered by sun.

Beth warned her pets to be good, apologized to him for talking to them as though they were human, then they headed out to his rental car, parked at the curb.

"A convertible?" Beth said, her eyes wide with delight. "I haven't been in a convertible since high school."

Score. And worth the top dollar he'd paid for it, too. He'd figured it would make the evening special—something she might include in her column.

Before he could grab the door for her, she'd opened it and wiggled appealingly into place. The woman made sitting in the car a sex act.

"And the weather's perfect for it."

She was right. The spring evening was comfortable, with a heady floral sweetness in the air he recognized from his years in Florida as citrus in bloom. The white flowers were everywhere on the waxy-leafed trees.

He started the car and they headed down the street. Once on the throughway, he glanced at her. The wind whipped her hair, but she looked happy. "Is the wind too much?" he asked.

"Who cares?" she said and leaned back, eyes closed, to relish the experience. "Breathe in the spring."

He sniffed. "Not bad, except for the fumes."

"Ignore that. Focus on the mesquite grill and garlic from restaurants, creosote from the desert, orange blossoms and green things, and, something's baking— bread, maybe? I think there's a bread factory around here."

He grinned and sniffed again. He couldn't get much beyond the sour diesel of a bus and oily exhaust from a badly tuned engine. She had quite a nose, Beth did.

He realized that the world had become a blur to him of late. He'd been ignoring his surroundings, even the weather. He'd rented the car just to impress Beth, not for the pleasure of driving around with the top down, which he used to love to do in his beat-up MG. At the stoplight, he turned to her. "Thanks."

"For what?" She blinked at him.

"For being you. For being interested in everything." He squeezed her knee through the flimsy fabric of her skirt in what was meant to be a friendly way, but her firm flesh felt good, and he flashed on the image of her legs wrapped around him while he moved inside her.

Growing hard at the thought, he pushed up her skirt to get at her knee, glad there were no panty hose in his way.

She made a little sound and her leg trembled. He looked at her face. He was only holding her knee, but she seemed ready to climax. Had they not been in an open car, he would have slid his hands under her skirt and stroked her to a quick orgasm. He felt a rush of impatience—a hopeless feeling that it would be forever until he'd be naked and inside her.

When had he last had this feeling? This desperate need bigger than hunger or thirst? He'd been much, much younger, for sure. Something about Beth took him back.

Being with her was so much like a first time. It made him remember his initiation at the hands of an older girl, who'd shown him the wonders of sex—and exactly what girls liked. The lessons had served him well over the years. He remembered driving home after that first time, the windows open, leaning back against the headrest, grateful for his mouth, his fingers and how incredibly soft women were.

The light changed and he accelerated away from the moment. They made small talk the rest of the way, discussing music and movies they liked, opinions on the news of the day. They shared an attention to detail, a love of the blues and movies that abruptly turned expectations on end. She was more optimistic than he, but she called him on every negative observation, insisting he defend his assumptions.

They shared a love of words, too. He confessed he'd once thought of becoming an English teacher, so they could discuss the joy of writing without blowing his cover. They agreed that the emphasis on profits over substance had deeply damaged the caliber and depth of news, both print and broadcast.

Whenever the topics got personal, he steered them to Beth's life, not his. She talked about her mother's tentativeness and her brother's generosity with friends.

She put the guy in the best light, but he sensed her frustration with him. Then she lectured him about talking to his parents more, getting past the bad memories to connect. *Family is important*. This made him smile. She was still trying to fix him.

By silent mutual agreement, they avoided the subject of relationships, past or current. He was glad. He didn't want to know about other men—especially about the guy who'd made her feel bad about herself as a lover—and he certainly didn't want to discuss his track record of short-term hookups.

They were so busy talking that he drove a half mile past the bar before either of them noticed.

Damn, he liked this woman.

He backtracked and pulled into the crowded parking lot of Zoot Suit. Recorded music—a torch song from the forties—leaked out, lending an old-fashioned romantic flavor to the moment. The neon sign above them made the curve of Beth's cheek gleam and her eyes glow. She was so excited. So happy and hopeful. And every word that came from her sweet lips, every glance of her gold-green eyes, made him ache with hunger for her.

But what if she expected more than was possible? She'd said he owed her no apology for the last-minute plans, seemed content just to be with him. But he should be certain she understood the limits, so she wouldn't get any wrong ideas.

Tell her who you are and you can have more time.

But that would ruin everything, make her question what they'd shared. Sure, he was lying by not telling her, but he was being honest about how he felt about her. That was what counted, right?

Plus, he was the perfect man for her column. Some

guys would object to their sex life appearing in a magazine. Others would turn the evening into a performance. And the rest would insist on approving what she wrote about them.

So he was helping her professionally—yeah, right—and they were both having a hell of a good time. When the moment felt right, he'd tell her the story about his "job" on the east coast and prepare her for the final goodbye. Prepare himself, too. He was unpleasantly aware that leaving her wouldn't be as easy as it should be.

7

BETH TRIED TO BE SUBTLE as she checked out the new
bar for her readers—not easy to do with heat waves
rolling through her body whenever she looked at AJ or
he touched her. She managed some furtive research,
though, and ducked into the rest room to jot a few notes.

> Cocktails from the '40s, boldly tropical decor...
> sluggish service, but to be expected with a new
> place...decent seating...generous dance floor...
> waitstaff in costume—men in baggy pants
> with suspenders; women in '40s-tailored suits...
> crowded after next to no advertising... Prediction:
> hot pickup bar in eight weeks.

Finished, she tucked her tiny notebook into her
equally tiny purse—essential for a dance club—and
emerged from the restroom alcove just as the band
kicked off with a hot, fast number that made her heart
jump in time. She saw AJ heading her way, smiling, asking her to dance with his eyes. They met in the spotlit
center of the dance floor and he tugged her into his arms
in a way that seemed choreographed. He swung her out
and in, then spun her, fast and tight, making her skirt
flare, then wrap around her legs.

Shyness threatened, but AJ pulled her close. "Every

man in this place envies me. Just relax and we'll show off a little."

So she gave herself over to the rhythm and AJ's hands, which held her confidently, sliding along her hips, bracing her at the waist, turning her, always protective, always possessive, placing her where he wanted her, and all in perfect time to the music.

Warmth from the lights above her and the flash and clash of colors and movement became a lush backdrop for more intimate sensations—the scent of AJ's cologne, the smooth silkiness of his shirt, the pressure of his chest against hers, the brush of his thighs, the way his gaze held her like a caress.

She lost her balance for an instant, but AJ pulled her against his body so that her stumble became a dance move, which he reversed into a turn. Abruptly, she found herself a breath from his face, then dropped into a dizzying dip. It was like some wild, human carnival ride. She laughed, breathless and powerless, but safe, too.

Dancing with AJ, she completely inhabited her body. The muscles in her calves tightened, her thighs tensed, her hips swayed…and her sex grew embarrassingly tight. Could people tell how turned on she was?

Dancing was sexual, of course—a civilized mating ritual—but she'd never felt it so vividly as she did in AJ's arms, with the jazz heat of the band making her body throb. The sax groaned like sex cries, the drums pulsed in a get-me-some heartbeat. The congas came after her, demanding satisfaction now. She was surprised people didn't just give up all pretense and go for it on the floor.

There was something so sexy about a man who could dance. It meant he was in touch with his body. And hers.

She should make a note of that. *Dance rhythm...
sex rhythm...chicken or egg?*

Only a few couples were dancing with them, including waitstaff doing showy moves. Dance skills must be a
hiring requirement. Very smart of the owner, she thought,
since having good dancers around you made you feel like
a better dancer yourself, almost part of a performance.

The band slid into a slow number and AJ pulled her
close, bending their bodies in a sinuous curve, his heart
pounding against her own in quick counterpoint. His gaze,
steady on her face, told her how much he wanted her. She
slid her hips against his groin to show him how much she
wanted him. They were one body moving to the music,
making love to each other in public. If only she could slide
her fingers under his shirt to feel his tight muscles, damp
from exertion. If only he could reach under her skirt to
cup her bottom. If only she hadn't worn panties. Oh, dear.

"What are you thinking?" he asked, interrupting her
wicked musings.

"What do you think I'm thinking?"

"If it's what I'm thinking, we could get arrested."

She laughed and kissed his neck. "Exactly."

"Have you seen enough of this place, because if we
don't leave soon, I'll have to take you right here, and I
don't think they'd let us stay in the same jail cell."

"Almost," she said in his ear, liking the tense-release
of his thighs against hers, his erection insistent against
her stomach. "Let's get a drink and rest for a bit." Holding out a little made everything more delicious.

Back at the table, they ordered drinks, then moved
their chairs as close together as possible.

"God, you're beautiful," AJ said.

"I'm a mess," she said, reaching up to push a strand
of hair behind the hairpiece.

AJ stopped her hand. "Just like this, you're beautiful. Flushed and sweaty, your hair flying loose." As he
spoke, he began to pull out the pins that held the hairpiece in place. Slowly, one by one, and with great care,
so that each pin was delicately dragged across her scalp,
tickling and teasing her skin. It was as if he were taking off her clothes. When all the pins were out, her hair
dropped onto her shoulders like a brush of hot breath,
and she gasped with pleasure.

"Much better," he said, combing gently through her
hair with his fingers, his tender gesture making her feel
both loose with pleasure and tight with arousal. He
cupped her cheek and brushed the pad of his thumb over
her lips. She kissed his thumb, then touched it with her
tongue.

"If you don't stop that I'll embarrass myself right
here."

"I like when you talk like that. You make me feel
sexy."

"You are sexy, Beth. And every man in this room
knows it."

She laughed, so happy about how this was going. Before she could say so, the waitress brought her gin and
tonic and AJ's Scotch. They took a sip, watching each
other over the glasses and she said, "I'm so glad we have
the whole night ahead of us. Maybe the whole weekend?"

AJ stilled at her words and the distance in his eyes
deepened. "Just tonight, Beth. I'm sorry. I need to get
back tomorrow."

"Oh, sure, no problem," she said, mortified that
she'd assumed more time and that her disappointment
surely showed in her face. So much for acting cool and
casual.

"I wish I could stay, Beth. I do. I just—"

"It's fine. This was a quick visit, I know. Maybe next time." She was just trying to save face, but he seemed even more uncomfortable.

"That's just it," he said, looking positively trapped. "After this I'll be heading to the east coast. For an extended time."

"Okay…"

"And I won't be back," he said in a rush.

Pain stabbed her, which she had no right to feel, but she fought to smile. "You don't owe me your plans, AJ. I wasn't asking for your itinerary."

"I just want to be clear. So you don't expect…well, just so you know."

He was looking at her with guilt and sympathy. She hated that. She'd only mentioned the weekend, maybe another date, not a wedding date. "For Pete's sake, you act like I'm clearing out a drawer for you. It's fine."

She busied herself scooping the hairpiece and hairpins into her purse to hide her hurt and irritation.

But AJ stopped her by taking her trembling hands in his. "That came out wrong. Being with you makes me want more time, too, but the thing is…I don't stick around. For anything. And you need to know that. And I need to remember it."

She managed a smile, grateful for his explanation—and his honesty. "So, okay. Let's just enjoy the time we have."

"Good. Great." He exhaled a great breath of relief.

Which hurt. AJ was relieved, while she felt a rush of sadness—she'd never see him again. To distract herself, she took a big gulp of her gin and tonic.

"You thirsty?" he asked, eager to change the subject,

it seemed. "I'll get water, so you don't chug that liquor too fast."

"Thanks." She was grateful that the neon-lit bar island was jammed with people, so he'd be a while, giving her time to settle down. She was here for her column and a little personal growth, not a relationship, after all. Still, the finality of it all made her feel cold inside.

Thankfully, the band started a song so rhythmic and fun she couldn't help moving in her chair. A man on the edge of the dance floor caught her eye. She smiled, then shifted her gaze, only to catch another man's approving nod.

How ironic. This wouldn't be happening if she were here alone, trying to look friendly and dance-worthy. She'd have to figure out how to bottle this confidence and douse herself with it when she needed it. After AJ was gone. That cold feeling hit again.

"Would you like to dance?"

Startled by the voice, she looked up into the face of the first man who'd smiled at her.

"Oh, I'm here with someone," she said, "but thanks."

He shrugged. "It's a great song."

He was right. It was fast and fun, with a salsa flair. And it wasn't like AJ owned her. He'd be out of her life in a heartbeat. "Sure. Why not?" She rose to her feet.

The guy was thinner than AJ and didn't hold her with the same assurance, but he was quick and a great dancer. She struggled to keep up, but he smiled as though it didn't matter when she flubbed, and took her on a dizzying ride. When it was over, he pulled her close enough to say thanks near her ear. She did the same to him, then headed back to the table, where AJ was scowling.

"What's wrong?" she asked.

"Did that guy get grabby with you?"

"Not at all."

"Because you don't have to put up with that."

"He was fine." She looked at him, puzzled by his tone, until the truth dawned on her. "Are you jealous, AJ?"

"Of course not. I just thought the guy was pushy."

"I appreciate your concern," she said, tickled by it, "but I can handle myself. If a guy gets out of line with me, rest assured he'll walk funny for a while."

"Just be careful. Guys can be tricky and aggressive. They misread signals, especially when they're drinking."

"I've been out of circulation, AJ, not in a coma. I understand the risks of dating. I slept with you, didn't I?"

"That was different," he grumbled.

As Neanderthal as it was, she enjoyed his protectiveness and jealousy, and the fact that he was denying it even to himself. He wanted her all to himself, bless his primal heart, and she loved it. Even if it was just for tonight.

LATER, AT HOME, THE DOGS galloped around AJ as though he were family. Even the cats climbed down to pretend they didn't care if he petted them, which he did, soberly and each in turn.

"I can't believe you scored with Frick and Frack," she said. "They don't warm up easily."

"They're just kissing up for a gift next ti—" He stopped talking, realizing, she knew, that there would be no next time. Ever since his announcement, he'd seemed more distant than ever.

And now he seemed uncomfortable in her home. In fact, he'd suggested they go to his hotel, making it sound as though he couldn't wait to get her naked, but she was sure he wanted the neutrality of an anonymous place.

That saddened her, but she pushed the feeling aside. She was determined to enjoy every minute they had together. She put her arms around AJ and pressed her body against his to remind them both of the magic between them. *Remember me? Remember this?*

He relaxed against her, tightening his hold, then slowly stroked her backside. Oh, yes. He remembered.

The sex would be different this time. Instead of the thrill of newness, she felt the delicious excitement of picking up where they'd left off. And going further.

She kissed his neck, sliding her tongue across his skin. "Mmm, you taste good. Salty and warm."

"You have the best tongue."

"All the better to lick you with," she said.

"Feel free to keep going."

Uh-oh. "Um, I should warn you that I'm not sure I'm very good at oral sex." She always felt disoriented, afraid she'd bump the guy with her teeth or not use the right tongue action.

He chuckled. "If this is the same as you not being good at orgasming, then I can't wait for you to try," he said, his eyes twinkling at her. "You're a natural, Beth. Don't worry."

He was so good for her confidence.

He bent to kiss her, but she had to put the final touches on everything in the bedroom, so she braced her arms against his chest. "I have to change."

"No, you don't. What you have to do is get naked." He reached for the buttons on her top, but she slid away.

"How about if I put on something else you can take off?"

"I prefer a blouse in the hand to one in the bedroom, but okay…." He stepped forward and captured her lips, cupping her face and kissing her as though he meant business.

This was so, so, *so* good…. "Take the dogs out," she murmured, pulling away with reluctance.

"Huh?"

"They need to go outside. Nature calls."

He looked down at the dogs. "You'd better whiz faster than you've ever whizzed before, guys. I've got business in here with your mom."

He headed off and Beth snatched up the jazz CD she'd been playing before AJ arrived, then rushed into her room, where she slapped it into her boom box, setting the volume low. Then she tore off her clothes.

She donned the simple pink silk chemise and high-cut shorts she'd bought for tonight, lit candles with shaking fingers, opened the bottle of wine she'd set on a tray with two goblets, then spritzed the pillows with rose-scented linen mist.

Back in the bathroom to comb her hair, she sprayed perfume into the air and was walking through the cloud of scent when she noticed AJ leaning on the doorjamb, legs crossed, feet bare.

"What are you doing?" he said, looking amused.

"Getting ready for you," she said, going to him and putting her arms around him.

He nuzzled her neck, then looked her over, his expression making her knees wobble. "You look great in this," he said, "but you'll look even better out of it." He slid the thin straps off her shoulders, each in turn, tickling her skin, then kissing the places the straps had covered. After that, he pushed the chemise down over her hips and to the floor, where it whispered into a soft pile on her insteps.

The brush of air on her naked torso made her feel exposed, but AJ's eyes told her she was beautiful. His hands, too, gave her that message when they cupped her breasts, hefting each as if it were a lovely weight in his palm. He brushed her nipples with his fingertips and they tightened into eager knots.

His eyes, so blue, held hers, gauging her response. She had the flickering thought that she would miss this so much. After only two nights together, she'd become attached to the searching stare that almost made her want to confess all her secrets.

She breathed in the vanilla-spice candles, let the sensuous jazz fill her head. The golden light of the lamp made the room glow like a dream.

Now AJ ran a finger along her bare skin at the waistband of the silky shorts. Her stomach jumped. "Ticklish?" he mused.

"A little."

He moved his hands so that his fingers brushed the fabric between her legs, making her sex twist into an aching knot. She made a sound and he touched her gently through the cloth. "You're swollen," he murmured.

"Because of you."

"I like knowing I make you hot."

"You do. Very." Now she needed to touch him, too, to feel his skin and muscle against her own. She undid his shirt and pushed it off his shoulders, as he'd done to her chemise. The silky fabric slithered off his straightened arms and dropped to the floor. There was his broad chest, soft hills of muscle, and his swelling biceps, open to her gaze and touch.

She spread her fingers on his chest, kissed the light

sprinkling of hair in the middle, breathed in his cologne—clean and musky and male. Then she slid her fingers down to unhook his belt. The latch snagged.

"Allow me," he said and finished the job, shoving his pants and boxers to the floor. There he was, ready, and she took him in her hand, tightening her fingers around the firm shaft with its familiar velvet surface. He pushed into her palm.

Because she knew him and trusted him, she felt free to try something she'd read about. With her other hand, she gripped his balls and tugged gently on the sac that held them.

His breath hissed inward and a tremor passed through his body. "Like I said, you're a natural."

She liked that she had him shaking with desire. She was so wet she had surely soaked through the silky shorts that were the only clothes remaining between them. She should take them off.

Reading her mind, AJ tugged the cloth at hip level so they dropped to the floor, and she stepped out of the puddle of satin. He looked at her body, wonder in his gaze. "I thought I'd made you up, but here you are, just as beautiful as I remembered."

He traced the skin of her upper arms with light fingertips, then circled her nipples. He ran his hand across her stomach and lightly brushed her pubic hair, setting the nerve endings there on fire.

She needed to lie down before she sagged to the floor. So she moved into his arms and pushed him into stepping backward to the bed, which she'd turned down to reveal satin sheets the same pink as her abandoned lingerie. Somehow, that detail meant nothing now.

They lay down, AJ half on top of her, his body heat like a warm bath she was sliding into. Beneath her, the sheets were silky and cool. He kissed her, his mouth as warm and wet as she felt between her thighs. She ran her hands down his back to his buttocks, loving how powerful he felt, the muscles tensing and rippling.

His fingers found her cleft with a gentle stroke, zinging her with electric need. She moved against his fingers, knowing she would soon be swept into a climax. But she wanted to do something new—to taste him— so she stopped his hand.

"My turn," she said. She shifted down so that she rested her cheek on his lower abdomen and took hold of him with her hand.

She was aroused enough that she didn't hesitate, just took him into her mouth. He tasted lightly salty and warm and right.

He made an incoherent sound; his body tensed, then relaxed into what she was doing.

She moved up and down slowly, breathing through her nose, relaxing her throat to bring him in more fully, surprised that she didn't feel choked or lost at all. She tightened her lips and continued moving up and down, again and again, more confident with each stroke.

"That feels great," he said.

Wanting to cover him completely, she gripped him below where her mouth could reach, again cupping his balls with her other hand.

He groaned. "Yeah, that's good." She was obviously doing this right. Even better, the act was arousing her. She gripped one of his thighs between her own, sliding against it in time with the movement of her mouth. As she felt AJ's climax approach, along with her own, she was so happy and so proud. Em was definitely on the town. She wouldn't need to write down a word to remember every second of what was happening now…or whatever happened during the rest of their night together.

RAFE COULDN'T REMEMBER when a woman's mouth had felt so perfect on him. For someone who claimed to not be good at this, Beth was pretty much sending him to orgasm on a bullet train. She'd locked her knees around one of his legs and the slide of her wet warmth aroused him even more.

He looked down at her as she moved on him and felt a flood of tenderness. This was confusing in the face of his lust. He wanted to simultaneously take her fast and hard, and be as protective and careful as possible.

She was so sweet and cautious.

And so hot and wild.

He wanted to please her, too, and he knew just how. He touched her head to warn her that he would be shifting, then removed himself from her mouth so he could turn his body and get at her, too, with his lips and tongue. He gripped her backside and blew a stream of hot air on her spot.

"Oh!" she said and her hips jerked in his hands.

He dabbed her with his tongue and she writhed and called out his name.

He dabbed again and a quiver ran through her body. It was so great making love to her. She was so eager, so surprised by the pleasure of it. And he wanted to surprise her over and over.

She seemed to remember what she'd been up to and took him into her mouth again, warm and hot and soft. The woman had an amazing tongue, as inquisitive as her mind. The connection of mouth and sex was lush and overpowering. New, almost invented, amazingly intense.

She moaned, even as she mouthed him, then paused to run her tongue up his shaft and swirl around his crown.

After that, they found a nice rhythm, tongues and fingers, lips and heated breath. He stayed with her, moving himself in her mouth while he used his fingers to spread her, touching her over and over with his tongue, lapping, dabbing, gently sucking. She gasped and quivered and squirmed against his mouth.

In minutes, they built to a peak. When her climax arrived, it pushed him over the brink with her. He knew then, as he came into her mouth and she did the same against his tongue, that he did not want this to be over, even if it had to be.

Beth released him and took a few breaths before she shifted her body so she was lying against him, her cheek on his chest. "That was amazing."

"I know," he said, overwhelmed by the flood of emotion passing through him—release, joy, tenderness.

"I've never…um…done that before."

"What? Both at once?" He smiled and hugged her against him. "Nice, huh?"

"Nice? I'd say it was pretty close to an out-of-body experience."

"You're right." He stroked her hair and held her tight.

The click of metal on metal made him look over to see all three dogs in an attentive row at the foot of the bed, solemnly staring at them. "Lord, we've got furry voyeurs," he said. "Enjoy the show, fellas?" Even the cats were on hand, he noticed, decorating both arms of the chaise.

"Don't worry," Beth said. "I think they gave you a nine-point-eight."

"You mean they rated me, like the Olympics?"

"Exactly."

"So, how come only nine-point-eight?"

"You have to have something to shoot for."

He chuckled. "It's a good thing I didn't know I was being scored. I might have folded under pressure."

"I don't think you have to worry about that," she said, grasping him. He was already thickening, readying for more.

"Could we have some privacy?" he said in the direction of the animal gallery. "I'm going for that extra two-tenths."

Surprisingly, the animals dropped out of sight at his words and Beth laughed, a lovely sound he wanted to hear again and again.

"Now go to sleep," Beth commanded the dogs through her laughter. She rested her chin on her fist on AJ's chest and looked into his happy eyes, loving the cozy intimacy of the moment, the way his chest rose and fell steadily under her. "That act should have a name, not a number. It sounds like taking a turn at the post office. 'Sixty-nine. Number sixty-nine. Who has number sixty-nine?'"

"I believe it's officially called mutual oral stimulation."

"That sounds like sharing a cigarette."

"Who cares what it's called when it feels that good?" He stroked her back with his broad hand, soothing and arousing her at the same time.

"Something that fabulous should have a fabulous name. I like things to be special."

"No kidding. Look at this place." He moved up onto the pillow in a half recline, pulling her with him. "Everything's all arranged. You've got wine over here and a little bowl of condoms like party favors. And candles everywhere. Even the sheets smell like flowers."

"You don't like it?" He'd sounded uneasy, not pleased.

"It's nice. And it's you, but I would have been happy with a threadbare sofa and a condom, as long as you were there."

He pulled her more fully onto his body and wrapped his arms around her. "You're enough, Beth. Just as you are. That's what I'm trying to tell you."

For just that moment, she melted into the feeling of being human and sensual and basic, with no frills or decoration. That was nice, too. It was kind of a relief, really.

She so liked this man. After just two intense nights, she felt closer to AJ than she had to Blaine after a year. Sex was a powerful bond, of course, which she hadn't realized before. Plus she knew more about him—his condo, his habits, his opinions, even a little about his family. That made the connection even stronger.

And the fact that he'd soon be gone even sadder. Misery seeped into her, like snow through leaky shoes.

She was exaggerating her emotions, no doubt. She should address this in her column—how good sex could make you feel deceptively close. Physical intimacy could lead to false emotional intimacy. Sex as a Trojan horse, so to speak. Trojans could be for protection or for risk. Hmm. Not bad. If only her heart would stop throbbing.

Then AJ's hand on her backside began to move more

deliberately and his eyes sparkled with renewed heat, warming her right out of her sadness.

"Toss me one of those things in your candy dish," he murmured, "and we'll go with a familiar favorite."

She reached for a condom—a mint-flavored one— and decided to try something else she'd read about. She peeled it open, put it in her mouth, then took the tip of his penis into her mouth so she could unroll the condom with her lips and tongue.

AJ gave an aroused groan. "Oh, yeah…something else you're not good at." He gripped her hair. "I can't wait for you to show me more."

She intended to do just that…all night long. No sadness, no worry, no concern would keep her from wringing the pleasure out of every minute that remained to them. She had one night, so she would make it the best night ever.

8

RAFE WOKE IN BETH'S BED the next morning feeling itchy, smothered and trapped. These were real sensations, it turned out, not his response to having accidentally stayed the night. The itch came from Beth's hair under his nose, the smothering from Ditzy, who was lying on his head, and the trapped sensation was due to Spud's bulk stretched across his legs.

He hadn't meant to stay, but the hours had passed in a feverish haze of thrusts and kisses and strokes and moans. They'd crammed an entire affair into one night. And now morning sunlight washed through the sheer curtains.

He could have left, of course. There'd been a distinct moment when it would have been easy. But she'd felt so good in his arms, so right, with her legs twined with his, her cheek on his collarbone, her breast soft on his chest, that he'd just let his eyes drift shut. She'd wanted him to spend the night, he'd sensed, and that should be okay. She knew he'd be leaving in the morning. Where was the harm?

To restore circulation to his numb legs, he gingerly moved his feet. Spud groaned, Ditzy made a lip-smacking noise and Beth's eyes fluttered open.

"You stayed," she said, giving him a dreamy smile and cuddling against his chest.

"Your dogs trapped me," he said, wanting to keep things light. "I should get going, though. Get some work done before my plane leaves."

"Sure," she said, but he felt her disappointment in the stillness of her body. "I'll run the dogs outside and fix some breakfast for you." His big mouth had just lost him morning sex, he realized, and she slid into her robe so fast he didn't get a farewell glimpse of her gorgeous body. He caught her hand before she hopped off the bed. "I had an amazing time, Beth."

"Me, too," she said with a tentative smile. "I learned a lot."

"Oh, me, too," he said, untangling her soft hair with his fingers. "That swirly thing with your tongue…you could patent that."

"Glad you liked it. A friend described it to me."

"Described it?"

"It's a long story." She blushed so sweetly he just wanted to drag her back into bed and make love to her. But that would be stupid. "Don't bother with breakfast. I should just go." How else could he avoid temptation? They'd both gotten what they needed. It was time to move on. Why prolong the inevitable?

"Sure. I understand." Sadness flickered in her green eyes before she bounced off the bed. He watched her wiggle away, trailed by her dogs, and felt a little sad himself.

He threw on his clothes and was waiting in the living room to say goodbye when she brought her dogs in from the backyard.

"I could still make waffles," she said hopefully.

"Better not."

She went to him and put her arms around his neck. "I've enjoyed knowing you, AJ."

"Me, too, Beth."

"If you're ever in town again…"

"You wouldn't have time for me. You're back in circulation, remember? Some guy will snap you up in a heartbeat."

"Who says I want to get snapped up?"

"One day you will. And the guy you choose will be one lucky SOB. I'm just glad I was in that bar the day you decided to get back in action."

Then, before he blurted something he shouldn't, he kissed her, cupping her face so that his fingers also touched her neck, felt her pulse throbbing there. He memorized her scent, the swell of her lips, the shape of her tongue, the particular curve of her neck, the incredible softness of her skin. Finally, he had to end it. "You're a great lover, Beth. Don't forget that."

"You sure made me feel that way." Her eyes gleamed with pride, gratitude and sadness.

"It's true. And it will be true with any man." Hell, here he was shoving her into some other guy's arms, dammit. But it was the right thing to do, so he smiled and walked away.

At the door, he patted her dogs, waved at the cats sulking in the shadows, smiled one last time at Beth, then headed out to the rented convertible. Seated, he looked up at the house and saw that Beth was standing in the doorway with the dogs. "Drive carefully," she called to him. "Have a safe flight. And a good life."

"You, too, Beth," he called back.

She waved him off as he pulled away, as if he were a family member she wanted to watch until he was out of sight. His throat tightened with emotion. He had the urge to turn around and stay a little longer. What would one more day hurt?

No, you idiot. Quit before you ruin it.

He could still reach her as Em, online. At least that. And he wasn't even going to think about how that could go wrong.

AFTER AJ LEFT, BETH ate a quick bowl of oatmeal with the strawberries she'd bought for the waffles she'd hoped to cook for him, then took her dogs out for a walk. She refused to be sad. They'd made an agreement that had served her as well as it had him. She'd needed sexual experience from him—and a column—and she'd gotten that. In spades.

The sex had been so powerful, though, and she did like him. She enjoyed his wit, his ability to distill the key points of an argument, his focus on detail and description. Hell, he was a frustrated writer, so they had that in common, too. She even liked his cynicism, which challenged her every premise.

He'd been so thoughtful, too, and sensitive and kind. Even to her pets. But, everyone was OBB—On Best Behavior—at first. It took time to discover the everyday person with all his moods and warts and insecurities, pettiness and annoying habits.

She thought about the distance in his eyes. He'd kept space between them always. Clearly, that was a key to AJ's personality. *I don't stick around. For anything.* He meant it, she knew, because he'd been up front with her from the beginning. That was something she valued most from him—his honesty.

When she was ready to be "snapped up," as AJ had said, she wanted a man who would be wholly hers, not distracted or distant or guarded. She didn't even know his last name. She had no phone number, nothing. They'd been just ships—make that sex maniacs—passing in the night.

Maybe she'd use that in her column—sex maniacs passing in the night. She sighed. At least she wasn't too sad to be clever. As soon as she got back from the walk, she'd put all her energy into her next column, "Second Dates and Déjà Vu Delights." She wasn't really in the mood to write, but that had been her whole reason for seeing AJ. She had to make it count.

HOME FROM HIS FLIGHT, Rafe unlocked the door to his place and found it quiet, open and orderly. The scent of lemon oil and disinfectant told him Alice, his cleaning lady, had been here recently.

He thought about how Beth's place smelled—homey and sweet. And how it looked—bright with color, rich with texture, loaded with treasured objects and comfortable furniture. A complete reflection of her personality. It had made him feel claustrophobic.

His place was tastefully expensive. Sleek furniture, abstract art, valuable sculptures. It could appear in an architectural magazine, but nothing here meant much to him. He loved the openness and the views, that was about it.

Beth would think it stark. She'd want to fill it with pillows and candles and flowers and dogs. He imagined Boomer, Ditzy and Spud jumping onto his furniture. They'd slip right through the open backs of his ultra-modern chairs.

Who was he trying to impress with this place? Not women. He hadn't brought a woman here in…well, a long time. He became aware of the echo in his living room, the chill in the lemon-and-pine-scented air.

His gut felt hollow. He must be hungry. The refrigerator was in its usual bare state. Alice always tossed the wilted leftovers from his takeout meals. He could make a sandwich—there were deli meats and a loaf of bread—but the intense emptiness he felt inside convinced him to go for something more substantial.

He grabbed the stack of delivery menus he kept on hand and flipped through the brochures, settling on the Middle Eastern place he'd mentioned to Beth. The food would remind him of her.

While he waited for the delivery, he turned on his computer and went online, wanting something to erase his listlessness. Out of curiosity he logged on to a Web site for editors and writers and scrolled through the job listings. Lots of editor slots. But he wanted the freedom to write, the challenge to create, not the task of improving, revising and deciding placement.

His eye caught on an ad from the *Miami Tribune*. The contact was his old editor there. What the hell. He dashed off a catch-up e-mail. He didn't want the job—he was way overqualified—but he had the urge to touch base with his past.

When the food arrived, he paid for it, then started for his office with the containers. Except this was a meal, after all. He might as well be civilized about it, so he backtracked for a plate. He used dishes so infrequently he had to rinse dust from its surface—Beth would have been horrified. In her honor, he made an appealing arrangement of dolmades, couscous, spanokopitas and souvlaki before he loped back to his computer and ate while he checked e-mail.

He was surprised to find a message from Curt Paterson, the CEO of *Man's Man*, asking for a meeting to discuss Rafe's "future with the company." He had a feeling he knew what this was about. Curt had been making noises about retiring. He suspected the man wanted him to take over.

He'd be a fool to say no. This was what he'd been working toward for the last five years. But if he took the job, he'd be locked in for another five. At least. Despite the challenge, the idea had zero appeal. What the hell was wrong with him?

So write something on spec. Beth's pragmatic suggestion played in his head. As simplistic as the idea sounded, it had more appeal than his meeting with Curt. He wondered what she'd say about that.

Without stopping to think, he clicked on Instant Messenger. To his delight, he saw that Beth was indeed online. His heart lurched with pleasure.

Em: What are you up to? he wrote, keeping it simple and light. It was hard to resist calling her *Beth.*

Rafe! Hello! I'm being a good girl and working on my next column. It's just flying out of me.

He couldn't help being flattered. He wondered if she'd written about the sex yet…and what she'd said. Smiling to himself, he typed, *I take it the dancing went well?*

Fabulous, she answered immediately. *Mr. Perfect Timing came after all for a First Date Redux. He turned out to be a great dancer.*

And lover? Did she think he was a great lover? *Glad to hear it.* Maybe he shouldn't keep this up, but it was damn fun to tease out her reactions. *So I was right about him wanting to see you again?*

Okay. You were right. He was delayed by a change in plans.

He smiled. This exchange was easing his loneliness, so he refused to feel guilty about continuing. *Have to earn my keep as your male perspective source.*

So, what are you up to? she wrote.

Eating. Greek food. He took a bite of souvlaki.

I love Greek food!

He knew that, of course. *I'd love to share,* he wrote, biting into the delicate crust of a spanokopita. If only she were sitting beside him, feeding him as she had just last night. Maybe on his lap…naked. He swallowed the spicy bite, remembering how he'd licked the oil from her fingers. It was ridiculous to get a hard-on over a nibble of ethnic food and a memory.

So, how's the boredom factor? she wrote.

Funny you should ask, but I think the publisher's about to offer me his job. He'd hit Send before he realized how risky it was to share that kind of secret with an employee. In his mind, he was writing to Beth, though, not Em. *Listen, keep that between you and me, please,* he added quickly.

My lips are sealed. I'm honored you'd tell me. How do you feel about it?

Mixed. It would be a challenge. But I've been scanning for freelance writing jobs. E-mailed a guy I used to work for to talk about old times.

Sounds like you've already decided.

Trust Beth to cut to the chase. *Should I lie down on your couch, Dr. Em?* He pictured Beth's green eyes, focusing in, sorting through options, wanting to fix whatever was wrong with him. He remembered her lecture about calling his parents.

My couch is open, she wrote. *For you.*

And he'd love to lie down on it—with her. Naked. He had to stop turning everything into sex. He tried to picture her. Where was she? Not her bedroom—no computer there. A second bedroom, maybe, that she'd turned into an office? Her animals were with her, too, he'd bet, punctuating the quiet with doggie sighs, grunts or collar rattles. One of them had been on her lap the last time they wrote—must have been Ditzy.

Those dog biscuits had practically blown his cover. He'd remembered about the dogs from her e-mail. Luckily, she'd bought his lie about hearing them over the phone. Whew. It was good that he'd ended things before he had a chance to slip again.

Maybe I'm just delaying the inevitable, he wrote now, getting back to the discussion. *I've invested years here. There's income to consider. I'd be going backward in my career.* He ate a forkful of couscous and waited for her reply.

How can doing what makes you happy be going backward? This is your life. The only one you get, as far as we know for sure. Life's too short to be bored or miserable.

He wiped his fingers on a napkin then typed, *How'd you get so wise, Em?*

Habit. I'm my family's unofficial advisor.

He thought about what she'd told him about her mother not bouncing back from the loss of her husband. And about her flaky brother. He wondered if Beth took on too much responsibility for them. And at what cost to herself.

Do they need advice? Your family, I mean?

My mom's a little shaky about practical things and my brother's a dreamer. He means well, but he gets lost in his plans.

So you take care of them?

As much as I can.

And what about you? Who takes care of you? Lord. Now *he* was offering therapy. But he wanted to look out for her. If not in person, then this way.

I'm fine. Really. I manage. Thanks for the concern.

She'd answered exactly the way he'd responded to her advice—a kind of "hands off, I'm fine." Maybe

they were a little alike after all. *The least I can do.
You're letting me complain about my work. And I trust
you to be discreet.*

*You can absolutely trust me. And I'm happy to be
your sounding board.* He could imagine her sober expression as she typed, the slow blink of her lids, the fur-
rowing of her forehead while she considered his
predicament.

You're easy to confide in, Em.

As soon as he hit Send, he realized this was entirely
too personal a thing to say. The problem was that he
could still smell her perfume on his clothes, still remember holding her in his arms, touching her softest places.

*Don't want to overstep things here...get too per-
sonal*, he quickly wrote. *You have a column to finish.*

*Actually, maybe you can help me. Want to tell me
what you think of the first half of my column?*

I'd be honored. He couldn't wait, in fact.

It's just a draft, but you'll get the feeling of it.

When the e-mail arrived, he skimmed it quickly,
grinning. She'd skillfully described the bar, capturing
the ambiance with a few quick lines and careful adjec-
tives. She was good.

One sentence made him smile.

Tip for first dates: Test-drive your guy on the
dance floor. He'll likely do the mattress mambo
with the same grace he shows there.

Good observation. Then it got better.

Second sex doesn't hold the new thrill of the first
time, but it has its charms. You've gotten are-we-
good-together? out of the way, so you can scale

new erotic heights, try new fabo techniques. It's like a second trip to Oahu—you visit the same papaya stand, but try the coconut smoothie this time. Mmm, mmm, good. Better, even.

The "new fabo techniques" had to be the mutual oral thing she'd wanted to give a better name. He wished she'd written more about that. Probably she'd do so in the second half. He was uncomfortably erect.

Great start, he wrote, keeping his editor's hat firmly in place. *More unified than the last piece, with a more confident voice. Nice transitions between the bar review and the date dynamics. Can't wait to read the rest.* No kidding.

I'm so glad.

He felt her relief even through cyberspace.

Any suggestions for the rest? she wrote.

He wanted to tell her to write about everything…in detail, include every thrust and kiss, just so he'd have something to remember for the lonely nights ahead, but he restrained himself. *Just keep it up. Keep the detail and tone and it will be great.*

Will do. Thanks.

He could have said goodbye, of course, but he'd lost his appetite and his place was empty, as was his calendar, and he just liked talking with her. So, he asked her about how she'd first gotten her entertainment column, what she'd liked about it and why. And she asked about his career history. Her questions made him realize he'd always gone with the flow, moved to the next thing, the next challenge, without considering what he was giving up. Interesting…

Some time later, a crick in his neck reminded him that he'd been hunched over the computer for hours.

He'd barely touched the food he'd thought he was starving for—obviously, his emptiness hadn't been hunger—and an afternoon fog had dimmed the view outside his window. *I should let you get back to work, he wrote. I believe you have a sex scene to write?*

But that's the easy part. GRIN, she typed back, flirting with him.

For you, I'll bet, he wrote, flirting back. Dangerous territory.

If you want to talk more about your job...or anything, shoot me an e-mail. Or call if you'd rather. Then she typed in her phone number. Which he could never use. Ever.

You've been great, Em, he wrote, needing to back off fast. *Good luck with your column. I look forward to the rest.*

They signed off and he felt abruptly alone. For all the coldness of reading words on a computer screen, their conversation had been a mind-to-mind connection almost more intense than talking face-to-face. He'd been playing with fire, but he was just transitioning out of his time with Beth. In a day or so, he'd be back to normal.

RAFE'S REACTION TO THE first half of her column made Beth want to do a knock-kneed victory dance. Only the fact that her animals would think she was gearing up for an early walk kept her from hooting and leaping around the room.

There was more to her glow than the column approval, she realized. She liked Rafe. He'd confided in her about his promotion and his doubts. They'd chatted about their respective careers and the exchanges had been so relaxed and natural, they'd seemed like friends.

Was it easy because of her newfound confidence with AJ? Or was there real energy between her and Rafe? Of course, Rafe probably had regular liaisons with the models and writers and photographers that worked at *Man's Man*. The place was sex, sex, sex, after all.

Still. She liked his spare messages. *Who takes care of you*? The words had hit hard. As though he'd reached across the cyber miles to embrace her. Ridiculous, really, to read too much into it. He was her editor, after all, so he was probably just being encouraging.

Motivated by Rafe's praise, she wrote until her pets were restlessly circling her for their now-overdue walk. She stood and stretched, her neck tight, her butt sore. She hit Print so she could read over the column once she got to the park and let the dogs off-leash.

The printer was still humming when a car pulled up outside. The tappity-tapping feet could only belong to Sara, who raced everywhere she went. Beth grabbed her column and headed for the front door.

"So how was it?" Sara whispered, looking past Beth as if she expected to see AJ behind her.

"He's gone," she said. "But it was great."

"Sooo, are you going to see him again?"

"Nope. He's off to the east coast," she said, wishing like anything he'd stayed just a little longer.

"So, if it was great, he'll be back."

"Nope. He was very clear about that."

"Airplanes fly both directions."

"Only if you know where to fly. Or at least have a last name."

"Maybe he's married," Sara said. "Did you think of that?"

"No way. He's not the kind of man who cheats."

"But maybe it's like *Jane Eyre*—he's got a crazy woman in the attic he can't quite divorce."

"Oh, please," she said, then noticed that the dogs were poised on their haunches. Boomer and Spud held their leashes between their teeth, and Ditzy's lay at her feet. "I've got to walk these guys. Want to come with?"

"Sure, if we go to dinner after. Rick's at his parents' tonight." She bent to pet Spud, scrunching up her face. Sara felt obliged to love the little guy, but said she didn't have to like his looks.

"So, the exclusive is working out?" Beth asked, clicking the leashes onto each dog, who whined piteously to get going.

"I guess." Sara went pink with embarrassment and stood up. "I promise we won't become Siamese twins joined at the hip, wearing the same shirts and finishing each other's sentences."

"However you want to be will be fine. I'm just happy for you." She handed Ditzy's leash to Sara.

"I don't want to jinx it," she said slowly, oblivious to the fact that Ditzy was winding her leash around her legs, "but I have to say that he's smart and funny and devoted. He puts up with my crazy stuff, and his crazy stuff doesn't bother me too much."

"That's probably as good as it gets with you, Sara."

They both laughed. Ditzy lunged toward the door so that Sara, her legs bound, wobbled into a fall. Beth caught her and helped detangle her.

"It sounds very promising," Beth said.

"What's that?" Sara nodded at the printout Beth held.

"A draft of my next column. Want to read it?" She opened the front door.

"Love to."

Before she could hand it to Sara, Boomer and Spud

lunged out, yanking her forward. "When we get to the park," she called over her shoulder.

Beth and Sara concentrated on following the eager dogs around telephone poles and fire hydrants, and steering them away from traffic as they galloped toward the park. A few blocks from their destination, a car's honk made them look up and see Heather, *Phoenix Rising's* receptionist, waving madly out the window as she drove by. She kept threatening to get a dog so she and Beth could walk them together. Beth hoped that never happened. She saw plenty of Heather when she dropped by for a beer or to borrow something. Occasionally, they rode to the magazine office together when Beth had a meeting.

Finally, they reached the park and freed the dogs to run in the nearly empty common area. Beth found a bench and handed Sara her column, holding her breath, watching for every smile or nod.

Finally, Sara looked up. "This is really good. Charming, sassy, edgy. You're hitting your stride."

"I'm glad you think so. It's my first test piece. It has to be great."

"Though you need more detail about the sex. It's a little fuzzy about who's doing what to whom."

"It was kind of fuzzy last night, too." She sighed, awash in sense memory. "It was actually amazing."

"So, tell me everything…no twitch too tiny, no moan too minor, remember?"

"You'll have to settle for the column. It's too embarrassing to actually talk about."

"Come on. Hasn't Em rubbed off on you at all?"

"Not enough, I guess. I wish I'd had more time with AJ. I know that's not very Em-like, but it's true." She looked out at the horizon, where the sunset's orange was fading to pale yellow. The day had ended. That seemed so sad. Lord, she was getting wistful about a sunset? She watched the dogs chase a trio of ducks who flapped a few feet into the air then landed in the lagoon. Ditzy yipped, Boomer gave a deep answering woof and Spud a sharp bark. At least the dogs had each other. *Get a grip*.

Sara studied her. "You like this guy, don't you?"

"What? No. I can't like him. He's a source. He's research."

"But you do anyway," Sara pressed.

"I'm just grateful. He's helping me with my column and he's helping me feel more confident with sex. It's like the first guy you kissed. You always feel something for him."

"He'll be back."

"I don't think so. I think being in my home made him—I don't know—uncomfortable."

"You fussed, didn't you?"

She shrugged.

"Of course. You're you. Fussing makes men feel trapped."

"Yeah. And AJ likes things simple." *I would have been happy with a threadbare sofa and a condom, as long as you were there*. His remembered words made her shiver. "So, I'm sure he thinks I'm more invested in this than he is. But I'm not. Not really. We were just good together."

"So the sex was better than okay?" Sara teased.

"Yeah. You were right. *Okay* and *sex* don't belong on the same continent, let alone in the same sentence."

"So, now you know. Now you can get out there and live your column. Without all the angsty hand-wringing. Set Em free."

"Sure. Yeah." At the moment, the idea made her tired. "The main thing is that I got two great articles out of what happened with AJ. And I'm close to winning my column for good. I showed Rafe the first half of this and he loved it."

"Rafe? Isn't he the hatchet man? And you're calling him by his first name? You look…wistful. What's that about?"

"We've been e-mailing. Just friendly stuff about work and our lives. He offered to be a resource for me—a man's view—and since then we've just… talked."

"Oh, you have?"

"Yeah. We did the instant messaging thing for almost two hours this afternoon. I think he's flirting with me. A little."

"Well, well, well. You're just reeling 'em in, Bethie."

"Hardly." But she felt a tickle of excitement. "We have our profession in common. He's smart and thoughtful and interesting."

"What does he look like?"

"Heather says he's mid-thirties and hot…but she has boyfriends with tongue studs."

"Is he single?"

"Heather says no wedding band. But who knows?"

"He'll be back to Phoenix soon, right? So, ask him out. You need a new date anyway."

"But I work for the man. Kind of."

"Even better. Ask him for coffee, to discuss your column."

"I could do that, I guess." The idea made her smile. It would be an Em thing to do. And Em had way more fun than Beth.

9

THE NEXT NIGHT, BETH woke to find herself sweaty and aroused, a pillow between her knees. She'd been dreaming about AJ, and it had been hot. She'd had sex dreams before, but only mildly arousing ones, not this aching hunger that actually woke her up.

Her whole body felt swollen and itchy and desperate. She tossed back the sheet, pulled off her nightgown, then flung her bare arms and legs straight out across the mattress to cool off. That didn't help much. Most of the heat she was feeling emanated from between her legs. She should do something about that. She'd never had much luck with self-pleasure, but right now she longed for a tasteful vibrator that could put her out of her misery in a few battery-driven moments.

Still wide awake and restless a half hour later, she decided to get something to drink. She sat up, prompting Ditzy to lift her head from the other pillow, smack her lips, then drop back onto the mattress. Ditzy wasn't losing any sleep over Beth's restlessness.

Naked except for panties, Beth didn't bother with her mules or even her robe, preferring the air on her body. This was unusual. She never walked around naked. Had to be sexual frustration at work. She stepped over Boomer, who didn't stir.

Spud was the only dog devoted enough to follow her

wearily into the kitchen, where she made herself some iced tea, holding the glass against her hot cheek. The surface of her skin felt chafed and sore. Inside, a furnace churned heat in rolling waves.

Something stronger than tea might numb her enough to sleep. She opened the cupboard where she kept her cookbooks, took out one with drink recipes and flipped through the pages. Long Island Iced Tea. Hmm. That sounded cool and summery and strong. Too strong. It called for four different liquors and a splash of cola. She settled for just two—vodka and gin—with diet cola in a tall glass with lots of ice.

Her first swallow rushed down her throat—warm, but soothingly so, unlike the heat her body was producing. While she waited for the liquor to relax her, she decided to take advantage of her mood to fix the sex part of her column. She felt sexy, so she'd surely write sexy, too.

She strolled down the hall. The ice cubes rattled against the sides of the tall glass like wind chimes. Air brushed her naked body as she walked, and her thighs brushed each other. *I should lose weight, exercise more.* That was her automatic thought, since thighs weren't supposed to brush.

But then she realized she liked the feeling, found it slightly stimulating. She should enjoy her body, after all. Maybe it was a little flabby, but it was also sensitive and lush. AJ certainly hadn't complained about the wobble in her thighs when he was kissing her down there. AJ…oh, man. She could sure use him in that vicinity right now.

In her office, she turned on the green-shaded desk lamp and lit the cluster of cinnamon-vanilla candles. Spud, always good writing company, curled up on the sofa beside her desk.

She opened the curtains a bit so she could see into the night—lit by the lights on her neighbors' landscaping. The mesquite trees that hid her from the view of anyone passing on her quiet street shivered in the light breeze, making the night seem mysterious.

Breathing in the candles' spicy sweetness, she turned on her computer, listening to its start-up music, watching the colorful icons jump into place. To add to the moment, she clicked on her serenity water feature.

She sighed, enjoying the steady bubbling, the squeak of her chair, the fabric against the underside of her bare thighs, the air on her naked breasts. She'd never written nearly nude before, and everything seemed more vivid. The cool ridges of her keyboard, the curve of her mouse, almost like a body part—a breast or a small abdomen. She remembered how AJ had cupped her stomach, as if he liked the bulge of it.

That gave her sex a little charge. She sighed and took another long swallow of the smoky-flavored drink, and the sweet burn eased down her throat and pooled in her stomach.

Even though her computer was automatically online, she wouldn't bother with e-mail. Every person she knew should be asleep, including the technical writers on the listserv she subscribed to. Instead, she opened her column and read through the first part, which was in decent shape.

Guys love the second time, but only when they know we gals aren't ordering wedding invites and sampling groom cakes. Ensure Passion's Peak Redux, ladies, by clarifying up-front that you're just sex maniacs passing in the night.

Then, get exploring. Now that you know each other's A-spots, G-spots and every spot to

Z-spots, you have carte blanche to try new things.
Or old things in a new way.

Time Two is Exploration Time—like the star-
ship Enterprise, you'll go where you've never
gone before.

She drank more of her cocktail, liking that she'd
begun to relax a bit. She let an ice cube rest on her
tongue, enjoying the way it melted and trickled down
her throat, cool fingers of relief. Ice was nice. She ran
the tip of her tongue along the top of the cube. Chilly
and slick. Mmm. Ice was a recommended intensifier for
oral sex in one of the books she'd read. If only she'd
thought of that the night before with AJ. But they'd
been too busy in bed to run off for things to play with.

She dropped the cube into her glass and returned to
the part of her column that needed more detail.

Confession: Never been wild about the oral thing.
The rhythm's weird, and where do your hands
go? Not to mention your teeth. Plus, there's jaw
fatigue, gag reflex and other issues too indelicate
to mention.

After a round with Mr. Perfect Timing, however, I see the appeal. And let me say this about
the mutual oral thing: Re-mark-a-ble. No tacky
number is an adequate moniker for this complex
pleasure. Like riding a tandem bicycle—you can
take turns pedaling or pedal together or just coast
for a while, but the ride's breathtaking…an entire
amusement park in a two-tongued package.

She added some details, then read it over. Maybe a
little too frank. Maybe too much of a reflection of her

currently aroused state. She would reread the piece in the morning to make sure she hadn't overdone it before she sent it to Will.

And Rafe.

What would Rafe think? She got a little shiver of anticipation thinking of him looking it over, a wry half smile on his hard-but-handsome face, pipe smoke curling above his head—why did she think he smoked a pipe? Surely he wasn't *that* old. Plus he liked her work. A top editor liked her work. That was a delicious feeling she tucked away tight. If she could just keep it up, she'd have her column for good.

She was about to shut down and go back to bed when her computer emitted the tinkling instant-message sound. She looked at the talk box. Rafe Jarvis.

He'd written, *What are you doing up so late?* A zing shot straight through the calmness the alcohol had finally given her. Rafe was awake, too, and writing to her across the cyber miles.

Couldn't sleep, she wrote back, her heart pounding. *How about you?* Strangely, the sexual feelings for AJ she'd been fighting shifted suddenly to hot thoughts about Rafe. How could she be lusting for two men at once? The Em factor, she realized. Em enjoyed the sexual buffet.

Or maybe it was being up late, aroused, and drinking two kinds of liquor. Whatever. She was dying to be touched, dying to touch someone.

Insomnia, Rafe responded.

Something wrong? she wrote back.

Frustration, I guess. You?

Me, too, she typed, excitement surging. Maybe he felt aroused, too… Was she nuts? He was her boss and nearly a stranger, even though they'd flirted a bit.

Maybe she was turning into Sara, who could go to bed with a man if he merely had expressive eyebrows. In her case, it was sexy keyboarding?

She should go put some clothes on and stop jumping to conclusions. She held her damp, icy glass up to her temple to jolt herself into typing a sensible question. *Have you talked to the publisher yet? About the promotion?*

Met with him today. It would be a challenge. For a while.

You don't sound excited about it, she typed, keeping her sensible confidante persona firmly in place. She had the urge to write *I'm nearly naked, how about you?*

Good point. I don't know what to say to the guy.

So try the coin-flip test. Heads you take the job, tails you decline. Your reaction to the toss will tell you what your heart wants.

Very wise, Dr. Em. Looks like I'm back on your couch.

She smiled. *Glad to be here for you. You've helped me with my column, after all.*

I haven't done much except praise you. Ask me a male perspective question so I can feel useful.

She did have a question, now that she thought about it. It had to do with why AJ had been so firm about ending things. Had she acted clingy or was there some gender thing going on?

Okay. I'm thinking about a column comparing men's and women's attitudes about sex, she wrote. *In your opinion, how much significance do men attach to having sex with a woman?*

There was a long pause. *That depends on the man. Some men are looking for a relationship and then the sex is a first step in that direction. For other men—like me—sex is an intense physical pleasure two people share. And they have to be clear that's all they want with each other.*

AJ had wanted to "be clear," too. *So sex is just sex?* she typed back, a little disappointed. Spud groaned in his sleep as if to agree.

Nothing *just* about it. When it's good, when the chemistry's right, sex makes you feel very alive.

She thought about being with AJ. *Oh, yeah. Absolutely.*

You felt that with Mr. Perfect Timing?

That was an intimate question, but she didn't hesitate to answer. *Very much so.* She wiggled in her chair, relishing the slide of her thighs against the fabric. She felt vulnerable somehow, and open, even though Rafe couldn't see her. The candlelit dark was romantic; the only sounds were the clock ticking, the computer humming and the water bubbling.

Then he's a lucky man, Rafe wrote.

I don't know about that, she typed, blushing. *I think I'm the lucky one. Being with him was good for me. For my column…and in other ways.*

How so? he wrote back.

She considered writing, *For one thing, I'm so hot now I'm ready to proposition you online,* but not even Em would do that. *How about I send you the rest of my column and you can see for yourself?*

Can't wait, was his reply.

Her heart pounding, she attached her piece to an e-mail, telling herself she only wanted his professional opinion. But it was more than that. She wanted him to find it exciting, to react to it—to react to her. What was she doing?

The alcohol and late night had loosened her up too

much to question her impulses. While she waited, the waterfall's music tickled her ears like a lover's whisper, and she watched the candle flame teasing the air like a lover's tongue. *Oh, stop it,* she told herself. *Everything isn't sexual.* She tipped back her glass for the dregs of her drink and caught an ice cube on her tongue. This time, ice water leaked down the sides of her face and onto her shoulder, giving her a delicious little shiver. And an idea…

She lifted out the cube and touched it to her chest. She gasped at first, but then the chill became stimulating. She slid the ice slowly down her chest and onto her nipple. It burned cold—a shivery little thrill—and leaked water in trickles that traveled down to her belly and pooled between her legs, dampening her panties, tickling her sex.

This would have been fun to do with AJ. Maybe with a blindfold, so she wouldn't know when or where the shock and chill and wet, slippery feeling would touch her.

The ding of Rafe's reply made her quickly drop the ice into her glass, as if he'd caught her fooling around with it. His response to her column was one word: *Wow.*

What does that mean? she wrote back, quick as thought.

Very hot.

That little three-letter word—hot—flew through her like electricity. *And that's good?* Okay, she was fishing….

Very. Why did his answers have to be so short? She could read anything into them. Or nothing.

She wanted to write, *How so?* but settled for, *I just hope I can do as well with my next column.*

What will you write about next time? I'm curious.

And aroused, she'd bet. He was definitely coming on to her. This was fun. And a little scary. *Not sure. I'm wondering a little about online sex. What do you think about that?* She couldn't believe how bold she was. Of course, she could easily pretend she was referring to her column, not what they might do *right now*.

There was a long, long pause before he answered. *Not sure. I've never done that. You?*

Not yet, she answered, leaving the possibility open. Her whole body vibrated with interest. Her words were bright on the white screen, practically pulsing at her. Here she was, aroused, tipsy, nearly naked and damp in a romantically lit room, with her cursor throbbing like her heartbeat. And other parts.

More silence. More waiting. Finally, he wrote, *I guess I prefer the real thing.*

Me, too, she wrote, relieved and disappointed, too. She couldn't resist a little teasing. *Like, for example, I am playing with ice right now—running it over my body.* She wouldn't tell him she was almost naked. That was too direct.

That's a great picture, he wrote back. *You're making me reconsider that online idea. What is ice like on your body?*

That gave her a zing. *Very nice*, she wrote. *Shocking, then refreshing and always very, very wet and slippery.*

I think I need some ice right now—poured onto my lap. We'd better stop.

At least she'd gotten him going, too. *Just a little research*, she wrote, being playful Em. *The point is that cybersex can be fun, right? Phone sex, too. Maybe I'll write a column on out-of-body intercourse. How's that sound?*

Interesting.

What's the appeal, do you suppose? The fantasy of it? A faceless voice, a bodiless keystroke.

I guess. And I'm sure it has to do with the skill of the participants, their chemistry, their imaginations....

She realized with a jolt that now was the perfect time to suggest what Sara had recommended—that they get together for coffee to discuss her column. She had to meet him now, to see if he was as fun and friendly and sexy in person as he was online. Her heart pounding, she typed, *Maybe we could have coffee when you're next in town. Discuss my next column in more detail.*

Another long, long pause. She rested her chin on her hands staring at the screen. Had she blown it?

Finally, his answer came. *My schedule's pretty unpredictable.*

Her whole body flushed with mortification. He didn't want to meet her. *Sure. I understand*, she wrote, but she didn't. He'd flirted with her like mad and now he'd slammed down like a car hatch.

If I can swing it, I'd love to, he wrote.

Bull. He had no intention of meeting her. She was mortified. She shouldn't have let the hyper-fueled tea, the late hour and the residue from the sex dream goad her into being so suggestive. Except she'd been Em, and Em wouldn't even blink when a man turned her down. His loss. Right.

Before she could redeem herself with a quip, he wrote again. *If we didn't work together, Em, if things weren't complicated, I'd be at your doorstep as fast as a man can fly. With an entire bag of ice—crushed, cubed, shaved. Believe me.*

Maybe he was just saving her pride, but she'd take it. *Such is life*, she wrote. *Getting sleepy. Must sign off.*

She'd better, before she inserted another foot in her wicked mouth.

Don't stop writing, Em. You're good company.

You, too.

'Night. He disappeared from her screen.

She exited e-mail and rested her head on her folded arms. She was a little relieved, really. She hardly knew the man and she'd been ready to jump into Internet sex with him. It must be leftover urges from AJ.

She took a shaky breath. She missed him. Where was he tonight? Alone in his big-windowed apartment? Packing for the east coast? Did he think about her? It didn't matter because he was gone. He was not going to magically appear on her doorstep in time for her next column. That would be impossible.

And too wonderful for words.

RAFE SIGNED OFF HIS computer and guilt flooded him. What the hell had he been thinking with all those hints about online sex? Beth had tossed out the idea and he'd snapped it up like a bass with a fat fly. In his own defense, her column had aroused hot memories, and he could picture exactly how she looked with ice cubes sliding over her body.

That was entirely inappropriate for their work relationship. From now on, he would send professional e-mail only—bodiless and voiceless, a private clicking of keys, throwing businesslike symbols through space. He certainly couldn't meet her when he was in town. At all costs, he had to avoid that.

But AJ could call her. The thought struck like welcome lightning. He'd told her he wouldn't be back, but that didn't mean they couldn't talk on the phone. About their time together. And about those ice cubes. Even better, he'd be giving her material for the out-of-body sex column she'd proposed.

No. Bad idea. Wrong on so many levels.

Too restless to sleep, Rafe channel surfed for a couple of hours on his barely used plasma TV. He woke up on his uncomfortable sofa with a kink in his neck. The same pain he'd gotten over their e-mail marathon the other day. A warning. He had to cut this out.

He did fine all the next day. But when he returned from a cocktail party, a couple of martinis under his belt, he found Beth had e-mailed him the final version of her column, and he was a goner.

Her words vividly captured their night together. Reading the piece, he was with her again on her slick pink sheets, in the candle-scented dark, hearing her soft moans, enjoying her restless fingers on his most sensitive flesh. Heat burned through him. He had to reach her somehow. It was a raw, primal need.

He found himself sitting on the bed, beside the phone. It was late, but her e-mail had arrived just a few minutes before, so he knew she was still up. He opened his wallet to fish out the paper with her number, then realized he didn't need it.

He knew it by heart.

10

BETH ANSWERED ON the first ring. "Hello?" She sounded startled and her voice was husky.

"It's AJ. Did I wake you?"

"No, no. I'm awake," she said. "I'm in my office."

"I know it's late, but I was just thinking of you." That sounded lame and lovesick, but he didn't care. He was so damn happy to hear her voice, he just flopped back onto the bed.

"Are you in town?" Hope rang like a bell in her voice.

"Sorry. Wish I was." He reached under the spread and pulled out a pillow to ball under his head. "How are you, Beth?" he asked, wanting very much to know.

"I'm…fine. You?"

"Fine," he said. Now that he was talking to her, he was. Her voice restored some kind of balance in him. Neither of them spoke and heat pulsed through the phone.

"You're up late," he said, just for something to say.

"I'm having trouble sleeping lately."

"Why is that?"

"I've been restless…preoccupied, I guess."

"Me, too," he breathed, wishing she were there with him. He imagined her standing in his doorway, the light from the hall revealing her body under the silky thing she'd worn that night. He'd love to walk to the window with her and look out at the lights and the bay together. Then he would slide her clothes off her body and carry her back to bed…

"I keep remembering our nights together," she said, soft as a confession, her voice huskier still—from memory and desire, he guessed.

"What do you remember?"

"Do you really want to know?"

"Oh, yeah," he said, hard as a rock. "Every detail. Maybe talking about it will help us both."

He heard her catch her breath. "Okay. I'd like that."

"Why don't you take the phone into your bedroom and get comfortable?"

"Good idea." Her voice jogged as she walked and he heard the rattle of the dogs' tags.

"The dogs on your trail?"

She laughed. "They're worried about me not sleeping, so they follow me around."

He was sorry about the insomnia, but not sorry that she missed him. He heard rustling, then she spoke, her voice heavy, so he knew she was lying down. "There. I'm comfortable. How about you? Are you comfortable?"

"Sure," he said. "I'm lying down."

"What are you wearing?"

"I've got on a T-shirt and sweats." But that wasn't phone sex material. "Hang on." He set the phone down, tossed off his shirt and shoved off his pants. "Now I'm naked."

"That's better. I like thinking of you that way."

"How about you? What are you wearing? That little pink number from the other night?"

"Exactly. It reminds me of you."

He remembered her dashing through her bathroom with a perfume bottle in one hand, her breasts jiggling as she ran, the nipples visible through the thin fabric, small tight berries waiting to be plucked. He hungered to touch them, kiss them, suck them until she moaned. "All I want to do is rip it off you so I can see all of you."

"I wish you could. I really do," she said, her voice so thick with longing she was almost crying.

Lust thundered through him. She wanted him as much as he wanted her. "So, why don't you take off your clothes for me now?" he said hoarsely. "And describe what you're doing."

"Okay," she said, and her voice wobbled as she shifted positions. "The chemise is slippery and cool. I'm pulling it down by the straps, but letting it tickle my skin the way you did with your fingers."

"I can see that."

"And now the top's off and I'm kicking off the shorts."

"So you're naked now?" He swallowed, seeing in his mind her pale and pretty flesh, accented by her brown nipples and pubic hair, the little swell of her stomach, her entire beautiful body spread out for him on her gleaming pink sheets. The picture and the aroused rasp of her breath made him hard as stone.

"Yes," she breathed, "but it wasn't like when you did it. Your mouth was warm and wet on my shoulders and your fingers were so gentle on my skin."

"I can see your breasts in my mind. And your nipples…so soft, they seem like they could melt. Until they knot up like hot little beads."

"That's when I'm excited," she breathed.

"Are you excited now, Beth?"

"Yessss," she said. "And I'm touching one nipple

now—pretending my fingers are yours—and it's all tight and achy."

He sucked in a breath. "I wish I could put it in my mouth, feel that knot against my tongue."

"Oh, me, too." She sounded almost in pain. "Your tongue is so wet and strong."

"Are you wet, Beth? I like how wet you get."

There was a pause and then she said huskily, "Very."

"Will you touch yourself for me? Bend one leg so that if I were there with you, I could see how you look, how wet and swollen you are, how much you want me inside you."

"Okay," she said.

"Are you doing it?"

"Yes. I'm touching myself." The words were a hungry sigh.

"I love the way you feel—soft and slick and layered."

"You're making me ache." She sounded so needy, he was desperate to be there to hold her, kiss her, replace her fingers with his own. But all he could do was close his eyes and picture her finger stroking her delicate flesh. "You're so swollen that your clit is peeking out, ready for more. Am I right?"

"Yes. Yes. Oh." Each lust-laden breath made him want her more.

"You're stroking yourself. I can hear it in your voice."

She gasped into the phone. "It feels good—because you're talking to me."

"That's why I'm here…to make you feel good. So good that you explode with it."

She took a shuddery breath and he pictured her mouth, soft and willing, wanting him to invade her, stroke and nibble and suck her. "Now you, AJ. Are you hard yet?"

"Are you kidding? I could hammer nails, thanks to you."

"Hold yourself for me. I love how you feel."

"I'm doing it." He gripped himself tightly, a poor substitute for her hands and body, but it would have to do.

"Describe what you're doing," she said, her voice rough with emotion. She was moving faster, he could tell by the wobble in her voice.

"I'm holding tight, so it feels like when I'm inside you as far as I can go. Tight and hot." He closed his eyes, saw her body in his mind, her fingers on him, then her mouth on him, hot and wet. He pushed into his own hand, hard and fast.

"I'm getting close," she gasped.

"Good," he said. "Put a finger inside you…the way I want to be inside you, making you crazy."

"I want you here. Now. In me. Pushing deep."

"Me, too, baby. Me, too. I want inside you, too. So much."

He closed his eyes, listening to their harsh breaths over the wire, rhythmic as their movements. He sensed her fingers moving, pictured her knotted nipples, her head back against the pillow, mouth slightly open, restless tongue skimming her lips.

"I wish I could take you in my mouth," she whispered.

"Oh, me, too." He stroked himself, imagined her lips on him, squeezing, sliding, her teeth gently teasing him.

"You're getting close, aren't you?" she asked.

"Yeah."

"Me, too. I've never felt so good by myself before."

"That's because I'm with you. For every second. I'm your finger inside you. I'm sucking your nipples, pushing into you."

But he wanted more. Bad. And now. *He could be on a plane in an hour.* No.

He stroked faster, focused on his image of her in her silk sheets, surrounded by pillows, her nimble fingers on her softest place, sliding in and out, gasping as she approached the peak.

And in her arms in three.

He forced himself to stay with his fantasy, imagined the flush on her neck and face, the glitter in her eyes, the bruised look of her lips after he'd kissed her hard.

"Are you…close?" she said, clearly struggling to speak. Her soft moan told him she was on the brink.

"Oh, yeah. I'm inside you now, Beth, pushing deep. I can feel all of you, all the way. And you feel good, so good, so…"

She cried out sharply and there was a clunk. He didn't have time to wonder what had happened before he climaxed into the sweatpants he'd grabbed at the last instant.

His body shook from the power of his release. He couldn't believe talking about sex with her could move him so strongly. And make him wish like hell he had her in his arms, was inside her, where it felt right, where he could lose himself in her.

Something was going on inside him because of her, something a little out of control. He'd been ready to run to the airport and fly to her.

There was a rustle in the phone. "I dropped the phone. Sorry," she said breathlessly.

He chuckled. "I was hoping you hadn't fallen off the bed."

"I almost did that, too." She laughed, mellow and rich. His Beth. He remembered their last night together, the post-orgasmic flush that spread across her upper body, her sweat-damp limbs twined with his, her cheek on his chest, her fingers reaching under him to hold on tight, as if he might slip away.

"Never in a million years did I imagine I'd do *that* on the phone," she said more lightly. "My friend Sara won't believe it."

"You'll tell her?"

She paused. "Would that upset you, AJ? To know I shared our, um, experience with someone else?" There was a thread of worry in her voice. She meant her magazine readers, he knew, not just her friend, and this was his chance to reassure her.

"Not a bit. I'm honored you consider it worth sharing."

"Good. That's good."

He smiled, knowing he'd relieved her. "Where's the animal crowd? Were they on hand for the action?"

"Sound asleep. Boomer's on the floor of course. Ditzy hates when the bed jiggles, so she's down there, too. And Spud's on your side."

He had a side? He didn't want to think about the fact that that didn't bother him.

They breathed at each other for a few more seconds, neither feeling the need to speak, the soft flow of air holding them together, suspended in time. He could almost feel the throb of her pulse against his ear.

"I know I shouldn't ask this," she said finally, "but is there a chance you'll come back to Phoenix?" She rushed to finish. "For work, of course. Because there's this thing with an ice cube I'd like to try." She was hiding the need he'd heard in her question.

"Hard to say." He had no business seeing her again. Every contact increased the risk that he'd reveal himself and was one more strike against his integrity. If only things were different. If only they hadn't started on a lie. But untangling the fiction would tangle everything else.

"Just throwing that out there." She was embarrassed. She thought he didn't want to come.

"I want to, Beth. I do. But there are things in the way."

"Sure. I understand," she said.

"I wish I could hold you now." What the hell was he saying?

"Me, too." There was a silent beat while emotion passed between them across the miles and wires. He missed her. And the soft sadness in her voice told him she missed him, too.

The climax had eased his tension, but he didn't feel better. He'd never thought of himself as a lonely man, but just now the lights out his window seemed hard and distant instead of cheerful and promising. Of course, if Beth were here, looking out there with him, it would be a whole different deal.

"At least we have the phone," she said. "Phone sex is better than no sex…. So don't hesitate to call." She stopped short, as if she'd said too much. "Until I'm back in circulation, I mean."

"Sure," he said, the idea of her in another man's arms making him feel cold. "Get some sleep," he said, closing the call. He wanted to talk more, to ease this empty feeling, but she might ask for his number. He didn't dare give it to her and hoped like hell she didn't use the telephone service to retrieve it. He shouldn't have admitted he wished he could be with her. It was cruel and just plain stupid.

On top of that, he'd lied to her again. He *would* be back in Phoenix. In just a few days. With a pang of guilt, he remembered that she'd asked him for coffee, as Em, online, and he'd shut her down cold. What a complete jerk he was. An A-one ass. This had to stop. He would make absolutely certain to avoid her at the magazine, make no more phone calls, and send no more risqué e-mails. It would only hurt her feelings, and it sure as hell didn't help him a bit.

THE FOLLOWING FRIDAY, Rafe pushed through the glass doors of *Phoenix Rising* to be greeted by Heather. "Well, hello, Mr. Jarvis! How was your flight? And you? How are you?"

"The flight was fine and so am I. You?"

"Bored brainless," she said with a dramatic sigh. "Nothing fun ever happens around here."

"Sorry to hear that. Is Will in?"

"Except when you come, of course. Then it gets exciting. Everyone scurries around trying to look hard-working and essential."

Everyone except Beth, he knew, who wouldn't be coming in today. He'd e-mailed her that he'd be here Monday, so she wouldn't pop in to try to meet him for coffee. He hated misleading her, but better a little disappointment now than the huge shock of discovering her online editor and out-of-town lover were one and the same first-class jerk.

"You say Will's waiting for me?" he said, to keep Heather on track.

"Everyone else, too. You make them all nervous."

That was an unfortunate side effect of his job. Today that bothered him. Everything about his dealings with people seemed more significant lately—maybe because he'd been worrying about the effect he was having on Beth.

"You don't make me nervous, though," Heather continued. "I know you're a big softie."

"Oh, you do?"

"Oh, yeah." She winked at him, flirting with all her might.

He smiled to acknowledge her efforts, but ignored her intent. "Would you buzz Will for me?" How did anyone make it on time to an appointment with Heather out front?

"Hey, I know what will help. Stay for our potluck and show people the real you. It's Administrative Professionals Day. So zip into the kitchen about eleven-thirty and say hi. The food will be outstanding."

"That's possible. How about if you buzz Will and—"

"Ironic, isn't it? We secretaries work our asses off all year long and they give us one day. Better than nothing, I guess. Though some office-chair massage wouldn't go unappreciated."

"I'll just head back to Will's office, okay?" He tapped the counter and turned to go.

"It's at eleven-thirty," she called after him, "in the kitchen."

Still wearing a smile—Heather was a trip—he breezed into Will's office. They discussed the transition for a bit, and the need for two replacement writers. Then Will led him down the hall to the graphics department to check out the changes in the magazine's design.

Lively conversation spilled out of the offices they passed, along with phone conversations and clicking keys. It was a friendly place and the halls were lined with dozens of framed magazine covers, evidence of the staff's pride. They passed the kitchen, which kicked out the scent of garlic and an oven's heat, then turned into a huge room flooded with mid-morning light—the graphics department.

While Will requested printouts of a makeready, Rafe wandered from workstation to workstation to comment positively on whatever he saw on the screens or worktables.

Will called him over to see the mock-up. Rafe suggested minor adjustments to the front page template, then spoke loudly enough for everyone to hear. "Everything looks great, Will. You and your crew do solid work."

Will grinned, and Rafe felt the rest of the room exhale with relief. For whatever reason, the human aspects of his work seemed more important to him now.

He flipped to the page that would hold the "Sex on the Town" column, and couldn't help smiling.

"You liked Em's new column, huh?" Will asked.

"Very much. It's fresh and strong."

"I'm pretty proud of her." The managing editor's almost paternal affection for Beth was touching. "She'll be here for the Admin's Day luncheon, and to pick up her fan mail. Why don't you stick around and meet her?"

"She's coming in today?" *Crap*. "I'd like that, but I made other, um, plans for lunch."

"At least say hello. She'll be here any minute."

"Sure. Great," he said, but he grabbed at his pocket as if his phone had vibrated. "'Scuse me while I take this." He whipped out his duck-Em device. "Yeah?" he said, speaking into the dead phone. "Sure…right…right away." He gestured at the phone for Will's benefit and headed for the door.

Knowing Will must think him insanely jumpy, he darted into the hall, where he saw that Beth stood at the reception desk talking to Heather. Lord.

At least Heather would hold her for a bit. He lunged across the hall and opened the door to the room next to the kitchen. It turned out to be a janitor's closet and catchall. Bare pipes, a furnace, fuse box and deep sink shared space with stacked cases of soda and beer, utility shelves laden with paper goods, serving bowls and trays, a helium tank and boxes of balloons.

Once inside, he realized what a mistake it was to hide in a room that everyone had to pass to get to the luncheon. He'd never escape. Sure enough, he could hear a steady stream of people walking by. If he popped out, what would he say? Just checking the plumbing?

This was insane. He was a vice president at a major men's magazine. He shouldn't be hiding out in a utility room to avoid a woman.

But that's just what he was doing. Because it was Beth. Vice president or not, he'd acted like a fool with her, and above all, he couldn't make it worse. For now, he'd stay the course.

"DON'T YOU LOOK HOT," Heather said to Beth. "Hair up and major makeup." She leaned over the counter to check out what Beth was wearing. "Great pants and I love your shoes."

"Thanks," she said, resting her potluck dish on the reception counter. She'd decided that if she was going to be a sex columnist, she'd better spiff up her look. She'd donned her fake hairpiece and an ensemble her mother had bought her and she'd never worn—formfitting chinos, a spaghetti-strap top and strappy sandals.

She looked far different from the woman in a tie-dyed jumper and a braid who usually popped in for checks, mail or to meet with Will.

"And is this your seven-layer bean dip?" Heather asked, lifting the foil and dipping in a finger, which she licked. "Delish. You should have told me you were coming in today and I'd have given you a ride. I'm going home right after the luncheon."

"I didn't think about it."

"Can I have this recipe? I'll trade you for my Bundt cake one. It's heaven. People practically pass out from the taste."

"You can have the recipe, no problem. You don't need to trade a cake for it, Heather. It's not exactly a secret."

"Are you sure? Tell you what, let me borrow your Bundt pan and I'll make you a cake so you can see what I mean."

"You don't have to—"

"I insist. And, hey, Will showed me your new column. Excellent. I know exactly what you mean about…" She mouthed, *blow jobs*. "*Très* ick until you care about the guy. And I'll tell you what I hate—when they push on your head like you don't know what's down there."

"Right. So true." Beth felt her face flame. She'd have to get used to trading sex stories if she intended to keep her column.

"So, Will says you're having to, like, audition to keep your column? That's heavy pressure. And they're nuts. You're too good to lose."

"I appreciate the support." Maybe she should get Heather's take on the topic of her next column, "Long Distance Hot Stuff." "What do you think about phone sex, Heather?"

"*Phone* sex?" She gave Beth a withering look. "I'm a telephone receptionist, sugar. When I'm off work I never want to *see* a phone, let alone have an orgasm with one in my ear. Though maybe with a speakerphone it wouldn't be so bad."

"Good point."

"Yeah. Hands-free phone sex. Not bad." Heather beamed at her own joke. "Here's another one. What's the best thing about phone sex? You never have to look your best. Funny, huh? Put that in your column."

"I just might."

Heather grinned, then seemed to remember something and leaned over the counter. "The *Man's Man* stud muffin is on site."

"Beg your pardon?"

"Rafe Jarvis, the cold-blooded, job-whacking corporate bastard who makes my pubes curl. He's here. Have you met him yet?"

"I didn't realize he'd be in today…." He'd e-mailed her that he was coming Monday, not Friday. Hmm.

"He's with Will. Go get him. You look great."

The rush of pleasure at finally meeting him conflicted with her hurt that he'd lied to her. But maybe his plans had changed at the last minute.

She left her bean dip in the kitchen and when she emerged, she saw that Will was motioning to her from the graphics department doorway. She joined him.

"I want you to meet Rafe Jarvis," he said.

"Sure," she said, smoothing her hair, her heart racing.

"He stepped out to make a call. Should be back any second."

They made small talk, speaking to people heading to the potluck, until *any second* had turned into a quarter of an hour.

"What's with this guy?" Will frowned. "I told him you'd be here and he whipped out to take a call."

"It must have been important." He was obviously avoiding her. What did he think she was going to do, throw herself at him? That stung.

"Hey, if it isn't *Phoenix Rising*'s newest star."

She and Will turned to see Garry Voss, the magazine's music critic, heading their way. The guy was a babe hound who dated models and singers, so Beth had the urge to turn to see if he meant someone behind her.

But he reached for her hand, shaking it while gripping it with his other one, making deep eye contact the whole time.

"Thanks," she said. "Just doing my job."

"You're too humble. Everyone I talk to is jazzed about your column. Women especially. Quite a departure from your old work—excellent in its own right, of course—but with the new direction, the new take fits well. What can I say? You're good."

"Why, thank you. I enjoy your work, too."

"Changed your hair, too. Very flattering."

"Watch out for this guy, Em," Will said, and shot Garry a warning look. "I'll get your fan mail and track down Rafe." He pointed at Garry. "You behave."

"I'm harmless," Garry said to her after Will left, lifting his hands in surrender. "But the rumors keep life interesting." He leaned against the utility room door, giving her a friendly up and down.

"I can imagine."

"You should stop by more often. We have similar beats, you know. We could compare notes."

"I work out of my home. I don't even have a desk here."

"I bet we could scrounge up a computer if you wanted to improve the scenery." He paused. "Actually, what are you doing tonight? There's a jazz fusion group at the Celebrity Theater and I've got an extra ticket. Want to come with?"

"Thanks, Garry, but I don't think so." The man was asking her out. He was handsome and funny and smart, and he dated beautiful, sophisticated women, not librarian types with secret lives.

"Come on. We'll make it a working date," he coaxed. "Don't you have some new club to review? The menu at Quiero is killer."

"Nuevo Latino, right? I'm dying to try the ceviche."

"Perfect. We could go to Axiom after that, check out the new DJ."

"True…." Why not work with a colleague? Six weeks ago, she would have been intimidated by his reputation—and his wily grin. But now she saw the invitation as a new column offered to her on a silver platter. What would she call it? "Tag-Team Dating"? Knowing Garry, maybe it should be "Dating with a Pro—Kids, Don't Try This at Home." "Okay. Why not?" she said.

"Great. We can do pre-post concert stuff and kick around our commentary."

"Sounds good." And what about sex? Could she go to bed with Garry? She didn't feel the vibe right off, but she was nervous.

What better way to prove she wasn't hung up on AJ? And if they slept together—eventually—that would verify that it was *sex* that was exceptional, not one particular, remarkable man.

Heather emerged from the kitchen, looking annoyed, and headed for them. "I need in there," she said to Garry, gesturing at the door behind him. "It's supposed to be my friggin' day and I have to set the buffet."

Garry pushed away from the door and cupped Beth's elbow, helping her out of the way.

11

RAFE TRIED TO dive behind the stacks of soda cases before Heather burst in, but she was fast. So he ducked behind the door to keep Voss and Beth from seeing him, then shoved it shut once Heather was inside.

"What are you doing in here?" Heather said, sounding more amused than startled.

"Shh," he said, motioning her away from the door so they wouldn't be overheard.

"What's going on?" she said, delight in her voice. Some people loved trouble.

"This is embarrassing." He rubbed the back of his neck, wracking his brain for a decent reason to be in here. "The thing is that I was headed for the luncheon and turned in here by mistake. Now I feel stupid coming out. I mean, how would it look?"

That was lame, for sure, and Heather didn't buy it. "What's the deal? Who are you hiding from?"

"Hiding? Why would I be hiding?" He tried for his no-nonsense tone, but Heather had already identified him as a pushover. His cell phone sounded and he slapped it on. "Yes?" he whispered.

"Where are you? Em's waiting to meet you."

"I'll meet her another time. I got tied up. Can I call you right back? 'Bye." He clicked off.

"I heard that, you know. Your phone spills sound. You're hiding from Em, aren't you?"

"Why would I do that?"

"Exactly. Why?"

What could he say that she would buy? His gaze fell on the helium tank and balloons. "Okay. You got me. The truth is that I have a surprise for Em…that I didn't want to tell her yet."

"A surprise? What surprise?" She crossed her arms in doubt.

"You can't say a word, Heather."

"My lips are sealed," she said, pretending to zip her mouth.

"I'm about to give her the column, but I have to wait for the official okay. Which I expect later today."

"She gets to keep her column? That's great. And that audition idea was insulting, if you ask me."

"The point is I plan to tell her later…over dinner," he improvised. "So don't spoil it for me, okay?" The lies were rolling off his tongue, but he knew Heather would never keep a secret this juicy without a solid story to go with it.

"You can count on me," she said. "And you're taking her to dinner to tell her? Very sweet. I knew you were a teddy bear. If you'd just tone down the icicle eyes."

"I'll try. Look, what did you need in here? You'd better get back before they send a search party."

"Cups, plates, napkins, forks. The whole shebang."

Rafe piled the supplies into her arms, then held the door for her.

"Want me to sneak you out some food?" she whispered.

"I'll be fine. There's plenty here." He grabbed a bag of potato chips off the shelf and showed it to her.

She nodded and left.

He closed the door behind her, half expecting her to trot back with security guards to escort him out of the building as a closet-lurking nutcase. Which he was. Absolutely.

When the door remained closed, the hall quiet, he figured he was safe and sank onto a case of soda to eat stale chips and wait for the clear sign from the ever-helpful Heather.

Now he had to give Beth her column, of course, forgoing the remaining trial pieces. She had a virtual lock on it anyway, so that was not a real problem. He'd have to e-mail her, or, better yet, let Will tell her. He wished he could see her face when she heard the news.

He sighed, munching the last crumbs from the bag. Then he remembered the weasel of a music critic asking Beth out. *Working date, my ass.* What an opportunist. Voss was a good critic, savvy and hip, and his tone was right, so he'd kept his column—a fact Rafe now found irritating. He'd met the guy and recognized him as a social opportunist.

So the bastard had finally noticed how hot Beth was. Surely she'd see through his lines. Except she was so trusting, so earnest, giving everyone the benefit of the doubt. Damn.

Before long, the hall was filled with the sound of people walking away, talking, and the rumble of voices next door thinned to nothing. Finally, Heather stuck her head in the door. "Beth has left the building. Along with Elvis."

"Thanks," he said, quickly emerging from the storeroom. "And I appreciate your continued discretion."

"I'll be cool, don't worry." She winked at him. "I knew you were a marshmallow." She jiggled off down the hall.

He sighed. What was he doing? He'd piled the lies so high it was only a matter of time before they crashed on top of him. He headed to Will's office to apologize for his disappearing act, but on the way, a tuneful whistle drew his attention to the music critic leaning back in his chair, feet on the desk, reading the liner notes to a CD.

Maybe he would just check the guy out. For Beth's sake.

The second he saw Rafe, Voss dropped his feet from the desk and stood. "Mr. Jarvis. Garry Voss." He shook Rafe's hand and met his gaze. "We met on your first visit."

"I remember."

"I like the changes you've made in the pub. We all do."

Fairly kiss-up, but not completely smarmy.

"What are you working on?" Rafe asked, indicating the guy's computer screen.

"A review of new jazz releases." He handed him the CD he'd been looking at. "These guys are great."

"I know this group." He tapped the case.

"You like them? Because I've got an extra ticket to their concert tonight. It's a decent venue. Intimate. Good sound."

"Thanks, anyway."

"No, I insist." He pulled an envelope out of a drawer and handed it to Rafe. "This is from a radio station promo. I'd invite you to sit with me, but I have a date."

With Beth, he knew. And the guy looked as smug saying it as a cat on the verge of swallowing a bird whole.

"I wouldn't want to interfere with your date," he said, wanting to do exactly that.

"You wouldn't be. We're a few rows down. Critics' seats, of course."

"Of course." The guy was so full of himself. He wouldn't know a sincere emotion if it punched him in the jaw, which was exactly what Rafe suddenly wanted to do. Beth would never sleep with this guy.

Would she?

"We could meet you for drinks afterward," Voss said.

"I doubt I'll make it," he said, trying to hand him back the envelope. "Thanks, anyway."

Voss held up his hands, refusing the ticket. "In case you change your mind."

The guy wasn't as sleazy as Rafe thought, he had to admit. And Beth was an adult. If she wanted to sleep with him, she had every right to. She could "make a guy walk funny for a week" if he got out of line, she'd told him. He'd love to see her put this joker in his place.

For a fleeting instant, he thought about going to the concert just to keep an eye out for her, check on the interplay. Too risky, even if he stayed in the shadows. If Beth saw him, she'd think he was the opportunistic rat, not Voss. She just might be right.

GARRY VOSS TURNED out to be a delightful companion. He was less flamboyant than Beth had expected, with an easy laugh and an open smile. He listened intently to her, asked pertinent questions and kept the conversation flowing. Very charming.

She'd never worked on a column with a colleague before, and it was a blast. As they ate at the Latin restaurant, sampled desserts at a famous resort, then headed to the concert, he quizzed her on how she would describe the food, the ambiance and the prices.

They left at intermission to check out the dance club,

and talked the entire time about how they went about formulating their respective columns. All in all, it was a lovely evening.

Except now they were pulling up to her house and Beth broke into a sweat. What now?

She'd enjoyed Garry, but she didn't want to have sex with him. His guiding hand at her back as they moved from place to place had been pleasant. She'd even felt flickers of arousal, but they'd been muted, as if her attraction muscles were tired.

That was too bad, because Garry would be the perfect next sexual adventure. He knew about her column, too, so there would be no secrets to keep. But she just wasn't, well, interested.

He pulled up to her place and braked.

Taking a deep breath, she turned in the narrow seat of his sports car to end this quickly. "Thanks for a lovely evening. It was a great working date. I—"

With no warning, he cupped her cheek and kissed her softly, then stilled, waiting for her reaction. She felt…nothing. Her bloodstream, which bubbled like seltzer whenever AJ kissed her, was as thin and still as two-day-old Seven-Up.

Garry pulled back and smiled. "So, not tonight, huh?"

"I don't think so. I'm sorry, Garry."

"Not a problem. But when you write about me, and you will write about me, be kind."

She grinned at the paraphrased line. "I had a great time."

"I thought there was chemistry, but you seem… preoccupied."

That was exactly it. She felt *unavailable*. As though her libido wore a No Vacancy sign. Because of AJ?

That would be a disaster. He was completely out of the picture. There was Rafe, too, she reminded herself. Except he was just faceless keystrokes she'd flirted with. Plus, he'd ducked out on the mere possibility of meeting her. How could she have a thing for him?

"Sorry," she said to Garry. "It's not you."

"Oh, I know that," he said, then grinned, as if making fun of his own arrogance. "Maybe next time." He brushed a hair from her cheek. Again she felt nothing.

"Maybe."

"And if not, then we'll be work compadres."

He was so easygoing. No ruffled feathers, no wounded ego. He would be a good man to interview for her column. "Could I ask you some questions, Garry? About dating? About how you decide to sleep with someone, what women consider charming, all that?"

"Zo, I am to be a re-zearch subject, hmm?" he said in a bad German accent. "You got coffee?"

"I grind my own blend—Hawaiian and Jamaica Blue."

"I knew you'd be good. At coffee…and much more. Too bad we didn't click."

Too bad, indeed. She knew that attraction was not something you conjured up on demand. But maybe she just needed time to cleanse her palate from AJ. Maybe next time she'd want more from Garry than conversation and professional rapport.

She could only hope.

RAFE JERKED AWAKE TO the sound of a siren in the distance. He'd fallen asleep in his rental car, waiting for Beth and the weasel to get home. He just wanted to see her safely in her door. And see Voss *leave*. What was that about?

Pain shot through his neck. He'd kinked it again. Damn. The pattern was clear: fall asleep thinking of Beth, wake up in pain. When would he get the message that this was bad for him?

He blinked and checked his watch. Midnight. He looked up the block at Beth's house. He'd parked a distance away to be sure Beth didn't see him, even though he'd rented a nondescript sedan—this time he'd just wanted a way to get to her. He saw that a silver Mazda RX8 rested smugly in her driveway. Exactly the car a trendy jerk like Voss would drive.

He'd missed their arrival, and judging from the last time he'd looked at his watch, they could have been inside for as long as an hour. Had she decided to sleep with him?

Alarm hit him in a wave of cold heat. What if she'd asked him in for coffee…and meant *coffee*? Was she nervously fending off roving hands? Delivering a knee to a randy crotch? Rafe could hardly peer into her window to check. He was already a stalker. He wasn't going for Peeping Tom.

He had to make sure she was okay. He opened his cell phone to call her, despite the risk to his cover, but then her front door opened and Voss stepped onto the porch. He walked backward toward his car so he could face Beth, who was watching him leave, smiling, just as she'd done for Rafe the last time he'd seen her.

She and Voss had had a good time. Had they had sex? Not even a player like Voss could move that fast. And what man could settle for just once with a woman as much fun in bed as Beth?

Unpleasant emotions roared up like a stoked fire— emptiness, anger, envy, loss. And raving jealousy.

What the hell was wrong with him? This was nuts.

He was hanging out here like a lovesick idiot. Beth didn't need his protection. She was perfectly capable of looking after herself. She already had.

As soon as she'd shut her door, he turned on the car and drove off, fast, cursing himself all the way back to his hotel.

He would take an early flight back to San Francisco and forget about Beth. Stop talking to her—or e-mailing her. Well, except to tell her she'd earned her column. But that was absolutely it.

She no longer needed him for her column or anything else. He'd helped her into circulation, as she'd wanted. He'd been her sexual Henry Higgins, and the newly erotic Eliza was off on her own. With that frickin' music critic.

That thought made him grind his teeth. What if the guy hurt her feelings? What if she got too attached to him? He was definitely a player.

Get over it, pal. She's fine. Let go.

All the same, he lay awake most of the night.

The next morning, Rafe stood at the ticket counter for his flight to SFO and accepted his ticket envelope from the counter attendant.

"You're all set," she said, smiling. "Heading home?"

Home? To his empty condo, smelling of Lysol and lemon oil? He thought about Beth in her pink silk bed, surrounded by pillows and her menagerie. He thought about her sweet mouth and eager eyes. If it weren't for the lie about who he was, he'd see more of her for sure. He hadn't felt that way about a woman in…well…

Hell, he'd never felt like this about a woman.

How could he just walk away?

"Sir?" the woman said. "Is there something else?"

People behind him were waiting to check in, but he

couldn't move. *If you tell her the truth, you can keep seeing her.*

Okay. He'd do it. He would explain the misunder-standing and why he'd kept up the charade. Surely, she would understand his predicament. She was a reason-able woman.

"Sir?" The ticket agent sounded impatient now. "Is there something else?"

"Yes. I need to cancel this ticket. I forgot something important." The idea sent a flood of happiness through him. He would just tell her the truth. Get out from under the black cloud of the lie. She would be upset, of course, at first. But she had a secret, too, about using AJ for her column. They'd get through the tension somehow and start over fresh.

There would be no pressure, because she wouldn't want that—she was just getting back into circulation—but they could see each other openly. Well, more or less openly. There was the problem of working together, but that would be over soon enough.

All he knew was that he craved her company. He wanted to talk about the things that were going on with him—as Rafe. Kick around the job prospect with her in person, watch her eyes as she pondered his options and gave him her gems of advice. Find out more about her. Find out everything.

He drove like a maniac straight to her house. He couldn't wait to see her face when he showed up on her doorstep.

BETH WOKE TO THE SOUND of her dogs barking and bounding on and off her bed as though it were a tram-poline. Through her haze, she realized that her door-bell was ringing. She looked at her clock and blinked.

Seven in the morning? Who could possibly be here this early?

She'd fallen asleep at two, a sex manual on her chest, after interviewing Garry and keying in her notes. She threw on her robe, slipped on her mules and trudged to the door, groggy and cranky. This better be good.

She looked through the peephole. AJ? She rubbed her eyes and looked again. Yes. It was him. On her porch. Impatiently leaning from foot to foot, arms akimbo, looking straight at the peephole.

She threw open the door. "AJ? What are you…? You're here!"

The mess his hair was in and the dark circles under his bloodshot eyes suggested something awful had happened, but his face was full of hope. "Can I come in?"

She backed up to make way and he entered, holding her gaze, oblivious to the dogs swirling around him. "I just want more time, Beth," he said, as if he were confessing some great sin.

"Me, too," she breathed. It crossed her mind that she should run and make herself presentable, but instead she threw herself into his arms and kissed him.

He held her tight and kissed her back, slow and deep and relieved.

After a long, lovely time, AJ tore his mouth away. "I know you don't know much about me, so I'm here to fill in the blanks."

"It's okay," she said. She'd alarmed him before with her fussy arrangements, so she wasn't about to grill him now. She knew the most important thing—that her feelings for him weren't crazy. The man had flown across the continent to be with her. "Take me to bed," she whispered. "Now."

"Are you sure?"

"Completely." For once in her life, she would be spontaneous. No second guessing, no elaborate preparations and no explanations.

Without a word, AJ swept her into his arms. She laughed with delight and put her arms around his neck. He carried her off toward the hall. She looked down to see all three dogs trotting happily behind, as joyful as she was about AJ's return.

Her self-consciousness wasn't totally gone, though. "I should brush my teeth and my hair, and wash my face, at least."

"I like you like this. No makeup, no perfume. Just you." He kissed her and she melted in his arms, weightless with joy. Weightless except for the arousal settling in her abdomen, locking her firmly into the reality of what she was doing—going to bed again with AJ.

Once in her bedroom, she spotted the book she'd been reading—*The Idiot's Guide to Amazing Sex*—smack-dab in the middle of the bed, the bright cover a bold contrast to the bedspread.

The instant AJ set her down among the crumpled sheets, she shoved the book out of the way, hoping he hadn't read the title. Her dogs, sensing the bed would be busy, had the decency to remain on the floor.

AJ wouldn't have noticed, though. He was too busy pulling off her clothes, and his. "I want inside you," he said.

"Yes, yes, please," she said. She flailed for the nightstand, where the condoms were, but AJ stopped her hand and took care of the problem—grabbing a packet, opening and applying the condom with swift efficiency. Then he hovered over her, so big, so there.

She took in the strength of his shoulders, the play of

early morning light on his smooth skin and rounded muscles, the glint of mastery in his eyes.

He would not be denied. She liked that…the feeling of being captured by him. She stretched her arms over her head. As if he'd read her mind, AJ reached up and pinned her wrists to the bed, as if to force her to hold still for him. She felt helpless, completely in his power, and she went liquid inside.

"Is this what you want?" he said, possessing her with his hands and eyes, trapping her legs between his.

She nodded. "And you inside me."

He held her gaze for a moment more, tenderness and arousal flickering in the clear blue of his eyes. They were warm and open and focused on her and—*oh, man.* He pushed into her with a strong, slow thrust, saying her name, as if he'd waited forever to have her.

"Oh, yes. That's it," she said, so thankful. She'd been starving for him. She wanted to touch him, but he'd pinned her with hands and penis, and that turned out to be fine. He thrust into her with perfect force and exquisite rhythm. She lifted her hips to meet each stroke. They didn't talk, letting their locked eyes and eager bodies speak for them, and she climbed steadily toward a climax.

When she was just seconds away, AJ slowed his thrusts and looked deep into her eyes.

"Please," she said, desperate for more. She strained against his grip on her wrists, wanting to grab him, to force him to keep moving.

"Let it build," he said, still pinning her. His face was tense with the effort of holding back. Why struggle? She lifted her hips, squeezed him with her internal muscles, tried to wrench her hands away.

But he held on, making her want him even more.

When he finally moved, it was with tiny jolts, giving her barely a sliver of the relief she craved. "Please," she begged. "More. Do more." *Take me*, she wanted to say. So wanton, but perfect for how she felt—craven with lust, every primal instinct sharpened to the fine point of a feeling she was depending on him to reach.

He was trying to hold out, to intensify the release, she could tell. But he couldn't do it, and with a desperate gasp, he rammed himself deep into her, filling her. At last. At last. At last.

She opened her legs more, thrust upward, her hips pivoting wildly. With one more push, AJ sparked her climax. Her entire body rocked with the force of it. She felt lifted off the bed, held in place only by AJ's hands on her wrists. He said her name in a desperate way, then came inside her.

Afterward, he kissed her face all over—her mouth and cheek and neck—as if he couldn't get enough contact with her. She did her best to keep up, kissing wherever she could reach—unshaven jaw, soft lips, straight nose—reveling in the intimacy of the moment.

Then he collapsed to the side and pulled her onto his chest. He flopped his head back on the pillow. "Ow," he said, and reached behind his head to pull out the sex manual she'd tried to hide from him. "Studying up, are we?" He grinned.

"A little," she said.

"You have the best ideas." He rolled over her, trapping her beneath him and resting the book on her chest, the spine a hard line between her breasts. "Anything in here you want to try?" He flipped through the pages. "Hmm, tantric sex. This sounds good. Step one…"

She closed the book with both hands. "Only when we get bored."

"Oh, that'll be a while. A long while." He tossed the book to the floor and looked at her. Lust flared, then affection, then caring…and then a flicker of the old distance. "We should talk."

"A man who wants to talk? Uh-oh. Before you confess all your flaws, how about I fix some breakfast? I make killer waffles."

He hesitated, seemed to change his mind. "That sounds great," he said on a huge exhale. "But then we have to talk."

"Sure. But on full stomachs. I'll get started. You just rest up. You looked beat when you arrived."

"I couldn't sleep because I was thinking about you."

"I'm so glad," she said, feeling like she was in a dream. "I'll bring the food back." She stood, but he caught her hand and pulled her down for another promising kiss. "Hurry back," he said. "Maybe I'll pick up some tips." He nodded at the book on the floor.

She reached for her robe.

"Don't do that. I want to watch you walk away naked…and know that you'll be coming back that way, too. With food, no less. Talk about a dream come true— a naked woman and hot waffles. Mmm."

"Okay," she said, letting her robe drop to the floor. She turned and walked away, not a bit mortified by her jiggles and the crinkles in her behind. AJ appreciated her body. He cared for her. She didn't use the *L* word, not even to herself. It was too soon for that. She at least had to know his last name, for heaven's sake.

He wanted to tell her about himself—where he lived, where he worked. Fill in the blanks, as he'd said. But she already knew a lot about him, she realized, from their nights together. She knew he was considerate, passionate, intelligent and witty. These were far more important than his job or income or the other facts he planned to share with her.

Don't push, don't rush, she told herself. They enjoyed each other; he'd come back for more, and if a relationship grew from that, good. She would not get her hopes up. If she had them.

I don't stick around. For anything. But that was before he'd come back to her. Things were different now.

Okay, she had hopes. She'd just hidden them behind lust. Now they could peek out, stretch and maybe grow into something real.

A few minutes later, Beth closed the griddle on the first batch of waffles, breathing in the sweet steam. She couldn't believe she was standing naked in her kitchen making breakfast. Spud and Boomer didn't seem the least bit puzzled by her nudity. They were more interested in what she might spill as she cooked.

She'd bring whipped cream with the waffles, in case they wanted to do some body tasting, like she'd read about in the book. She'd protect the sheets with towels, of course. You could plan a little spontaneity, right?

What about the column? She hadn't thought once about that since AJ had arrived. "Third Time's the Charm" would be a good name for a piece based on this visit, but the idea of describing these magical hours for the magazine felt wrong.

That made her realize she had a truth to confess, too—her column. What if AJ didn't like the idea that she'd been writing about him to fifteen-thousand readers? She doubted any secrets he had to share could match that one. He might be shocked or hurt or even angry. Her stomach jumped at the thought.

He was an easygoing guy. Surely, he'd take it in stride.

12

RAFE SLID HIS ARMS across the sheets, reveling in the smooth, silky expanse, then connected with curly fur. Ditzy groaned and looked at him, giving a snort before she dropped her head back to the pillow. Having dogs everywhere was annoying, but he'd been pleased at how happy to see him they seemed. Since when had being a hit with pets been a big deal?

Since Beth.

He shoved a pillow behind his head and looked around her fussy room. The place was filled with furniture and every surface was covered with objects—delicate glass bottles, framed photos, fresh flowers, candles, books. It was very Beth.

And a little overwhelming.

He liked how it smelled, though—of candles and fresh-cut flowers and Beth—a residue of her perfume and a sweetness all her own.

Drifting over that was the aroma of the waffles she was cooking in the kitchen. They smelled like Christmas to him. Growing up, breakfast had been cold cereal or bagels—his mother had had a busy career and lots of social engagements and his father didn't cook. But during holidays, his mom would make a big breakfast for the three of them—pancakes or waffles or crêpes or French toast.

So that smell spelled holiday to him. With Beth, every day was a holiday. And fussing was a way of life. He wasn't entirely comfortable with that. It made him feel closed in, struggling for breath in air thick with emotions and ties.

Maybe after he'd straightened out their misunderstanding he'd be less bothered. He'd go help her now—get past the worst of it fast.

He patted the bedclothes for his boxers—no luck—then surveyed the floor around the bed. Not there. He leaned down to look beneath the bed, where he found his shorts resting on a flat object. He pulled it out. It was a framed photograph of Beth standing before a travel poster advertising a Caribbean cruise. She wore a wide grin and a straw hat, and her arm was around someone who'd been neatly blocked from view by two strips of masking tape on the photo glass.

Had to be a man. The boyfriend she'd referred to in passing? The reason she'd been "out of circulation"? The picture obviously had meaning or she wouldn't have kept it, and since everything had a place in her house, its location—shoved under the bed—meant something, too. The guy had dumped her, no doubt. Protective anger flared in him.

Beth was so tenderhearted, so generous.

And so different from the women he usually spent time with. Women who never wanted more from him than he could give. Beth would want more. Beth would want it all.

He cared about her, wanted more time with her, but beyond that he couldn't promise anything…or predict it. Commitment wasn't in him. Would he hurt her?

She seemed okay with what they'd shared so far, but how long before he let her down? The picture in his hand was a gold-framed warning under glass.

"How do you like your coff—"

At the sound of Beth's voice, he looked up. She was so beautiful, standing there naked in the doorway, staring at what he held. What a way to ruin the moment.

"I reached under the bed for my shorts and found this," he said, extending the frame. "Sorry."

"It's okay." She took the picture, her face pink, then shot him a tentative smile. "We're going to talk, right? I might as well start." She looked down at the picture and the curve of her smile dropped to a sad, straight line. She pressed the frame over her naked breasts, arms crossed as if over a schoolbook.

"You don't have to say a thing, Beth," he said, going to hug her, the hard square a barrier to her body. He focused on the soft warmth of her back under his palms. "It's none of my business."

She pulled away to put the picture face down on her bureau. She tapped it. "My old boyfriend, Blaine Richardson. We were planning a cruise a year ago that fell through. He turned out to be a different man than I thought he was."

So was he. The thought chilled him.

She walked into his arms, her eyes hopeful and honest. Holding her, sensing her vulnerability, he felt an urge to protect her that was so strong it made him shake inside.

She leaned back to look at him, a rueful expression on her face. "He cared about me. That I know. And I think he was going to suggest getting serious while we were on the cruise." Her chin dipped in hesitation. "But something happened. I think his business floundered and he was ashamed to tell me. That's my theory anyway. I keep thinking I should have known something was wrong."

"Didn't he explain himself?"

Her face took on a distant expression. "No. The last time I saw him, he was headed out of town on a quick business trip. But he never returned."

Like her father, he realized with a jolt. The guy had disappeared like her dad. "He left without a word?"

She nodded. "It seemed so out of character. I was stunned. And then later it got worse…when I found out—" she swallowed "—that my savings were gone, too."

"He stole your money?"

"Evidently. I knew he was anxious about investors for his business. He didn't like to talk about it around me, but he was worried. I knew the project was risky but lucrative."

"How did he get the money?"

"Forged my signature on a check. I never hid things from him. My statements and checkbooks were easy to see on my desk. I remembered afterward that he'd once admired my handwriting, commented on my distinctive signature. I thought it was odd at the time, but the police said forgers are experts at mimicking handwriting. I just never suspected he'd do such a thing."

"How much did he take, if you don't mind my asking?"

"Twenty-thousand dollars—almost my entire money-market account." She tried to smile. "Maybe I trusted him too much, but Blaine was devoted to me and I know he was happy being with me. It was strange. Like I said, something must have happened with his business."

"Some very smart people have been tricked by con artists, Beth, so don't blame yourself. They're experts

at faking emotions. Their secret is that they truly believe
their lies."

He'd done a story on con rackets, working with the
U.S. Postal Service, and knew the skill and cleverness
this brand of criminal employed. "Did the police search
for him?"

"Nothing came of the investigation, except they said
he'd worked in Florida under a different name—Bill
something…Donaldson, I think. They warned me the
likelihood of getting my money back, even if they found
Blaine, was low."

Rafe felt sick thinking of that rat seducing Beth just
to steal her savings. He could picture her innocently
awaiting the guy's return, calling his cell, his home, not
getting an answer, but still believing, because she was
so trusting. Then the shock of learning he'd taken her
savings along with her heart.

Rafe wanted to hit something. Blaine Richardson.
"I'm sorry that you had to deal with that…scum."

"He wasn't scum. Something went wrong and he
must have panicked and took the money. Maybe he
owed someone dangerous. I'll never know. That was a
year ago and I'm over it. I was hurt and pretty stunned.
And I guess I was hiding out for a while—emotionally,
I mean. But now, partly thanks to you, I'm out again,
living life, getting involved."

Getting involved. Lord. She put her arms around his
neck and looked up at him, hope in her eyes. "That's
why you've been so good for me. You're honest and direct. I think it's sweet that you want to tell me everything about you."

"Yeah, I do," he said, his gut tight with guilt. Now
he had to tell her about his panic and lies, and see the
hurt and shock in her earnest eyes.

And then what? Assuming she forgave him, it wasn't like he would marry her or invite her to live with him. That was what she would want, what she deserved. Despite his good intentions, he'd be another man who would let her down.

He held her gently, preparing himself to tell her the truth. Was there some way to ease the blow? He breathed in her sweet smell—flowers and vanilla and…

Burning waffles. The acrid smell swept through the room.

"The waffles!" Beth jerked out of his arms and ran for the kitchen. Rafe followed, relieved to have a moment's respite before revealing the truth about who he was.

They were soon busy rescuing breakfast. Rafe scraped the ruined food out of the waffle iron, waiting for the right moment to start his sad tale. Beth made coffee, then poured more batter into the waffle iron. When she smiled up at him, he knew it was time to start.

"Beth, listen, I need to tell you—"

The doorbell rang.

"Oh, no," Beth said, reflexively crossing her arms over her bare breasts, her eyes wide in alarm like a kid caught doing something wrong. She rushed to the door and peeked out. "It's my brother," she whispered to Rafe. "Just a sec," she called through the door, then scampered to the bedroom.

Rafe followed her pale and lovely backside and found her rushing from closet to drawer grabbing clothes in a panic.

While he watched her struggle into shorts—foregoing panties, he was delighted to notice—and a shirt, he pulled on his boxers, then his pants.

"This is so awkward," she said. "What am I going to say? What will he think about you being here?"

"Shall I hide in the bathroom?" he teased.

"That's silly," she said, but he could tell the idea had a momentary appeal. "I'll just say that you're…that you came to… Oh, I don't know what I'll say. And, for God's sake, put your shirt on."

"I could pretend to be a missionary," he teased, buttoning his shirt. "Trying to convert you to something."

"That's not funny," she said, misbuttoning her top.

"How about a Fuller Brush man?" he said, hooking his belt. "Do they still do door-to-door sales?"

"Cut it out, funny man."

"Just tell him I'm a friend." He captured her for a hug and a steadying look.

"That's true, isn't it?" she said, pink and panicked. "But put on your shoes."

"You're an adult woman, not a nun, Beth. You get to sleep with men. He knows about your column, right?"

"I just don't want to have to explain, or have him read more into this than there is…." She studied his face. *Is there more?* The question was as plain in her honest eyes as their shade of green.

Was there? He got that now-familiar ache in his chest and had no idea how to answer her. "It'll be fine," he said and undid her wrongly buttoned blouse.

As he concentrated on getting her buttons right, Beth straightened his collar and ran her fingers through his hair. "You look fine. Do I look okay?"

"You look freshly laid, darlin', but I'm sure your brother won't notice."

Her blush brightened. "God, I hope not." She took a deep breath, then led the way to the living room. With a final glance at him, as if to be sure he was still there, she opened the door.

"What's the holdup?" the guy at the door protested. "I've been standing out there for—" He stopped at the sight of Rafe.

"This is my friend AJ, Timmy," she said. "AJ, my brother."

"Nice to meet you," her brother said, shaking his hand. To his credit, he didn't look shocked to see a barefoot stranger in his sister's house, as unusual as that had to be. "What's cooking?" He sniffed audibly. "Or should I say, burning?"

"Waffles," Beth said. "I burned the first batch."

"I love waffles," Timmy said, rubbing his hands together. "Okay if I stay?"

"Actually…" Beth said.

"Sure," Rafe blurted. "No problem." It was stupid, but part of him welcomed the delay. Maybe it would be easier after breakfast to tell Beth what he had to tell her.

"I'll set the table," her brother said and headed for the kitchen. Beth frowned at Rafe and he shrugged sheepishly before they followed her brother into the kitchen.

Timmy had come to borrow Beth's car to make some deliveries for a deli, it turned out. He told a story about metal shop fees for a friend that irritated the hell out of Beth, Rafe could tell. Then he asked Rafe what he did for a living and he was forced to repeat the lie about being a transition expert. After that, the guy pitched him about an invention, asking if any companies Rafe worked with might want to "snap up the idea." Rafe bluffed his way through the discussion and accepted Timmy's card.

As pushy as her brother was, at least he helped with

breakfast preparations, and soon they sat down before plates of fresh waffles with strawberries and whipped cream and steaming mugs of Beth's delicious coffee.

Beth kept giving Rafe wistful looks as they ate and as soon as Timmy had taken the last bite of the last waffle, she said, "Hadn't you better get going on the deliveries?"

"I'll help with the dishes," Tim said. "Why don't you give me a hand, AJ?"

"Sure."

Beth sighed. "I'll go brush my teeth."

"I got some freebie floss from Dr. Dave," Timmy called as she left. "I'll bring that over when I bring back the car. And Julio says I can have the leftover sandwiches, too."

Beth called back her thanks and Timmy turned to Rafe. "She likes you." His expression was a mix of curiosity, pleasure and concern.

"And I like her." Rafe carried the plates to the sink and began running water.

Timmy followed with the coffee mugs. "She's not as tough as she seems." He reached under the sink for soap and squirted it into the filling sink.

"I realize that," Rafe said, knowing he'd be testing her toughness the minute her brother left. He began washing plates.

"She got involved with a creep who did a number on her." Tim took the washed dishes and rinsed them, putting them on the drainer.

"Look, the last thing I want to do is hurt your sister." More guilt knotted inside him and he scrubbed harder.

"Just so you know… I think that one's clean."

"Oh, right," he said, handing the over-scrubbed plate to Timmy.

"You do know, then?"

"I know." Her brother's heart was in the right place where Beth was concerned. His was, too, and he just hoped Beth would see that when he finally told her the truth.

BETH HEADED BACK INTO the kitchen, her mouth minty fresh, her hair combed and makeup on, determined to shoo Timmy out the door. She didn't know how long AJ was staying this visit and she wanted him to herself for as long as she could have him. They had to have that talk, after all, and she had to explain about her column.

She marched up to Timmy, ready to order him out, when he tossed her his towel. "Sorry, gotta skate, Beth. I need the keys. When I bring back the car, you can drive me home for dinner. Ribs in the slow cooker. Why don't you bring AJ?" He said it casually, but he was clearly fishing for their status.

"Timmy…" she warned.

"Why don't you come?" Timmy said to AJ. "Food's good."

"It depends on a few things." Something passed between the two men. AJ looked tense. What had they talked about while she was gone? Rafe wouldn't quite meet her gaze. Did he think this was a meet-the-folks deal? She was far from ready for that.

Maybe the Blaine story had bothered him. Did he feel sorry for her? It was probably a mistake to tell him so soon.

She walked Timmy to the carport to find out what had happened while she was innocently brushing her teeth. "I hope you didn't grill the man."

"Of course not. I just wanted to get to know him."

"Really?" There was more to it than that, she suspected.

"He's cool, but be careful, okay? Guys can be tricky."

"I'm an adult, Timmy. I know what I'm doing."

He pulled the car door shut and looked at her through the open window, one eye closed against the sunlight. "Thanks for the car. We can take the wheel off my bike and fit it in your trunk when we go to Mom's. I'll fill the gas tank. And I'll be paying you back for everything. Don't forget that."

He gave the side of the car a slap for emphasis, his expression grim and determined, as it always was when he made that promise. Ever since Blaine had left. He seemed to think he single-handedly had to make up for Blaine's thievery.

"The money will work out fine. Just please—" *Get a real job. Quit bailing out your friends.* But he looked so determined and so hopeful, and she had AJ waiting inside. "Never mind. It'll work out."

"I think he liked my idea, don't you? You think he'll hook me up with someone business-wise?"

"It's a long shot. Just like it is with Thompson Manufacturing. You have to put together—"

"A prototype, yeah, yeah. I'm working on it. Like I said, Dr. Dave is letting me use his metal shop stuff. Have a little faith."

"I do." As much as she could manage, though lately it seemed more difficult. Something needed to change with Tim, but she wasn't sure how to make it happen.

She returned to the kitchen, which AJ had made spotless. The man had manners, though that could be because they were still in OBB mode—On Best Behavior. She went to where he stood by the sink and put her arms around his neck. "Thanks for cleaning up. Sorry about Tim."

"He had to check me out." But the distance in his eyes had doubled. He was definitely bothered.

"Whatever he said about me, forget it. And forget the Blaine thing. Let's get back to our morning."

"Yeah," he said, gripping both her hands and kissing her knuckles. He was acting casual, but she felt trouble in the air, like rumbling clouds rolling across a sunny sky.

Maybe if they made love, they could start over mood-wise. She kissed him soft and slow, coaxing him to relax, sliding her hips against his. "We could try something in the book," she murmured. "Like that tantric thing maybe?"

He hesitated for a second, then kissed her back, deep and strong. She reveled in the familiar heat, relieved to know they'd soon be back where they'd so joyously been two hours ago.

They'd start fresh and *then* have their talk.

Except the doorbell rang.

Again.

Her place was Grand Central today. The dogs erupted in barks and yips and leaps.

AJ didn't seem to want to release her, but the bell rang again, so she pushed reluctantly out of his arms.

Through the peephole, she saw that it was Heather. Damn. She'd come for the Bundt pan, no doubt. Except she had something…balloons? What the hell…?

Beth opened the door and Heather rushed in.

"Congratulations!" she said and threw her arms around Beth, which made the balloons bounce against her head.

AJ inhaled sharply from behind her.

"Congratulations? What for?"

"Your column, of course. I was at the store getting

cake ingredients and these were on sale." She held out the balloons, which said Get Well Soon, Congrats, Graduate and Happy Valentine's Day. "So I thought, why not? I had to borrow your pan anyway."

"My column?" she repeated, staring at the gleaming balloons, then at Heather.

"Don't you know yet?" Heather looked uncertainly at AJ. "Didn't you tell her?" Heather knew AJ?

Beth whirled to look at her lover's startled, sheepish face. "Tell me what?" Her mind was working slowly, as if running through sucking mud, trying to understand all this—balloons, congratulations and Heather knew AJ?

"Am I too early?" Heather said. "You said you were telling her last night, Rafe. You have no shoes on... Uh-oh."

"Rafe?" Beth turned to AJ again. "You're Rafe?"

He gave a short, pained nod. "Adam Rafael Jarvis. AJ with friends, Rafe with everyone else. That's what I wanted to talk to you about."

"I see," she said, barely beginning to.

"Anyway, the important thing is that you got your column," Heather said, thrusting the balloon ribbons into Beth's hands, smiling uneasily because of the tension beginning to crackle in the air. "Rafe had to tell me about it when I caught him in the utility room yesterday."

"You caught him?"

"Yeah. He was hiding from you...to keep the surprise until later...." Her words faded away.

"You were hiding from me?" Beth repeated, staring at AJ. Through her shock, anger began to swell.

"Look, if you two are busy, I can get the pan later," Heather said. "Give me a call, Em, when you can."

Heather backed toward the door, opened it, caroled her usual, "Bye-eee," and slipped out, leaving Beth and AJ-slash-Rafe staring at each other in a silence that snapped with so much electricity the balloons seemed to sway.

"When we met at Grins, you pretended not to know who I was?" she said, slowly putting the pieces together.

"No. I didn't realize you were Em Samuels until Will showed me your column the next morning. Then I didn't want you to think I'd deliberately come on to you."

"The way I think now?"

"At the bar, I heard you saying you didn't know how to pick up a man, and that intrigued me."

"So you decided to help the poor loser out?" This got worse with every word he said.

"I was attracted to you. You know that. After I found out who you were, I thought you might not believe me."

"You got that right."

"So I thought the simplest thing was to disappear, avoid you at the magazine and let it all fade away. Except then you needed a second date and—"

"You did me a favor? Please."

"I wanted to see you again, too."

She shook her head, hurt and angry and stunned all at once. "And all those e-mails, where you—as Rafe—asked me about my column and told me about your job offers…and the ice… You were *playing* with me?"

"No. I knew that if you knew who I was you might be angry and that would complicate things, so it seemed best to keep quiet."

"How can you say that? The truth complicates things? That's your excuse?" She couldn't believe what she was hearing. Everything she knew about this man had been turned upside down and inside out. No wonder she had felt like she knew Rafe online—she did. She'd slept with him. "But you said you prefer to be up front and direct."

"I do. But this situation…was different."

"And after that, there was phone sex? You didn't tell me then, either?" She noticed she was still holding the balloon strings. She released them and the gleaming air-filled wishes bobbed to the ceiling. "And what was Heather saying about my column?"

"It's yours. The column. I decided to give it to you." But his sheepish expression said there was more to the story.

"What about the rest of the trial pieces? When did you decide this? Exactly?"

"Yesterday, I guess…."

"Yesterday…when Heather found you hiding in the closet?"

"Yes," he said, flinching. "But it was inevitable. You're doing great. You have the right tone, the right take. You'd have gotten it anyway."

"You told Heather about the column to keep her quiet."

He opened his mouth.

"Don't. I won't believe it anyway." Her heart filled with a heavy pain. How could this have happened to her? She'd fallen for another guy who'd lied to her. Was she completely crazy? She'd been certain Blaine loved her, and that AJ was trustworthy. But she'd been wrong about Blaine and now she was wrong about AJ.

"I'm telling you the truth, Beth. That's why I came back. To tell you everything so we can spend more time together."

"Right."

"I know it's hard to accept this—especially because of what happened before with your boyfriend. But I'm not like him."

"Oh, no? What are you like, AJ? Or, I mean, Rafe? It's hard to know. Are you the editor who would be interested in me if I didn't work for him? The one who was coming to Phoenix on Monday, not Friday? Or are you the transition expert who flew all the way from the east coast to see me again? You sure spit out a lot of lies for an honest guy."

The bitter words stung her throat. She hated how she sounded. She was generous with people, gave them second chances and the benefit of the doubt. But uncovering AJ's lies made her feel stripped naked, and she wanted to curl into a protective ball somewhere.

Rafe reached for her, intending to hold her, she could tell, but she backed away. She didn't dare get warm in his arms.

"Handy how the truth didn't come out until Heather showed up with balloons."

"You know I've been trying to talk to you since I walked in the door. If your brother hadn't arrived, I would have told you everything. It was just bad timing."

"Oh, yeah. I think the whole thing is bad timing." She felt dizzy and disoriented, as if someone had tilted her house on its side, then righted it abruptly. "I don't want to talk about this anymore. Not now. I need to think. Alone."

"Don't overreact, Beth. I care about you. That's why I'm here."

"How am I supposed to believe that?"

"Because it's true." His laser blues dug at her, insisting she trust him. But she'd trusted Blaine, too. Wanting something to be true didn't make it so.

"I care about you, Beth," he repeated, low and urgent. "And I think you care about me."

She did. Entirely too much, she realized abruptly. "How could you be with me the *way* you were…and not be *who* you were? How is that possible? To be so separated from yourself…I don't understand." But she did understand, if she let herself. She'd seen the distance in his eyes from the moment he'd sat at her booth. *Don't get too close*. That was his first message to her. It wasn't because of the secrets he'd been keeping. It was a permanent expression—his warning to the world.

"I can't do this right now," she said, not wanting to cry in front of him. "I think you should go, AJ. Or Rafe…whoever you are."

"This is a shock, I know. But, look, you didn't exactly come clean about who you were, either. You told me you were a technical writer, remember? You never mentioned writing a sex column."

"You're right. And I was going to tell you about that—"

"Why should I believe you?" he said harshly.

Silence pulsed.

"You're right. Advantage, AJ," she said.

"I just mean there are two sides to this," he said, softening his tone. "I know why you didn't tell me. And I don't blame you. And I was as open as I could be, considering…everything."

She just looked at him. He'd been as open as he could be without being himself. What a painful thought. Yes, she'd lied to him and that was wrong, but her own culpability only made things worse. "So, we lied to each other. And now we know the truth and it changes everything."

"It doesn't have to."

"Yes, it does. I didn't know much about you, except that you were honest with me. I knew where you stood. But that's all gone now. I don't know what to think."

"Look, I made a mistake. A mistake I intended to correct today. Isn't that enough?"

"No. It's not enough. You're not the man I thought you were. And the man you are, well, I'm not sure I want to know him at all."

"You're upset. You're not listening. Think about what I've said and we can talk when you've calmed down."

"I am calm. Completely calm. And absolutely certain you should leave." She walked to the door, her legs as numb as her heart, and opened it for him.

He just stood there, hope in his eyes, but she had to stay strong. "You'll need your shoes—I think they're under the bed." Her voice cracked, thinking about how much she'd wanted to be in that bed with him just a few minutes ago.

She remained firm, though, and held his gaze, watching as the hope in his eyes faded to resignation and he headed down the hall.

She stood frozen in the doorway until he returned, shoes on his feet, departure in his bearing. He came to stand close. "You're wrong about me, Beth, but maybe it's right for me to go. I'm not the kind of man you really want. Not long term. I just wanted more time. That was selfish, I guess. I just…"

Before he could say anything insanely optimistic, she said, "You don't stick to anything, right? Ever?"

He looked at her, started to speak, then stopped.

"At least you were honest about that." How had she ever imagined they could mean more to each other? She'd been lying to herself, too.

He cupped her face in his hands. The warm comfort

of his palms against her cheeks turned her anger to an overwhelming sadness. She looked into his blue eyes, expecting to see goodbye in their depths. Instead, they held the look she hoped for from a man who would one day promise to love, honor and cherish her for the rest of his life. How could he do that to her?

She broke away from him so abruptly it seemed as though something tore inside her. She'd obviously misread him. Again.

"You're an amazing woman, Beth. You deserve forever with a good man." And then he was gone, leaving the heat from his fingers still on her cheeks.

Beth closed the door and stood there, completely immobilized. The dogs stood in a row staring at the door, poised for him to return. Then they looked at her. *Don't just stand there, go after him.* When she didn't move, they sighed in a chorus and slumped to their bellies at her feet.

Meanwhile, standing there numb and cold, the truth dawned on her like a sad sunrise.

She was in love with AJ. The feeling, sprouted in secret during their first and second nights together, had broken ground and stretched to the sky when he arrived this morning. Now, after he left, she felt the swaying bloom in her heart.

What a fool she'd been. She'd fallen for a fake and a liar and a stranger and her boss. She'd fallen in love with a fantasy.

She'd learned one thing for sure—sex was important in a relationship. She'd misunderstood it all along— first, by not having experienced it fully, and now, by underestimating its power. The way it could build false hope, trick you into believing it meant love when it only meant desire.

In a way this was all Em's fault. Em had had a blast. Like a teenager whose parents were out of town, she'd thrown a huge party, and left Beth to clean up the mess—the ashes on the carpet, the spilled punch, the crumpled napkins, the regret, the pain, the loss.

But Beth was back in charge. The parents had returned and Em had been grounded.

13

RAFE ROLLED HIS BAG to the wall of mailboxes in his building, weary to his bones. Two of his neighbors, Mrs. James and Mr. Cho, stood nearby, talking about Mr. Cho's daughter, who was homesick at college. Mr. Cho and his wife were headed there the following weekend to cheer her up. His mail in hand, Rafe said a few friendly words, then headed for the elevator.

He could imagine Beth jumping into this conversation with both feet, suggesting care packages and flight discounts.

Since he'd left her place a few hours ago, everything seemed to remind him of Beth. The flight attendant's smile, a column in a flight magazine, the dogs being walked down the block from his place, the perfume he'd picked up as he passed a woman on the sidewalk, and now this neighborly chitchat.

The breakup hurt like hell. It wasn't even really a breakup, since they hadn't really been together. Which made the intensity of his regret seem overblown.

Maybe it hurt so much because she'd assumed the worst about him. After her ex's behavior, she was understandably reluctant to trust any man, but it rankled him all the same. He wanted to redeem himself in her eyes, prove to her that he was an honorable man.

Ending it was right, though. Standing there, cupping

her face in his hands, seeing the vulnerability and generosity and plain goodness in her eyes, he knew he wasn't enough for her. She'd forever wonder about him, search for connections he couldn't make with her—or anyone. He'd feel trapped, then resentful, and then he would hurt her more than he already had. And he couldn't do that. Not to Beth.

He unlocked his door and found his apartment in order, thanks to Alice, and very empty. Maybe he should get a dog, as Beth had suggested. Something less yappy and frantic than Ditzy, and smaller than Boomer....

Who was he kidding? His travel schedule made a pet impossible, even if he did feel comfortable asking the Jameses or Chos to watch it while he was away. On the other hand, if he left *Man's Man*, went back to writing...? He'd still travel, no doubt.

He carried his bag into his bedroom and tossed his wallet, keys and the coins from his pocket onto the bare bureau top. Beth's bureau was full of glass junk and photographs.

He didn't even have a photo of his parents, he realized. Wait a minute. There was that shot he'd taken with him when he left for college. He'd snatched it from a photo envelope in his mom's desk. Maybe it was in that box of stuff from college?

On impulse, he took the cardboard container down from the back of his closet. He shuffled through writing awards, story clips from the college rag, research papers he'd been proud of, and found it—a yellowed snapshot of his parents on their honeymoon, smiling, their arms around each other tight.

In a rush of sentiment, he'd taken it with him. He'd liked the earnest glow in their faces. They were so young and hopeful and confident of their love.

They divorced just months after he left. Upset by the breakup, and in clear violation of the unspoken family vow to stay silent about conflict, he'd asked them each what had gone wrong. They'd blamed each other—no surprise—and it hadn't helped him a bit to understand.

His mother's words had stayed with him, though, because they included a warning for him. *Your father is a castle surrounded by a moat. When I met him, he was so intense, so attentive that I didn't realize there was no bridge across that moat. I pray you'll be different, Adam, but if you aren't, don't lead a woman on. Don't offer more than you have to give.*

The castle moat image rang true in his soul and he'd taken his mother's advice to heart, avoiding women who might mistake his friendliness for more than it could ever be.

Until Beth, of course. He'd slid into a relationship with her by complete accident. Against his better judgment, almost against his will.

Rafe carried the photo of his parents into his office and pinned it to the corkboard beside his monitor. He hadn't talked to his father, a busy attorney, in a year. The man had remarried years ago, but never sounded that happy about it. His mother, single and a fund-raiser for a small art museum, called every few months. Maybe he should do what Beth had suggested and reach out to them more. He loved them in his own way. Maybe they had more to say to him all these years later. Family should mean something.

With a sigh, he turned on his computer and checked e-mail to find another message from Curt Paterson, who wanted a decision about the advancement offer. Beth's advice came into his head: *Life's too short to be bored or miserable.*

Then he spotted a return e-mail from his old editor in Florida. Hadn't Beth's con-man boyfriend been active in that state? Con artists loved Florida—plenty of retirees to strip of their annuities. Maybe he could look into that. Ask his old friend to run down any clips about Richardson…Bill Donaldson, hadn't that been the alias?

He couldn't be what Beth needed, but if he could find out more about the rat who'd tricked her, show her she wasn't alone in falling for his lines, maybe he could help her and, at the same time, show her who he really was. It was a long shot, but it was something to do besides pour himself a Scotch and mope, which he was about to do anyway.

AFTER AJ LEFT, BETH allowed herself a single hour of self-pity. She buried herself in the sheets tangled by their lovemaking, still smelling of his spicy cologne, and dropped a few tears into her pillow. Her dogs lay in a sad row beside her, muzzles between paws, worry in their brown eyes. *Why are you in bed at noon, Mom?*

She could write a column about this. Yeah, right. Except Em didn't get her heart broken by a three-night stand. Em kept it light and breezy and sex-machine-in-the-night-ish. Em didn't fall for fake guys with commitment issues.

But then, it wasn't Em lying here soaking a pillow with tears. That was Beth. Completely Beth.

"WHAT THE HECK ARE YOU drinking?" Sara asked Beth a week later, sliding into the booth at Grins, eyeing her frosty drink.

"Tutti-Frutti Martooti," Beth said. "It's what I was having when I met AJ…I mean Rafe." It hurt to call him by his work name, but that's all he was to her now—a business associate.

"Oh, no. Not nostalgia drinking, babe. That is no good. And that is not Em."

"Good point. Time to move on." Sara had willingly listened to her angst since the breakup, for which Beth was eternally grateful. But tonight wasn't about comfort. Tonight was about her next column, which had become agony to write.

She'd decided to write about the two possible outcomes of great sex—it either frothed into a love frappé as it had with Sara and Rick or curdled like lemon in milk, as it had with her and AJ.

"Let's get started, before I can no longer feel my toes."

"One froufrou drink is making you numb?"

"I certainly hope so. Maybe I'll make the next one a double."

"So, that's the plan? Replace heartbreak with hangover?"

"Exactly. Serum of ipecac for a breakup. That sounds like Em, right?"

Sara patted her hand. "Hang in there, sweetie. It'll get better." Sara motioned for the waitress—the same woman whose pen had been the source of AJ's pickup line—and ordered gin neat. Sara liked her liquor the way she liked her men—straight up and to the point.

When the waitress left, Beth clicked on her tape recorder, picked up her pad and held her pen poised to write. "So, Sara, tell me everything about how you realized you were in love. Spare no detail. No sigh is too minor, no tender word too tiny."

Sara smiled and launched her tale. It had started with a fight over Rick's tightwad ways. He'd complained about the expensive restaurant Sara had selected to celebrate their three-month dating anniversary, so they had a terrible time, didn't stay for dessert and went to bed angry, back to back, only to be awakened when Rick became violently ill all over Sara's new handcrafted throw rug.

"First of all, I couldn't believe that I didn't give a damn about the rug," Sara said, eyes wide with remembered surprise. "I just wanted to help him. I held his forehead in the bathroom and cleaned him up afterward and curled up around him in bed when he fell asleep."

"That's impressive," Beth said. Sara was squeamish, adored her new rug and despised cheapskates.

"I know. So not me. I thought love was about him adoring me and us having a good time together. And great sex, of course. But it turns out to be about him mattering to me as much as I matter to myself. I want him to be happy and safe. And the cool thing is that the feeling hangs in there even when I'm pissed at him."

"And does he feel that way about you?"

"He's getting there. I mean he told me *I love you* weeks ago. He's one of those guys who blurt it when they want an exclusive. Primate stuff. Territory marking. But it's a start. He's growing. Like he's decided to set up a money-market account to fund gifts for me, so it won't hurt so much to spend big bucks. He's fighting his penny-pinching nature for me. That's love."

"You sound so certain, Sara."

"You know it when you feel it, I guess. Like a first orgasm."

"I'm so happy for you."

"You'll feel that way, too, Beth." She patted her hand again, like she was feeble or ill. "Have you at least talked to AJ?"

"You mean Rafe? He calls. I screen. He just feels guilty about lying to me and wants to be certain I'm not contemplating suicide by heartworm medicine or something."

"Maybe there's hope. At least hear him out."

"There's no point. He's not Mr. Forever. He told me so himself."

"He said that? 'I'm not Mr. Forever'?"

"He said I deserve forever with a good man."

"That's sweet. He sounds pretty good to me."

"But he doesn't stick to anything, remember? Or anyone."

"He's probably just scared. Reassure him. He's underestimating himself."

"He keeps people at arm's length. Doesn't even speak to his parents much. I want someone who'll be open, who'll share their lives, their feelings."

"Real men hate sharing. The ones who do it willingly have *issues*, if you know what I mean. They're either gay and won't admit it or are seriously into therapy. Talk to the man. Just don't use the word *share*. To a man, that's worse than fussing."

Beth shook her head, though the idea of talking to AJ made her heart pound with the desire to do exactly that. She missed him like crazy. But she thought she'd figured out why. "We were so compatible in bed that I just read too much into what was going on. Em wanted simple sex, but sex is never simple for Beth. Which brings up another problem. What business do I have writing a sex-is-fun column?" She went to take a swallow of her drink, but pricked herself with the umbrella pick. "Ouch."

Sara removed the umbrella. "That's the problem with these stupid drinks—not only are they deceptively high-octane, they can poke out your eye. You got out there and tried, Beth, instead of ducking behind a bunker, like after Blaine."

"Yeah, and look what happened. With Blaine I just felt stupid and blind. Now I'm in emotional agony." She pressed her hand over her chest. So dramatic. The liquor in the tiki drink had hit her hard.

"You'll get over it. This was just like training wheels. You'll meet a new guy and get right back on that ten-speed."

"I don't want to meet a new guy."

"Of course not. It has all the appeal now of a Brazilian wax, but—"

"Oooh, ouch." Beth wiggled in her seat.

"—eventually you'll want to get back in the game."

"That's the problem. It's not a game to me, Sara." Which more and more made the idea of her sassy, sophisticated sex column seem wrong, wrong, wrong.

"Okay, it's not a game. It's a war. On the dating battleground, you're wounded, but still standing—bloody, but unbowed."

"You make it sound noble. You should be writing my column."

Sara's cell phone rang. She answered it and her face lit up. "Rick," she whispered to Beth. "I can't right now, sweetie," she said into the phone. "We're still talking."

"Go see your guy," Beth whispered. "I've got enough from you for the column."

"Are you sure?" Sara said, her eyes shining.

"Positive." The look on Sara's face told the whole story of falling in love, even without the anecdote.

"Don't order another one of those umbrella thingies, and eat something, would you? And take a cab if you're unsteady."

"You know me. Always prepared. I've got a cab company number right next to my credit card."

Sara left and there Beth sat. She should go home and write the rest of her column. The part about Sara falling in love would be easy, but the rest of it—about sex going sour—would be hard to write as Em. She was feeling very, very Beth.

Was Beth done for as a columnist? She couldn't be. The one good thing Beth had gotten out of the whole achy-breaky mess with AJ was her column. She couldn't give it up without a fight. *Get back on the horse.* Wasn't that always the advice after someone got hurt or scared?

There was a cute guy at the end of the bar. A very cute guy. An Em kind of guy. Beth took a deep breath and blew it out. Okay…she'd start with this guy— launch a conversation and flirt a little. She'd apply a tourniquet to her bleeding heart, jump back on that horse and gallop back onto the dating battlefield. That could be her next column. Sure.

When the waitress approached, she ordered a double Martooti for courage and some stuffed wings to keep her stable. She downed the drink, ate a few wings, wiped her mouth and braced herself to set off.

When she stood, the pen she'd taken notes with rolled off her lap and into the aisle. Hey. She could use AJ's ploy. A great image for her column—passing the pickup torch, so to speak.

She bent for the pen but wobbled horribly. Her fingertips, toes and nose tingled. She was more looped than she'd thought. Luckily, a pant leg appeared before her hazy eyes and she grabbed it to keep from tipping over.

The leg's owner reached down and helped her to her feet. She looked into a familiar face. AJ.

"Are you all right?" he asked her, concern creasing his forehead.

"I'm fine." She blinked quickly and tried to settle herself. "What are you doing here?"

"Staying in the hotel. Why are you here?"

"You should know that," she said, winking—sort of. "I work this bar, remember?" she said as jauntily as she could manage with her smile so crooked—at least, what she could feel of it. She held up her pen. "I'm using your pickup line. You should be proud."

"It works better if you're not plastered," he said, sounding irritatingly amused. "You need to sit down."

"I'm fine."

He gripped her elbow anyway and helped her back to the booth, where he waved the waitress over and ordered Beth a cup of coffee. "Eat," he said to her, putting a cold wing under her nose.

"I already did." She took the wing and dropped it onto her plate. "I'm just feeling the rum a little. And maybe the vodka."

"You're drinking another one of those Rootin' Tootin' Toddies?" He nodded at her empty Martooti glass.

"Yes. A double. Or maybe a triple. I forget."

"This isn't like you, Beth," he said softly.

"No. It's like Em. You have a problem with Em? You never had a problem with Em before. Don't look at me like that." She struggled to get the ends of her words to come out.

"I'm just concerned about you."

"Oh, please."

"Whatever else you may think, you have to know I care about you." He put both hands on her forearms, which rested on the table. Even through the alcohol numb, she felt his warmth.

"Still? It's been a whole week. I thought you didn't stick to anything."

Hurt flashed in his eyes, so vivid she felt sick for having said it.

"I'm sorry. That was mean." She touched his cheek. "I don't know why I said that."

"Can I give you a ride home?"

"Please," she said humbly. "I think Em has had all the fun she can stand for one night."

He paid her tab, then helped her out of the bar and into the passenger seat of his rental car. "It was a mistake ordering a double," she said, flopping her head back on the seat, wooziness assailing her. "A single would have given me the nerve I needed without making me wobble."

AJ didn't offer an opinion, but after a few seconds of silent driving, he asked her softly, "How are you doing, Beth?"

"Getting along. How about you?"

"The same." But his tone told her he missed her. At least that. He stared out the windshield, driving steadily, and they sat in thick silence. They cared about each other, missed each other, but that wasn't enough.

Still, Beth was happy to ride beside him, aware of his strong, solid body, the muscular flex of his fingers on the wheel, the way his gaze flicked to the rearview, then the side mirror—to be sure they were safe—and then to her because he had to see her, be sure of her, too.

The last time she'd ridden with him, it had been in the convertible and they'd had a night of dancing and fabulous sex ahead of them. If only they had that night again. If only they'd kept things simple and sexual with no secrets or lies. Her eyes drifted closed.

When she opened them again, AJ was carrying her. "Where are we?" she asked.

"Home," he said, talking over the dogs' welcoming racket. She realized they stood on her porch. She could almost imagine he'd meant home as the place they lived together. But that thought made her hurt worse, so she focused on fishing her house key out of her purse. AJ held her so she could reach the keyhole.

When the door opened, her pets spilled onto the porch, eagerly greeting AJ, who spoke to them like family while he carried her inside. She couldn't help wishing they were a family. And that she and AJ would make love and fall asleep in a pile of people and dogs.

Even in her Martooti haze, she knew that was impossible.

AJ carried her down the hall and into her bedroom, where he peeled back the covers and helped her into bed. She wasn't ready for him to leave. "It's like not knowing it's the last Oreo," she murmured.

"Beg your pardon?"

"If you know it's the last cookie, you savor it…let it melt on your tongue and fill your mouth. You make it last."

"What are you talking about?" He sat on the bed and brushed a strand of hair from her face.

"We didn't know it was our last time together."

"Oh. I see."

"What if we had one last time? An Oreo for the road?"

He bent to kiss her cheek like she was his niece or something. "You're not thinking clearly."

"How clearly do I have to think for that?"

"More than you are. You'd regret it in the morning. Along with that double. Or triple."

"No, I won't."

"I'm lousy boyfriend material, Beth. That's the bottom line. You can't forget that."

She looked up at him, aching for him. "You could try a little, you know. Work at it. It's not like relationships come with instruction manuals. Nobody knows exactly what to do." She was speaking from her heart, which, of course, wasn't very smart.

"Remember my father? The castle with no bridge over the moat? That's me all the way. I couldn't stand hurting you."

"I'm a big girl," she said. But that wasn't the problem. The problem, clear to her even in her muddled state, was that he didn't care about her enough to want to try.

She deserved a man who would give his whole heart, not begrudge every connection, every bond, every shared emotion. He was right about that.

"I'll get you some aspirin. While I'm gone, do me a favor and get undressed—and covered up. I'm not that noble." He set off on his errand.

Maybe she didn't want him to be noble. Maybe she wanted one last cookie. If she was going to have regrets, they should be doozies.

ALL THREE DOGS TRAILED Rafe to the medicine cabinet in Beth's bathroom. They seemed to think if they kept an eye on him, he wouldn't leave, which made him feel guilty as hell. He had to laugh at himself. He was treating the dogs as human, the way Beth did.

Aspirin and water glass in hand, Rafe found Beth lying on her side, her cheek nestled into the pillow, her clothes in a heap on the floor. She was really drunk if she'd leave her clothes in such a mess.

"Here you go," he said softly, extending the pills.

She lifted her head from the pillow long enough to take the painkillers, then dropped back down.

"Good night," he said, and leaned down to kiss her cheek.

Except she turned her face to meet his mouth.

She tasted of liquor and coconut…and Beth. It took all his strength to break off that kiss.

She blinked up at him, sad and lonely, and his heart went out to her. "Could you stay with me for a bit? Until I fall asleep?"

He groaned internally. Crawl into her bed and not make love to her? Like he said, he wasn't that noble. But he couldn't refuse her, not after what they'd shared.

"Okay," he said. "But just 'til then." He stripped down to his boxers and slid into the bed. She jabbed her butt at him until he cupped himself around her, aching with the pleasure of feeling her naked body against him, but wishing she wore something granny-like and layered. Quilted…with barbed wire.

But no. She was warm and naked and smooth and soft, and he was hard as a rock against her back.

He wanted her, yes. Badly. But other feelings rose, too. Yearning, affection, an overwhelming protectiveness, the desire to stay with her, to never let her go.

He knew what this was, of course, even though this was the first time this particular emotional speedball had roared through him. It was love. He was in love with Beth.

So this was how it felt. Painful and wonderful and scary as hell.

"I thought you'd never get here," Beth murmured, getting cozy against him, tugging his arm around her middle, just under her breasts. She meant in bed.

"Me, neither," he breathed. He meant in love. He'd thought himself incapable of feeling this deep and steady connection with another person. Was it an illusion? The result of infatuation and the knowledge that he couldn't have her?

Before he could figure it out, she surprised him by turning to him and twining her legs with his, her body warm and lush against his. She kissed him, slow and serious, then looked at him, desire steady in her gaze. "I want to make love," she said, not sounding drunk at all. "One last time. To remember."

It was heaven holding her in his arms, her breasts against his chest, her legs between his, her clever fingers now holding him inside his boxers, and his brain shut down hard. "Beth, I…" He fought to be sensible, but all he wanted was inside her.

"I need you," she said, and placed his hand where she was wet and swollen and slick.

He stroked her, loving the way she moaned and moved against his fingers. Okay, one last time.

Within seconds, he'd applied a condom and slid into her, as natural as breathing, reaching deep where he belonged.

She gasped and lifted her hips, inviting him deeper. "Oh, I missed you," she said, the words both a cry and a sigh.

Rafe kissed her, trying to tell her he felt the same. With each deep stroke, each sharp lift of her hips, each kiss, he fell more in love with her. Her serious green eyes stared into his, shiny with love, shadowed by sadness.

She quickened the pivoting of her hips and gave sweet, gasping cries. He matched her rhythm, driving himself into her, deeper and harder. He stroked her to the brink of release and felt his own approach. Their eyes locked.

"I love you," Beth breathed so faintly she might have meant it for her ears only.

I love you, too. The words filled his head, rose to the back of his throat...and stuck. What good would it do to say them? It would make his leaving that much more painful. As corny as it seemed, he took his promise to his mother seriously. He never wanted to make Beth feel as lonely and lost as his mother had been all his grow-ing-up years.

So, instead of saying he loved her, he reached into her with all he had—giving her his body and, he knew, his heart.

Afterward, when he started to roll away, she held him in place. "Don't go."

"I'm too heavy for you."

"No, you're not."

But he was. He slid to the side and made her com-fortable against his chest. Lulled by her soft breath and the rise and fall of her chest, he let himself fall asleep.

Sometime later, Beth jerked up in bed, then stumbled to her feet to stagger to the bathroom. He followed and held her while she threw up, then helped her back to bed. He held her close, happy to be with her a blame-less time longer.

She was soon asleep, but he was thinking too hard to doze off. He began to ponder his other task—track-ing down Beth's criminal ex-boyfriend. He'd come to Phoenix on magazine business, too, but his more urgent purpose was to interview the detectives who'd handled Beth's case. He'd taken two weeks' vacation to track Richardson, telling Curt that he needed the time to think over his offer.

When he finished with Phoenix leads, he was head-ing to Florida to talk to the police about Richardson's crimes under other names. He'd already made some calls.

He couldn't tell Beth he loved her, but he could find her rat of an ex-boyfriend. He could damn well do that for her.

Still restless, he reached into his discarded pants to read the time on his cell phone. It was two-oh-four and he had a voice mail message. Hmm. Extracting himself from bed without waking Beth, he carried the phone to the living room, pleased that Boomer padded companionably at his side.

The message was from a detective from Miami, and it was good news. Blaine Richardson was in the Monroe County jail, due to be transferred within the week. The detective had arranged a visit the next day through Richardson's attorney, if Rafe could make it. Adrenaline surged through him.

He wouldn't miss it.

He didn't have the heart to wake Beth and wasn't ready to talk about what he was doing until he had some answers, so he scribbled a note, set it on her pillow, then kissed her cheek. She stirred.

"I have to go," he said. "But we'll talk."

"Mmm," she said in her sleep.

All three dogs walked him to the door, their eyes gleaming with a clear message: *You better come back.*

He would. One last time.

14

HE HELD ME while I was sick. That was the first thought in Beth's mind when she woke up—after she wondered why a construction crew was pounding away in her head and someone had filled her mouth with cotton balls.

Just like Sara had held Rick. If that wasn't love, what was? She reached for AJ, to reassure herself that she hadn't dreamed their lovemaking, but the bed was empty except for Ditzy, who oofed at being poked.

Beth jerked to a sit, then grabbed her throbbing head, noticing, as she did so, a note on AJ's pillow.

No regrets, I hope? Except for the liquor. Take two more aspirin and a cool shower—better for your hangover. I had to take off. Let me know that you're okay. We'll talk when I get back. AJ.

He'd left in the middle of the night? At least he'd left a phone number. *We'll talk.* What did that mean? Was this the old "tell her what she wants to hear" dynamic Sara had described? That didn't seem like AJ...but maybe that was how *Rafe* operated.

What had made him leave? Then it came back to her—fuzzy, but definite. She'd said *I love you*—sure to scare off a guy like AJ. The words had escaped like a long-held breath. His face had been so full of tenderness at the time, she'd been almost sure he felt the same.

Too many Martootis had made her misread him again. She'd promised the sex was just "one last Oreo" and then gone and confessed her love.

God. What if it had been pity sex? She *had* practically begged him. Did he feel sorry for her? The idea made her cringe. Now here was a topic for a column—Top Ten Things Not to Do with an Ex. Number one: Get drunk and have sex. Thank you, Em.

She drafted the column in her head.

Ladies, when you've fallen head-over-Achilles for Mr. Wrong-o, stay clear of Demon Alcohol. The words One More for the Road should never cross your lips—he'll assume you're not talking about another Tutti-Frutti Martooti. Which you shouldn't have anyway, because we young active singles never drink and boff, right? Right? Impaired judgment and all that...

She tried to smile at her cleverness, but the movement hurt too much. How was she going to work today—and she had to—when the keystrokes would be little hammers tapping her skull, which felt as fragile as an eggshell?

Ditzy licked her forehead in sympathy and Spud stretched across her midsection, a furry hot-water bottle on her queasy tummy.

An hour later, she managed to shower—cool water, as AJ suggested—and forced down some toast and tea. Walking gingerly, like a patient dragging an IV cart, she made her way to her computer.

And just sat there. She watched her two cats bat at

each other's tails. Outside, she tracked a quail couple and their six babies as they pecked the ground. A gecko skittered across her window ledge, pausing to look in at her in sympathy: *Never drunk, never sorry*.

Her notes swam before her eyes and it all seemed like too much work. Clicking gently, she switched to her e-mail, hoping that would stir her productivity. Will had forwarded her a piece of fan mail. She opened it and read:

Em:
Remember me, "Like a Virgin in West Phoenix"? I wrote you after your first piece about sex? About how you'd given me hope? Well, I took your advice and went out with the guy who so politely accepts my dry cleaning each month. We had a lovely time and the sex was such a surprise that I blushed the whole next day whenever I thought about it. I thought I'd discovered a whole new me. Then he didn't call. Ever. I told myself to keep it light and breezy, like you said, but I wanted more. I wanted it to mean something.

So I took in a dress that didn't even need cleaning just to talk to him. What a bad idea. What was my problem? he wanted to know. We had a good time. Why wasn't that enough for me? He was right, but what do I do now? My heart won't stop aching. I feel like something died inside.
Signed, Foolishly Heartbroken Virgin No More

Guilt washed over Beth in a sorry wave. Em's cheerily reported sexploits had caused Foolishly Heartbroken incredible pain. Were there others like her who'd taken Em's advice, only to pay the price later? Sure, she preached safe sex. But safe sex meant more than preventing pregnancy and disease. It meant that if you wore your heart on your sleeve, you at least gave it a protective fiberglass coat. Why hadn't she thought this through?

In the old days, if she accidentally misled readers, the worst that happened was they got a mediocre chicken Milanese or paid too much for an assertive pinot noir.

If she misled people about sex, they could get hurt. Badly.

Stirred by Heartbroken's words and oblivious to the throbbing of her head, Beth began writing her column.

I have been sadly remiss in not issuing a Surgeon General's Warning for my words. So, tardily, here it is. Caution: Sex can lead to love, and good bed-mates don't necessarily make soul mates. This intrepid sexplorer reached her Seven Cities of Cíbola to find them gleaming with fool's gold.

Yes, dear reader, I fell for the first car I test-drove.

Ladies, some vital information. Though plenty of men get hooked on the first babe whose morn-ing breath they can stand, research shows that women make a bigger deal of the sex act than men. Fifty percent of women need to feel affec-tion before doing the bedroom boink. Seventy-five percent of men, however, can have sex with their emotions in neutral. Or, as one crude but insightful male survey respondent said, "Frankly, sweetheart, I don't turn nothin' down."

The words trailed off. The piece wasn't breezy enough for Em and was too lighthearted for Beth. With an agonized moan, she dropped her cheek on the desk beside her humming computer. She had to do something for poor Heartbroken Virgin No More and all the readers like her that she'd urged into emotional white water. She just didn't have the strength, the courage or the verbal skill to manage it right now. She'd struggled and risked and changed herself, all to get a column she had no business writing. Em *was* a fraud.

RAFE SAT IN A METAL chair at the scuffed table in the interview room and waited for the deputy to bring in Blaine Richardson, aka Bill Donaldson. He'd been arrested for check kiting—a fairly low-rent crime for a master con marr, Rafe thought, but he was glad the guy had slithered into custody.

He would handle him with kid gloves, use his best interview techniques and try not to lunge across the table and slam the guy to the floor.

Ash-smeared ashtrays littered the table, and the smell of burned coffee, Lysol and old paper filled the air, along with a sour tang that was probably the result of accumulated misery and despair.

He felt good. Sharp. As alert as a predator about to nab a long-hunted prey. He'd enjoyed the job. Following leads, coaxing police officials to search their memories and their records, tracking down news clips with the help of his former *Tribune* editor—even a sidetrack of research into the newer scams—had filled him with energy and excitement.

And made him decide what he wanted to do with himself. When this was over, he was going back to reporting—investigative work. Forget the prestige and salary that went with the publisher's job. Forget taking the next step. *How can going backward be bad if it makes you happy?* Beth was right.

Pursuing this story had made him feel more alive than he had in years. It might just be because he was helping Beth, but that didn't change the result. Something in him had shifted. He'd neglected his creative side for far too long, gotten lost in the business of words, not the words themselves. It was time to connect with the rest of himself. Time to be whole.

He had changed. Enough for Beth?

Not likely.

And it probably didn't matter. She hadn't returned his second call this morning. No doubt she regretted sleeping with him. Damn.

At least he'd be able to give her the gift of the truth about her ex-boyfriend. After he talked to Richardson, he had a meeting with a couple in Hollywood, Florida, who'd lost money to the guy, and he'd been able to take notes on three other victims' cases. That ought to be enough to ease Beth's humiliation. She wasn't alone in falling for the man's scams.

His attorney claimed Richardson actually *wanted* to speak with him, though Rafe figured he'd been promised some deal for cooperating.

He heard footsteps and the door opened. A man in a jumpsuit entered, escorted by two uniformed officers. Blaine Richardson was medium build, medium height, medium brown hair, medium good looks. Way too medium for Beth.

Rafe stood. "Rafe Jarvis," he said, and the guy nodded, then dropped into the chair across from him. Rafe sat, too. "Thank you for meeting with me," he said, then pulled his tape recorder out of his pocket, along with his pad and pen. "I'd like to tape our conversation, if that's all right?"

Richardson leaned forward. "I'll answer your questions under one condition—you tell Beth that I did not steal her money."

"Excuse me?"

"You heard me. I did not take Beth's money."

"Okay…"

"Yeah, I ended up with it, but I didn't steal it. Her brother Timmy gave it to me—to invest in my partnership. I didn't know it was her money."

"Her brother? You're saying her brother robbed her?" This guy had balls.

"When my lawyer told me what you wanted, I realized the little bastard had let me take the rap. I don't want Beth thinking that. So that's the deal. Tell Beth the truth and you can tape every last word I say."

"And how will I know you're telling me the truth."

"Just tell her what I tell you, pal. Talk to her brother, her bank, whatever. This is the truth."

"Okay. Start talking." Rafe clicked on the tape recorder and prepared to take notes.

"I knew that kid was trouble from the beginning. Foaming at the mouth to get in on the deal. He was clueless about the investment, but I was leveraged big-time, so I took his money."

"What happened exactly?"

Richardson sighed. "The kid showed up with twenty K he said was from savings. I didn't blame him for wanting in. It was a sweet package…time-shares for singles…Club Med without the beaches, and completely legitimate. The deal was solid, so we'd all make money, so I figured he knew what he was doing."

"He's pretty young."

"And flaky. Yeah, I knew that." Richardson shrugged. He held himself in a way Rafe recognized as honest—calm, shoulders back, eyes steady, no nervous finger movements. Except he knew that con artists could pass lie detector tests. "He worshipped his sister, so I can't believe he didn't come clean with her."

"So what happened with the time-shares?" Rafe asked. "And why did you take off?"

Richardson shook his head slowly. "That was pure tragedy. The general partners churned the money, lined their pockets and sent the Limited Partnership belly-up, leaving the rest of us high and dry. When I told Tim, he freaked—said he'd 'borrowed' Beth's money and demanded it back, the idiot. Venture capital is not for sissies."

"But you didn't tell Beth."

He sighed, shook his head sadly. "I couldn't. I'd lost everything, including our cruise money, and I knew she'd blame me for letting her brother in on the thing. I couldn't face her. I left. It was too complicated."

"Without an apology? Or even a decent lie? A letter?"

"Put it in writing? Never wise."

"You could have called her, made sure she knew your disappearance wasn't her fault."

Evidently reading something into his tone, Richardson's eyes shot to his. "So, you're what, the new boyfriend?"

"I'm a friend," he said, clearing his throat.

"Sure you are. You came all the way to Florida because you're her friend."

"Yes, I did."

A slight smile curved the guy's mouth. Rafe fought the urge to wipe it off his face with his fist. "Beth knew I cared about her. Hell, I was in love with her. But the bubble always bursts, you know? I just can't give them what they want for long."

Rafe was disgusted to realize this lying, thieving sociopath was voicing his own excuse for running from Beth. *I don't stick around. For anything.* That sounded so ugly and cowardly and plain stupid to him now.

"I just want Beth to know I didn't steal her money. The deal crashed, yeah. That's the chance you take. But I didn't even ask her to invest. I wouldn't have. I kept her out of my business. She was…above all that, for me."

"But you managed to walk off with her money anyway."

"And that stinks. I thought we'd come through. We didn't. It happens. So…is Beth okay?"

"She survived. She's hurt and confused by what you did. She thought you cared about her."

The guy had the decency to cringe. "Yeah. I regret that. Big mistake, getting involved with her. Beth's a great person. She can make you feel bigger than you are. For a while anyway."

Rafe hated it when lying scumbag criminals were right. "So you want me to tell Beth that you're innocent?"

"Don't look at me like that. I know what I am. Can you say the same?"

He just glared back at the guy.

"Feel superior if you want, pal, but don't judge until you've walked in my Guccis. Just tell Beth what happened. You owe me that."

"I'll tell her what you told me," he said, "but she's not going to believe that her brother robbed her."

"She will if she talks to him." The guy seemed completely confident he would be proven right. "And, listen, take good care of her, would you?" Richardson's voice went soft, and Rafe saw for a second what might have attracted Beth to him. "She still have those crazy dogs?"

"Yeah."

"And the cats? They gave me the heebie-jeebies, staring down at me all the time from that archway like they wanted to claw my eyes out."

"Yeah. They do that." The flicker of camaraderie he felt creeped him out.

"Beth deserves the best," Richardson said.

"She does."

"She know you're out here? That you tracked me down?"

"Not yet."

"Hang on to her, pal. If I'd had the testicles God gave me, I'd be with her still. Women like Beth don't walk into your life very often."

No, they didn't. He couldn't believe a guy who lived off lies was delivering truths that struck Rafe like blows to the gut.

He left soon after, but the conversation kept playing in his head. *I know what I am. Can you say the same?… I just can't give them what they want for long…. Women like Beth don't walk into your life very often.* And Rafe hadn't even told her he loved her.

Beth's alcohol-slurred words came to him: *You could try a little, you know. Work at it.*

Could he?

He'd had feelings for the women he dated, developed friendships with some, but he'd never before felt this hunger to connect, this need to be near someone in order to feel right in the world. This was new. Maybe there was hope for him yet.

He knew one thing—if he let Beth go, gave up now, he'd be as much a loser as Blaine Richardson was.

He could at least talk to her about it. Tell her how he felt. See what happened after that.

BETH WAS WALKING THE DOGS a block away from home when all three exploded into barks, yaps and woofs and lunged toward the house, where a car was pulling up. She could barely keep a grip on their leashes as they all ran toward the parked car. From half a block away, she saw that AJ was climbing out of the driver's side, a thick manila folder in his hand.

The dogs jumped as high as they could reach on AJ's body. Boomer's paws on his chest sent him stumbling backward a few feet. "Hey, guys," he said, but even as he struggled with the dogs, he kept his eyes riveted to Beth's face.

"AJ." It had been five days since he'd left her his note. She'd avoided his calls and vowed to stay cool about what had happened. *Pay no attention to the woman behind the triple Martooti,* as Em would say.

"Beth." He didn't move to touch her. In fact, his face wore a confused expression, as if he were glad and worried at the same time. "I got your machine, but I took a chance you were home."

She grimaced. She'd been screening his calls. "You didn't have to come, AJ. There's no need to apologize about the other night. I was loop-de-looped. I don't remember a thing. Lord knows what I said." The lie hurt.

"I'm sorry to hear that," he said, low and sad, "because I remember. Everything. And it meant a lot to me."

"Oh, well…gee. I just…" What was he saying? A niggling hope rose in her. "What's up? What have you got there?" She nodded at the folder in his hand.

"I have news. That's why I came by."

"News?"

"Can we go inside and talk?"

He always wanted to talk these days. And so far what he'd had to say had been far from reassuring. She nodded and led the way inside.

"Can I get you something to drink?" she asked after she'd freed the dogs from their leashes. The dogs watched them like marriage counselors hoping for the best, but fearing the worst.

"Let's talk first." He went to the sofa and sat.

She sat in the closest chair. Despite herself, she was happy to have him in her house again. She breathed in his familiar scent and tried to memorize his face. "So is this news good or bad?"

"Both, I guess. The good news is that you were right about Blaine Richardson. He did love you."

"What are you talking about?"

"I found him, Beth. I talked to the cops on your case and tracked him down. He's in jail in Florida for check kiting. I was able to arrange a meeting…which is where I went when I left you the other night. I also talked to some people he lured into iffy deals, and got notes on others."

"I can't believe you did that. You went all the way to Florida? Why would you…?" Her heart skipped, her mind struggled to grasp what he was saying. It seemed so crazy.

"I did it for you, Beth. The guy trashed your self-confidence and I wanted to prove that it wasn't your fault, that he'd done this to other people. I couldn't get back your money, but maybe I could get you some peace of mind."

"Wow. I don't know what to say. I can't believe you

talked to him. Why would he even see you? He was in jail?"

"Yeah. He agreed to see me because he wanted me to tell you… Now this is the bad news…" He took a deep breath, as if to steel himself. "He claims he didn't steal your money. He lost it when the deal went south, but he didn't rob you."

"He what? I don't understand. If he didn't *take* my money, how did he *lose* it?"

"He says Timmy gave it to him."

"Timmy? Blaine blames Timmy?"

"Yeah. According to Richardson, Timmy was desperate to invest in his time-share business and Richardson didn't ask where he got the twenty K. He figured once they turned a profit, it wouldn't matter. Then, when the business went belly-up, he couldn't face you. That was why he left."

"Why would he make up such a lie?"

"I don't know that it's a lie, Beth. Talk to Tim. Or check with his bank about a large deposit."

"You believe him? You believe Timmy would do such a thing?" Her heart thudded in her chest. Her mind was fuzzy. She was safe in her own living room, her dogs at her feet, but what she knew to be true was being stretched and twisted into a shape she didn't understand.

"The guy made enough sense that I'd look into it if I were you. I thought of talking to your brother first, but that didn't seem right, so I came to you."

"How could you?" Anger rose in her. At Blaine for lying about Timmy and at AJ for believing him.

"I had no idea your brother would be implicated, Beth. I just wanted to find out what happened. I was sure you'd want the truth." He leaned forward and placed the folder gently on her lap. "There's a tape of my conversation with Blaine and reports from the other victims. Listen to it, read the file, then talk to your brother."

"No." She shook her head.

"And remember that you were right about the guy. He did care about you. That's the one good thing in all of this." AJ took both of her cold hands and looked into her eyes. "He might be a conniving bastard who bilks people out of their money, but he loved you. You weren't wrong about that."

"That's supposed to make me feel better?" Her voice wobbled and she swallowed hard. "I never asked you to do this."

"I know. But I wanted to help you. And for you to see me for who I am."

"And who is that?" she asked coldly.

"I…love you, Beth. I may not be good at it, but I want to try. Talking to Blaine, I realized that I couldn't let you go."

"Talking to Blaine? The man who stole my money and accused my brother of robbing me convinced you that you love me?" This was insane.

"He made me realize that a woman as wonderful as you isn't going to walk into my life again. And I can't let you slip away. I know you're scared. I am, too. But I'm willing to try. To work at it. Like you said."

She shook her head, struggling to sort out her emotions. Anger, shock, confusion, with a flicker of delight that was instantly snuffed by disappointment. AJ had announced he loved her and declared her brother a criminal all in the same breath.

He won't stay. The words rang clear and true in her mind, coming up from a deep scared place inside her, and she grabbed on to them hard. *He'll leave*. That's what she had to remember. No matter what. *He won't stay. He'll leave*.

"You make love sound like some kind of punishment," she said sharply.

"I'm new at this, okay? Like you said, there are no instruction manuals."

"Maybe not, but love is supposed to be joyful and rewarding, not a prison sentence, for God's sake." This was not how she wanted to fall in love—not at all.

"I don't get it," he said, shaking his head. "I do all this—track down the guy, tell you I love you, and now you're angry at me?"

"You just told me my brother is a criminal. You expect me to thank you?"

"Of course not. But set that aside, would you, and think about us…what's between us, what we want. I'm here, offering myself to you. Isn't that what you want?"

She paused and looked at him, letting the fear in her swell and fill her heart. *He won't stay*. "No," she said softly. "It's not. You think you love me, but what you feel is some kind of obligation. And this—" she waved the folder at him "—this is the last thing I wanted from you."

"The truth isn't always pretty, Beth. Sometimes it's messy and confusing. It gets served up on paper plates with napkins, not fine china and linens, but that doesn't change its value."

"I have no problem with the truth. And what's wrong with china? Are you criticizing me for liking nice things?"

"No. Except I guess I'm a paper plate kind of guy, and if you can't accept that…"

She just looked at him, knowing she should argue,

because he was wrong, but at least he was coming to the same conclusion she had—that this would not work.

"Don't hide from the truth, Beth. About your brother. And about us. Even if it's hard."

"That's rich, coming from a man who lied to me about who he was for weeks on end."

"That's not fair."

"It's more than fair. Too much has happened, AJ, and not enough has changed. About you or me."

He just looked at her.

"You said it yourself—you're not the kind of man I want. And it has nothing to do with paper plates or linen napkins. It has to do with the distance in your eyes. The castle and the moat, remember?"

Her words hit home, she saw in his face, which paled with pain. She wanted to take back what she'd said, throw herself into his arms and start over. She wanted to shout, *AJ, I'm lying. Can't you tell?*

But he believed her, dammit, and a resigned sadness clouded the crystal blue of his eyes. "That's all I've got, Beth. I can't take back what's happened between us. And if you can't see beyond it, what more can I do? We both have to want it." He held her gaze for a few long, sad seconds, then stood to go.

She stood, too, and followed him to the door. The dogs milled around them, whining, anxious about the quarrel.

"I hope you find what you're looking for, Beth," he said, then quickly left.

Beth stood still, letting her feelings tumble and swirl. The dogs remained staring at the door, waiting for AJ to return. "He's not coming back," she said to them. She'd been right to send him away. She didn't want a man who had to work so hard just to be in love with her.

He won't stay. That truth throbbed inside her like a second heartbeat, comforting her in her loss.

She looked down at the folder that supposedly held the truth about Blaine and her brother. This was garbage. She headed for the kitchen to dispose of it. She pushed the foot pedal on the trash can, tossed in the folder, then stared down at it as a fleeting memory crossed her mind…Timmy lurking nervously near her desk one afternoon, a few weeks before Blaine left, shoving something into his pocket before answering the question she'd asked him. She'd thought his behavior odd, but ignored it, the way she ignored so many annoying things about Timmy.

She'd been so sure Blaine had taken her money. He'd disappeared, for one thing, and made that comment about her handwriting.

Slowly, she lifted the folder from the trash can. AJ was wrong. She wasn't afraid of the truth. She sat at the kitchen table and opened the folder.

Ninety minutes later, she arrived at her mother's house to talk to Tim. She was diverted from her mission by the presence of George Nichols on the sofa, drinking iced tea and eating cookies, his toolbox resting on the table, beside the gold-rimmed plate of gingersnaps.

He stood to shake her hand. "I stopped by to tighten the hinges and knobs on your mother's cupboards."

"He won't let me pay him," her mother interrupted, her face bright with color, wearing a linen dress she usually reserved for church.

"It's a pleasure to help," he said, catching her mother's gaze. Beth watched her mother visibly soften. This was a good sign. But her head was so filled with what she had to talk to Tim about and what she was going to do about AJ, it was hard to focus on her mother.

"Would you like some tea, sweetheart?" her mother asked her and headed for the kitchen.

Beth followed her, intending to ask where Timmy was, but as soon as they were alone, her mother whispered, "He keeps asking me out."

"So, go out with him. He's a nice man and it's obvious he likes you. He came over here to tighten your hinges, for heaven's sake."

"I know, but…"

"Do you like him? Are you attracted to him?"

"It's never that simple, Beth." She brought the tea pitcher out of the refrigerator. "They expect too much or they get bored or I get bored or they go, for whatever reason." An expression came over her mother's face that chilled Beth. It was the one she'd worn when Beth's father disappeared—vulnerable and frail and so lost.

Her mother seemed to gather herself, and smiled. "It's just too much trouble." She went to the cupboard for a glass.

Her mother was scared, Beth realized. The same way she'd been scared when AJ told her he loved her. Seeing her mother's expression, thinking about that time, she realized she'd been feeling the same sick dread she'd felt when she realized her father wasn't coming back. The lonely loss. The betrayal and shame.

Her father's abandonment had scared them both, down deep.

Maybe AJ was right. Maybe she was hiding from the truth. Had she chosen Blaine because she sensed his impermanence? Expected him to leave her? She'd certainly picked AJ with limits in mind. Except she'd gone and fallen in love with him. Which was scary, but not as scary as knowing he loved her, too. *He won't stay*.

Her mother poured tea into the glass and handed it

to her. "How will you know unless you try?" she asked softly, accepting the tea.

"How will I know what?"

"If it could work. If you could make a life together."

"I just know." *He won't stay*, her mother's eyes said.

"He's not Daddy."

"Of course not." Her mother laughed. "George isn't like your father at all."

"But your expression is exactly the one on your face when Daddy left."

"It is?" Her mother frowned.

"Yes. Give George a chance to prove who he is. Give yourself a chance. You won't crumble. You're smarter and stronger than you were twenty years ago. You know yourself better. You know people better. Just see what happens."

Her mother blinked and pursed her lips. "You're making sense, I guess. I'll have to think about it." Then she studied her daughter. "What's wrong, Beth? You're upset about something."

"Maybe I should start taking my own advice," she said, smiling sadly. "But for now I need to talk to Tim. Where is he?"

"Out in his workshop. What's the matter?"

"I'll talk to you about it later. Or he will. For now, go make some plans with George. Go fishing or skiing or tighten some hinges at his place."

Her mother smiled softly. "A fishing trip wouldn't hurt, I guess." It was a first step.

Beth poured another glass of tea for her brother and set out to learn the truth, ready, this time, for all of it.

15

INSIDE THE STAND-ALONE garage Timmy used as a workshop, Beth blinked to adjust to the dim light, breathing in dust and the smell of heated metal.

"Hey, Bethie," Tim said, looking up from something in a vice he was hammering. He accepted the tea from her and took a drink. "Whew. I needed that. Want to take a look at the prototype blueprint?"

"Not right now. I want to talk about Blaine," she said.

His gaze shot to her. "Blaine? What about him?"

"I want to talk about how he got my money." She let the words hang in the air, remembering how furious Timmy had been at Blaine, how he'd repeatedly said he'd pay her back for all she'd done for him.

Sure enough, Timmy's gaze slid away from hers, first to the workbench, then to the wall—anywhere but her face.

"How do you think Blaine got my money, Timmy?"

"Blaine was a crook," he said, and his Adam's apple rose and fell in a hard swallow. "He lost your money."

She looked at him, realizing for the first time how she glossed over things about him, and even about her mother. How she saw only what she wanted to see. "But how did he get it, Tim?"

Guilt flashed across his face as vivid as a neon sign. "Are you accusing me of something?"

"Am I?"

And then he slumped onto the metal stool, elbows on the bench, head in his hands. "I wanted to tell you so many times. Blaine made it sound like a killer opportunity. I thought we'd double your money and then it would be like a gift to thank you for all the times you bailed me out."

"You took my money and let me blame Blaine? All this time?"

"He was a bastard for leaving you. And he didn't tell me the risks. He stole from both of us. I knew that if you knew what I'd done, you'd feel even worse. As soon as my invention sells, I'll pay you back. I swear."

"Oh, Tim," she said. Why the hell were they still calling him *Timmy*, anyway? He was a grown man. But he was also a child, she saw now. A dreamer and a bumbler like her father had been. He meant well, but he was completely lost.

"You should have told me. You should have been honest."

"I know. It's been killing me. I'm so sorry, Beth." He looked up at her, wretched and hopeful, wanting her forgiveness.

She was so disappointed in him. But also in herself. How had she been so blind?

"I'll make it up to you," he continued. "With this project. I know it will hit."

"No. That has to stop. This—" she motioned at the sad little workshop "—is a hobby. You'll make it up to me by going to college, getting a degree and a real job. Then you'll pay me back, month by month, like any loan."

"What?"

"You heard me. It's time you took some responsibility for your own life. Pay Mom rent or, better yet, move out on your own. Make things happen for yourself."

"I thought you believed in me."

"I do. I believe that you're smart and creative and you try to help, but you're out of touch and full of wishes and hopes, not action. Maybe one of your inventions will sell one day, but for now you've got to pay your own way like everyone else."

"That's harsh."

"That's reality. We've been kidding ourselves—all of us. Mom's been hiding from men. You've been hiding from adulthood. I've been hiding from what I want."

"Are you going to tell Mom what I did?"

"No. You're going to tell her. We're all going to start telling each other the things we need to hear."

She talked with him longer, encouraged him, while staying firm, and then left him sitting at his workbench, stunned and a little scared.

He'd come around, she knew, just as she was doing—opening her eyes to the way people really were, not how she wanted to think of them. AJ had been right. She preferred her reality dressed up and decorated—on the good china, not paper plates.

She'd been as scared as AJ, but hadn't realized it or understood it.

AJ believed he couldn't commit, but he'd hunted down her old boyfriend to help her feel better. Maybe it had been misguided and unnecessary, but he'd done it out of love. He loved her. The experience was new for him, but he was ready to work at it. She'd refused to even give him a chance.

And it wasn't just her love for AJ she'd been hiding from. She'd also been kidding herself about her column.

She was not a sexual adventuress. She was a shy, serious woman for whom sex was a way bigger deal than she'd pretended it was. She could no longer be the "Sex on the Town" columnist.

She'd lose that sense of importance the column had given her, but she'd find other rewarding work. She hoped Will would hire her to write features, but if he wouldn't, she'd freelance.

In the meantime, she had to give Will her resignation and write her last column.

It would be her best.

A WEEK LATER, AND JUST after his meeting with Curt Paterson, Rafe stopped at the Middle Eastern deli for a bottle of champagne and a package of baklava to take over to the Chos. Tonight was their anniversary and he thought he'd offer neighborly congratulations.

He felt like celebrating, too. He'd declined Curt's offer without a moment of regret. He'd taken a job doing research for a government watchdog group to pay living expenses, but he'd work as a freelance investigative journalist, too, building his business clip by clip. He'd scale down his lifestyle, live somewhere outside the city, or another state, for that matter. He didn't care. He was wide open.

He felt whole for the first time in a long time. He'd use his creativity and business sense together and end this split existence, this half life he'd inhabited. He felt complete…well, except for his heart. That was an empty, aching spot in his chest.

He'd love to share his news with Beth, who'd helped him make the decision, but that was impossible. Instead, he'd hang out with the Chos. He just knew he didn't want to be alone. Beth had shown him that about himself, too. He wasn't quite the loner he'd convinced himself he was.

He loved her, but he wasn't enough for her. And he didn't want to live his life trying to meet impossible expectations. He'd told her from the beginning he wasn't the man she wanted. Why had it surprised him when it turned out to be true?

He forced a smile, focusing on the things he had to celebrate, knocked on his neighbors' door and was soon welcomed into the fragrant warmth of their happiness.

TWO WEEKS LATER, RAFE stepped into the elevator of his hotel. He was on his way across the street to the *Phoenix Rising* offices for the changeover party. He'd intended to decline—not wanting to see Beth—but Will wanted him there, and he couldn't let the staff down. They were all proud of what they'd done and he wanted to make sure they knew how pleased *Man's Man* was with the transition.

So, he'd deal with seeing Beth as best he could. Maybe she wouldn't even be at the party. She'd resigned as a columnist. He'd felt guilty about that, but Will had assured him she was happy to be writing features for the magazine—the assignment Rafe had had in mind for her in the first place.

Exiting the elevator, he was heading across the lobby when a familiar voice called his name.

He turned. Beth stood in the entrance to Grins. She wore that same slinky blue number she'd worn the night they met, and was holding out a ballpoint pen. "Did you drop this?" she asked in a sultry voice.

His heart lifted at the sight of her. God, he loved her. He wanted to sweep her into his arms, forget everything that was wrong between them, and just hold her.

She wore a smile as broad as the bar's name, he was pleased to note, and her eyes twinkled as if she had a secret.

A secret he would really, really like.

"Sorry, not mine," he said. "I was heading across the street for the party. Want to join me?"

"How about a drink first? Tutti-Frutti Martootis all around?"

He smiled. "What about my masculinity?"

"I'm not worried. Are you?"

"Tiki drinks, here I come." He followed her into the bar, delighted to notice she wore the kitty-cat barrette again and still wobbled on those heels. She must have been watching for him—Will knew where he was staying. Was she recreating their first encounter? What did she have in mind? He hoped it was the same thing he was thinking: they had to find a way to be together. They had to make this work somehow.

No matter how hard it was or how ill-equipped he was for the task, he wanted to spend his life with this woman. For better, for worse, for richer, for poorer— and poverty was a distinct possibility with his change of career—for fantasy and reality.

Beth slid into the booth where they'd first talked about pickup lines, and AJ sat across from her.

She pulled a magazine out of her purse, opened it and slid it across the table. "I think you'll like my last column."

He looked into her smiling face, then down at her words, and began to read, feeling her eyes on him the entire time.

Your "Sex on the Town" reporter is a fraud. That's right. She is not the cool, smooth Em who's been dishing out glib advice on easy-breezy sex, lo, these past few months. No. She is a shy, repressed librarian-esque woman who fell in love with Mr. Perfect Timing. Remember him? Well. he turned out to be Mr. Impossible Love.

Rafe paused to look up at her. Her face was bright with hope and love and mischief. "Keep reading." So he read on.

Beware, oh, beware, dear readers. Good sex can turn into a great love when you least expect it, and if you're careless or scared, you'll chase it away. Which is exactly what your intrepid reporter has done.

So, here is Em's final advice: Forget the rules. Forget the perfect martini, the correct second-date ambiance, the decorative candy dish of condoms. Scrubbing rust stains from a laundry sink can be swooningly romantic when you do it with the one you love. The romance, the dancing, the champagne, the tender gifts…all just frosting on the love cake.

Go for the cake. The cake's the thing.

And so is a man who would go from coast to coast to help the woman he loves—even when she's an ungrateful brat.

You were right, Mr. Impossible Love. I was only seeing what I wanted to see. Life and love are just fine in the raw. All you have to do is open your arms and let it all in.

He glanced up at Beth. She wore her heart in her eyes, open and honest and offering forever.

Which didn't scare him one bit.

He looked down to read the last paragraph, surprised that he had to blink to clear something—dust?—from his eyes.

Forever's not so scary when you take it one day at a time.
Very truly yours,
Beth "Em" Samuels

WATCHING HIS FACE as he read her words, Beth saw the exact moment when AJ melted. Before he even lifted his eyes from the page, she knew it would be all right.

When he finished reading, he didn't say a word, just came around to her side of the table, pulled her into his arms and kissed her, long and slow and joyously familiar. "So we take it one day at a time?"

"Yeah. And that can add up to a fine forever, I think."

"That's what I want," he said, but there was a flicker of hesitation in his eyes.

"You can do it, AJ. I know you can. You chased down Blaine, for heaven's sake. Now that's commitment. And you tried to tell me the truth when I was busy ducking under the covers. After all that, a little thing like being in love should be a walk in the park."

"You told me some truths, too, Beth. You were right about me and the magazine. I quit *Man's Man* to get back to reporting. That's who I am and what I want. I was only using half my skills, half my heart. You helped me realize that."

"Whatever makes you happy, AJ."

"You make me happy, Beth. You and your crazy pets and your fussy house and your china plates and linen napkins."

"There's nothing wrong with paper plates," she said, tears in her eyes, "if I'm sharing them with you." Her heart squeezed with so much love she thought she might burst. "A threadbare sofa is all I need...as long as I'm sharing it with you."

At those words, another feeling eased into her awareness—desire—that raw hunger to be in his arms, naked, skin to skin. She smiled, realizing exactly what she should do about that. "I understand you have a room in the hotel? You know, I've been out of circulation for a while. Maybe you could show me the ropes? Help me get my feet—or whatever—wet?" She winked at him.

"Mmm. The advantage of hotel bars, right? One quick lift and we're bed-bound?" he said, quoting from her first sex column. "What about the magazine party?"

"Maybe later." She leaned in and kissed him, cupping his jaw, thrilled to know that she'd be able to do this very thing over and over for the rest of her life.

AJ broke off the kiss, took her hand and stood to help her to her feet. "I'm glad to see Em hasn't totally disappeared from the scene," he said, pulling her close.

"Oh, no. She and Beth are like this now—" She twined two fingers together. She would be sexy and sensible, wild and careful, spontaneous and fussy. She'd be the well-rounded woman AJ had helped her discover she truly was. She looked up into his blue eyes. The cool distance she'd always seen was gone, replaced by warm connection and deep love. That at-the-altar look, only more definite, more determined, more solid this time.

"I fell in love with AJ, but something tells me Rafe's got a lot to offer, too."

"Yeah, but wait'll you see them together. Unbeatable."

"I can't wait." She shivered with anticipation and

tucked her body against his, both arms around his waist as they walked toward the elevator. Making love now would be new, a blending of their separate selves, a bonding that only love could achieve.

"Maybe we can write a guest column together," AJ said when they'd stepped into the elevator. "Something about the bride wore red leather?"

"The bride?" She looked up at him.

"Just thinking ahead," he said, kissing her hair.

And so was Beth. To a future of learning each other inside and out. Beth and Em and Rafe and AJ all together. She wasn't sure she could write about that, though.

She'd be too busy living it.

If you enjoyed what you just read,
then we've got an offer you can't resist!

Take 2 bestselling love stories FREE!

Plus get a FREE surprise gift!

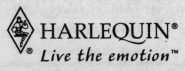

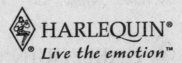